KISS CAM

● REC

KIARA LONDON

KISS CAM

subject to the condition that it shall not, by way of trade or otherwise, be lent, resold, hired out, or otherwise circulated without the publisher's prior consent in any form of binding or cover other than that in which it is published and without a similar condition including this condition being imposed on the subsequent purchaser.

Swoon Reads New York

A Swoon Reads Book
An imprint of Macmillan Publishers Limited

First published in the US 2016 by Feiwel and Friends
First published as an eBook 2016 by Macmillan Children's Books

This edition published 2017 by Macmillan Children's Books
an imprint of Pan Macmillan
20 New Wharf Road, London N1 9RR
Associated companies throughout the world
www.panmacmillan.com

ISBN 978-1-5098-1891-4

1 3 5 7 9 8 6 4 2

A CIP catalogue record for this book is available from the British Library.

Book design by Liz Dresner

Printed and bound by CPI Group (UK) Ltd, Croydon CR0 4YY

To my followers on Wattpad, this book is, and always has been, yours.

Also, to Stephanie and Isabel, my biggest fangirls. I love you both.

One

WereVloggingHere

I KNOW JAS is up to no good the minute he plunks his tray down across from mine and flashes me a mischievous grin.

"You'll never believe what I convinced Lenny to do," he dares after he's dropped his schoolbag to the floor and seated himself slightly askew on the other side of the bench.

I raise an eyebrow and tip my head sideways to search for Lenny among the lunch lines. "What's he going to do?" I ask curiously, and turn to face Jasper again when I've decided there are too many students blocking him from my sight.

His eyes glint, smile growing when he answers, "He's going to eat a nasty combination of whatever I want."

"That's disgusting," I comment, and snap off the cap on my flavored water. "He's going to puke."

"Who's going to puke?" Allison, my best friend and go-to history project partner, asks as she drops her tray beside mine.

"Lenny's probably going to eat mayo and peaches," I update her. And mayo and peaches it's likely to be. We always grab fruit cups for Lenny, and I dip my french fries in mayo.

"Ew." She grimaces and then shoots a look at Jasper. "And you're going to film it, aren't you?"

Jasper lifts his backpack into his lap, unzips the first pocket, and pulls out his video camera, which he, Lenny, and I all pitched in to buy but is technically his. "Yep!" he chirps, and sets the camera beside his tray.

Allison's eyes narrow at him, and she shakes her head hard enough to make her dark hair sway. "You guys and your vlog," she mutters to herself.

It's no secret that Allison hates our vlogging antics, and it's mostly due to her camera shyness—something I got over six years ago, and it's all because Jasper Lahey, self-proclaimed news broadcaster of his life and all with whom he decides to tangle fates. If it hadn't been for dorky twelve-year-old Jasper inviting me to join in on his and Lenny's shenanigans, I would have remained camera and people shy.

As for my history partner, no one is getting Allison Steele out of her tightly woven cocoon. After all, it is *I* who does all the talking during our history presentations. For now, the girl has decided to hate the player and the game—covering her face from every camera shot and kicking Jasper under the table for trying to include her.

Lenny now joins our group with a sour face, making Jasper grin wickedly. Looking at the assortment of odd things on Lenny's tray, I can already tell that this will end badly. Not only are there peaches and a glob of mayonnaise, but pickles, coleslaw, ketchup, fruit snacks, lime Jell-O, and a bag of croutons. Just the thought of all those things being combined and consumed is enough to make me gag.

"Oh, please don't eat that," Allison groans, and hides her eyes behind her painted fingernails. I nod in agreement and scoot away from Lenny when he seats himself on the other side of me.

"Puke in the other direction." I frown.

"Nah, man. Spray June. That's comedy gold!" Jasper cheers.

Scowling, I glance up at Jasper, who has now turned on the video camera and propped it up, waiting with a boyish grin on his face.

Jasper is all jokes, dark hair, and long legs. And he *would* sacrifice me for comedy, too. Back in the day, he almost used me as a guinea pig to see if Mentos and Coke would still fizz up if someone drank it. That was one of the first things he wanted to do after inviting me to join Lenny and him in their games. I was about ready to walk away from it all when Lenny took a bullet for me and did the experiment instead. And, yes, Mentos and Coke still fizz up. Lenny laughs about it now, but he still won't drink anything that fizzes.

"You're despicable," I tell him jokingly.

Jasper knows I'm wearing new leather boots I got for my birthday a few weeks back. It's evil of him to wish for me to get puked on when this is the first day they've made it outside my house.

"C'mon, June, take one for the team." Jasper laughs and turns the camera on me, the red light glowing in the corner. I should have known he'd document the moments leading up to the gross food challenge.

"I hope the splatter is so violent that chunks hit you," I deadpan, and Allison squawks her disapproval of my word choice while Jasper cracks up.

Meanwhile, Lenny mixes together the pickles, lime Jell-O, and whatever else is on his tray. Having gained confidence now that the camera is on, he begins talking smack and placing bets on how much he can eat.

There are two things one should know about Lenny. First, he can't say no to anything. Second, he's the easiest person to make laugh. The first one is relevant in this case.

"Just don't eat it," Allison whines, shielding her eyes behind her hand. I glance at her and laugh a little, thinking the only strong thing about this girl is her jawline.

"Twenty bucks I can eat all of it," Lenny barters, ignoring Allison's pleas. "Thirty if I can keep it down."

"Deal," Jasper chuckles, and then sprinkles ground croutons over the slimy and very chunky food combination.

Lenny leans down to take a whiff of the concoction but pulls back quickly, trying not to make a face. "Well, that doesn't smell poisonous at *all*."

"I'm sure it doesn't," Jasper comments, and then charmingly adds, "Juniper, darling, could you show the camera how absolutely revolting that looks?"

"Juniper, darling . . . ," I mumble under my breath, and give him the stink-eye while I accept the camera from him.

Lenny leans back while I scoot forward and bring the lens right up to the slightly green and watery mixture. The pickles, peaches, and fruit snacks make it extra chunky and colorful, while the Jell-O has been mushed into slime. It looks the same way it's going to look when it comes back up.

"Would you eat this for twenty bucks?" I ask the camera with a grimace. "I wouldn't."

Jasper snatches the camera away from me and looks up at

Lenny. "On the count of three you have to eat *all* of that for twenty bucks. Keep it down and it's thirty." Lenny nods and lifts his plastic spoon, looking nervous but still wearing a goofy smile for the camera. "One. Two . . . Three!"

I have to look away when Lenny dives spoon-first into the hearty-style peach-mayo-and-more soup. Like Allison, I can't watch him take that first bite, swallow, gag a little, and push forward. Unlike Allison, I sneak tiny peeks at Lenny, who struggles to spoon another glob into his mouth.

It proves to be too disgusting to watch, though. He spits up a little, and I shield my eyes while Jasper cheers. Lenny lurches forward like he's going to puke, and I ram into Allison to get into the splatter-free zone while Jasper closes in on him.

In the end, he eats it all.

"That was the grossest thing I've ever done next to eating those worms a couple years ago," Lenny moans, and buries his face in his arms to let the challenge try to settle.

Jasper's eyes light up, and he laughs. "Hey! I filmed that, too! Good times."

"Is it over?" Allison asks, hesitantly removing her hands from her eyes and peeking over at Lenny's blond head, red face concealed by his arms. Looking around, I can see we've attracted the attention of other students. Some of our peers are actually leaning across their tables to see if he'll spew.

"I might throw up," Lenny admits after a couple of minutes. "I feel sick."

"No shit, Sherlock," Allison snaps back, and drops her hands down on either side of her tray. "You guys are so *gross*."

Jasper and I share a look across the table, hiding smiles. She's always in a foul mood when one of us is doing something stupid.

I think she takes the hit for all the embarrassment none of us ever seem to feel.

After a few more minutes of filming Lenny groaning and bellyaching, Jasper decides to end the video.

Turning the camera around to face himself, Jasper salutes the audience, saying, "Well, folks, this is what we got up to today. So, stay out of the way. We're vlogging here."

Just as he presses the off button, Lenny blows chunks all over my new boots.

———

I fall onto Jasper's bed and flip onto my side when he turns on the box light in preparation for our weekly Q&A video on VlogIt. The bed shifts beside me, and I know Lenny sat down as well, leaving all the work to Jasper.

"I'm *really* sorry about your boots, June," Lenny apologizes for the hundredth time.

"It's *fine*," I say, trying not to laugh. "Besides, I blame Jasper."

My boots really are all right. They got a good scrub-down in the school bathroom. Luckily, Allison had some body spray in her backpack, so I didn't smell like vomit for the rest of the day.

After lunch, Lenny went to the health office and then home. He didn't look good before, but now he's looking chipper as ever. Good thing, too, seeing as this is the only night this week we can do our weekly questions video.

I turn over and watch Jasper bounce from his laptop to his camera, dodging electrical cords as he goes. If it weren't for his video setup, this room would be pretty tidy.

We're not the highest quality of video bloggers, yet we're one of the most subscribed-to vlog channels on VlogIt—which also means we've partnered with the site and get paid.

We *could* be a quality vlog channel, but Lenny's laziness, my spending tendencies, and Jasper's fondness for the "kids-next-door" feel keep us doing what we've been doing for three years. And, thanks to us being laid-back and random, our channel WereVloggingHere has made leaps and bounds since its start.

Our success has enabled us to set up meetings with other vloggers and meet-and-greets with our subscribers from across the globe, but in town we aren't well known at all. To our neighbors, we're just an eccentric group of teens with a camcorder. It does a good job of keeping us grounded.

One of the most popular things we do on our channel is answer our subscribers' questions on camera. There's a different theme for each ask, and tonight is Truth or Dare.

"You know," Jasper comments while he sets the camera on its tripod, "it kind of looks like we're filming a cheap porn video."

Lenny stares at him blankly for a second and then bursts out laughing. I sit up and purse my lips. "How do you figure?"

Jasper grins at Lenny's easy laughter and chuckles himself. "Oh, c'mon, June. How can you not see it? Lighting, a camera aimed at the bed, three horny teenagers. Things could get pretty risqué."

At this, Lenny laughs harder and falls back on Jasper's orange bedding to cover his red face.

I snort. "Speak for yourself."

"Meaning?" he asks distractedly while unhooking his laptop from his charger. He wiggles his eyebrows at me when he comes to sit between Lenny and me.

"I'm not horny," I reply simply.

"All teenagers are horny," he says with a shrug, and pulls up the comments from our last video on his laptop.

Lenny raises his hand. "I second that."

"Whoa," I laugh. "I don't need a mental image of what you two get up to in your free time."

"Not *together*," Lenny huffs, shaking his head as he sits up.

"Or maybe we do. . . ." Jasper winks and Lenny punches him in the arm, making him recoil and bump into my shoulder.

Laughing, I push him away and stand up, making to leave the room. "I'll leave you two to it, then," I tease.

"No!" Lenny wails. "Stop! Just sit down. We have to shoot this video tonight. I don't have time for it tomorrow. Baby-sitting the twins, remember?"

Lenny's excuse for everything is his twin sisters. Sometimes he doesn't want to tell us he'd rather not hang out, so he lies and says he has to babysit. Except he doesn't know we know his grand excuse.

It's Friday night tomorrow. He doesn't have to babysit. Jasper and I both know that *Desperate Housewives* reruns are on Friday nights, and Lenny has a crush on Eva Longoria. He can't trick us. We've known each other too long for that.

"Fine," Jasper sighs, and gives me a sly smile. I try not to grin too widely when I think about Lenny watching *Desperate*

Housewives and eating popcorn with saucerlike eyes, drooling every time Eva shows some skin.

"Any good questions?" I ask over Jasper's shoulder when I've reseated myself.

"Don't know, they've just loaded. Want to go in order?"

Lenny and I both nod, so he sets his laptop in Lenny's lap while he hits record on the video camera. When Jasper's sitting back down, we all look at the camera and smile.

"I'm Jas."

"I'm Lenny."

"I'm June."

"And we're vlogging here!"

Jasper takes the laptop from Lenny, and I remind the audience what tonight's theme is.

"Hey, guys. We asked you to send us Truth or Dare questions this week, and it looks like there's quite a few," I say, glancing over at the comment count. "We're going to go in order until we get sick of telling you our biggest secrets and eating questionable things out of Jas's pantry."

Jas snickers at this because the last time we chose the Truth or Dare theme, I had to eat raw macaroni noodles and cold goopy cheese.

"Lenny, would you like to read the first Truth or Dare? It looks like it's a top comment, too," Jasper notes while leaning back to make room for Lenny. "Should be interesting."

I rub my hands together like a super villain and wait to see who the Truth or Dare is directed at. I have my bet placed on Lenny, since he will do just about *anything*. He never uses his chickens.

"TeamJacob3012 says," Lenny reads. His eyes scan the

comment, and then he bursts out laughing. It's not until his laughing slows to spaced-out intervals that he can announce, "For all the Jasiper shippers out there, I dare June and Jas to kiss!"

Two

Avoiding Tongue

I CAN'T TELL if my eyes have widened or my brows have furrowed or even if I'm just sitting there staring at the camera blankly. I do know one thing, though. My insides are being tickled by the wings of a thousand butterflies.

Since the beginning of our video blogging days, I've found myself being paired up with either Lenny or Jasper as a couple ship. To make things clear, a ship isn't what one might think it is—at least not in this case.

According to any Internet slang dictionary, a ship can be described as:

1. an unrealistic relationship that makes your heart swell with all the "feels," causing you to pound your head against a wall, cry to the heavens, or dissolve into giddy giggles. May include "cannons" (confirmed relationships).

2. to support a romantic pairing. Shipping is often the purpose of many fanfiction stories. Used for characters in books, TV shows, movies, anime, manga, video games, etc.

3. Short for a romantic relationship followed by a fandom.

Ships are probably one of the most dangerous things on the Internet; well, that and the hundreds of porn sites waiting to poison the minds of our children.

Lenny, Jasper, and I didn't even know we were part of a large fan ship circle until our names started to be combined in the comments under our videos to show which couple one supported.

Our viewers have always been rooting for a pair of us to become a couple. Not only are there Jasiper (Jasper and Juniper) and Leniper (Lenny and Juniper) ships, but Jenny (Jasper and Lenny) ships as well. However, the most popular among our viewers is the fictitious romantic relationship between Jasper and me. And anything could set off our viewers, too. If Jasper and I look at each other too long or touch each other too often in a video, the fans of our ship will go crazy.

> You guys are such a cute couple!!!
>
> Admit it, you're a couple!
>
> Why are you hiding your relationship from us?!
>
> The love in their eyes is so obvious! Jasiper feels!!

Sometimes our viewers get carried away. Not all of them are like this, of course. Some people watch our videos simply because we're entertaining. But it's the crazy ones who stand out the most.

And it's not like we ever deny anything happening between us, either. In fact, Jasper and I joke about Jasiper quite often on camera. We think it's funny that some of our viewers are so invested in our nonexistent relationship. We tease them, which is probably what lead up to this somewhat uncalled-for and chicken-worthy dare.

I laugh somewhat awkwardly and turn to Jasper for help. "Kiss, huh?"

Jasper looks down at the computer screen to confirm Lenny's words. "Looks like it."

My insides knot up further, and I have to hold back a groan while Lenny muffles laughter on the other side of Jasper.

"I mean, it's *just* a kiss, right?" Jasper checks, nudging me in the side. "No big deal."

"Are you kidding?" I scoff in surprise. He's being remarkably cool about this whole thing. His expression remains neutral, his demeanor bouncy and excited. Kissing is *kissing*. It's intimate no matter how you look at it. With the opposite sex, friend or not, it surpasses all boundaries.

"Oh, c'mon, June," he says with a roll of his eyes. He passes his laptop back over to a still-snickering Lenny and turns his body to face mine. "It'll be a less-than-a-second, quick little lip touch. Besides, we kiss each other on the cheek all the time."

My mouth is still agape as I continue to stare at him in disbelief. I have previously saved my mouth kisses for those I had deep feelings for—relationships. What Jasper and I have is friendship. And sure, we're close. We're neighbors, have had sleepovers, slept in the same bed, changed in the same room. And it's because of this that I don't want to cross any boundaries. People have already considered us *too* close as it is.

"Chicken," I say simply, and turn my head away from him to look at the camera. "I totally chicken out of this one, TeamJacob3012."

Jasper makes a scoffing noise and slaps my shoulder. "Don't chicken!"

"Jas, I'm not kissing you," I say seriously, and cross my arms. "That's too weird."

"Oh, suck it up," Lenny chimes in. "I ate lime Jell-O in mayonnaise today. You're getting off easy."

Jasper raises his eyebrows, waiting for me to respond to that. I can't understand why he's so adamant about doing this dare. I mean, I guess we've all been dared to do grosser, stranger things. It's just that this goes against a lot of my personal rules, especially my rules about Jasper.

"It's just me." Jasper shrugs. "Could be worse."

Sitting forward, I put my head in my hands and let out a deep sigh. "This is ridiculous."

"Is that an okay?" Jasper asks, and I can *hear* the victorious smile on his lips.

"*Fine*," I groan, sitting up. "It's just a kiss."

"Exactly." Jasper nods. "It's just a kiss."

"Right," I say, because now it feels uncomfortably tense in the room, but maybe that's just me.

Before you're about to kiss someone, there is usually that *moment*. It's when you both realize you're thinking about it, you exchange glances, you lean in, lids flutter closed, and you wait for their lips to brush yours. It's romantic and sweet.

There is nothing romantic and sweet about this.

I turn toward Jasper and let my hands rest in my lap. He watches me settle in and I see Lenny peek around his shoulder to watch with a goofy half grin on his face—which is about as creepy as it sounds.

Jasper clears his throat then and runs a hand through his hair while I raise my eyebrows. "Okay, ready?"

"I guess."

"Ready . . . go!" Lenny cheers over Jasper's shoulder.

It's all so bizarre that I have to giggle, but I'm a bit too late because Jasper's already leaned forward and pressed his lips against my smile. It's quick, like he said it would be. A little lip touch that leaves me barely enough time to close my eyes. No goose bumps, no blush. Just a kiss.

Leaning back, Jasper grins and gives two thumbs-up to the camera. "Only took six years," he jokes at the camera. "There is hope for the friend zone!"

I roll my eyes and jab an elbow into his ribs. "Oh, stop. No sparks, everybody!"

He was right, after all. I had worked myself up over nothing. There was nothing no sparks I was afraid I'd feel. Simple. Easy.

Jasper shakes his head. "Lies. We all know June thinks I'm a babe."

"Jas . . . ," I warn, eyes hooding.

He sighs dramatically but gives in. "*Fine*, she's right. Sorry, guys, but no sparks. It was a ship effort, though. That's what matters."

Lenny glances between us and giggles. Then he looks down at the computer screen. "There, challenge complete. Next."

Jasper moves over to read the next comment. "It's truth."

He grins. "And this one is for June."

I make an unimpressed face at the camera. "Really, why is it always me?"

After filming, Lenny leaves with the footage to edit, but I hang around as always to do homework and hang out with Jasper. I like to stay away from my house as much as possible. It's small and empty a lot of the time. My dad works the night shift and sleeps most of the day, and my mom works during the day and doesn't get home until my dad is leaving for work. So when I'm home, I have to chill out and be quiet. It's boring, so I stay at Jas's to keep him company until his mom comes home from work.

Jasper's parents are divorced, but he lives exclusively with his mom, who works a thousand and one jobs while going to school for a business degree. That's why we mostly film at his house. It's empty and we can be as loud as we want. I know Jasper wishes his mom was around more, though. I can't really blame him. He's alone a lot, and that's why I tend to stick around.

When Lenny's gone, Jasper disappears into the kitchen and I settle into the overly furnished living room with my backpack and make myself comfortable.

"Dr Pepper or Fanta?" Jasper yells from the kitchen.

"Dr Pepper!" I call back, and pull out my calculus homework. I'm shit at numbers and Jasper's good at them and willing to help me with my math homework in exchange for history refreshers.

A moment later, Jasper enters the room with a bag of chips and two cans of Dr Pepper.

"Hey, did you get problem seven? I don't think Mr. Wright

even taught us how to solve this," I ask him as soon as he sets the snacks beside my feet on the coffee table. My fingers work around one of my strawberry-blond curls as I stare at the problem in frustration.

"I don't know. Let me check." He sits down next to me heavily and digs through his backpack stretched open beside his legs.

I tap my pencil against my lips and frown at my textbook, thinking how this problem is too hard to be on the upcoming test.

"Hey," he says suddenly. "Did we mention next week's question theme, earlier?"

I shrug. "I don't know. Maybe not. We'll just answer random questions next week. No biggie."

The pout in his voice is evident when he says, "It's more fun with a theme."

Dropping my pencil in my textbook, I glance up at him incredulously. "It's a recipe for disaster."

"What?" He pulls a notebook from his backpack and flips it open, not paying me any attention. "Because this time we kissed? So?"

"It doesn't bother you?"

He finally looks up, but slowly, skeptically, his brown eyes zipping across my haggard expression. "No? I thought we were past this. . . ."

"Our viewers won't be," I state bluntly. He lets out a breath and reaches for his soda to sip before answering.

"They know how we felt about it. Remember? No sparks."

"And that was true, right?" I clarify, now moving my schoolwork from my lap to make room for the bag of potato chips. If he lied about that, I don't know how I'm going to handle the situation. My gut says not well.

"Duh," he replies, and takes a large gulp of his soda. "We could kiss again and I'm pretty sure I'd still feel the same way about it—not that you're a bad kisser or anything, well, not that what we did could even be considered a proper kiss. But, yeah."

"It *was* an awkward situation," I add, and shove a couple of chips into my mouth to let the crunching fill the silence. He nods and reaches across me for my textbook to look for the corresponding problem to the answer in his notebook.

After a few moments, he suddenly dumps the books onto the coffee table and grabs the bag of chips from my hands. "Want to make sure?"

Frowning, I roll forward and reach for the chips. "What are you talking about?" I groan when he pulls the bag away from me.

"That there's nothing there—you know, feelings?" Like before, he's uncharacteristically calm about the subject. His eyes remain steady on mine; there's no involuntary charm. It's Jasper being serious.

"I'd rather not find out," I admit, because once upon a time fourteen-year-old me had a crush on Jasper Lahey, and eighteen-year-old me would rather not find out if it still exists. I'm sure it doesn't. We've grown too close for those kinds of feelings to blossom. My reluctance is based on the idea that this could create wiggle room our friendship probably doesn't need.

"You aren't curious?" he asks me.

I laugh a little at the absurdity. "Curious? Jas, bad things happen when friends experiment."

"Not if we do it right." He shrugs and then bumps his leg against mine. "So, what do you say? Want to make sure?" The usual playful twinkle is in his eyes when he says this, and I know I've got no choice but to give in. Now it's like a challenge to prove I'm wrong about experimenting.

I slap my hands on my thighs and turn to him with a pointed look. "All right, fine. Better now than never—because you know that's not the last kissing-on-camera request we're going to get, right?"

"That's why I want to make sure." He nods and then turns himself completely toward me. "Proper kiss."

"This is not normal," I remind him, and he chuckles.

"Have we ever been normal, June?"

I think about this, and well, maybe he's right. The dynamics of our relationship have been irregular since I can remember, and we're thrown into weird situations because of our chosen hobby—which is also not normal. I guess this was bound to happen anyway.

"Guess not," I say.

"All right then." He smiles, and with that leans forward to capture my lips with his own.

This time it's not a little lip touch. It's leaning completely forward, turning heads so noses don't bump, open-mouth kisses but avoiding tongue—because, yeah, that's going too far—and fingers tugging at the back of each other's necks. It's long, longer than anticipated, and I know because soon I don't taste Dr Pepper on his lips anymore. I just taste Jasper.

When we finally pull away, I'm startled to find that I actually don't mind kissing him—it's nice and comfortable. And the best part? I can look him in the eye, fingers trailing down his shirt, and say, "Nothing."

He nods with a cheeky smile and replies, "Me too."

Three

The Dance with No Pants

THE VIDEO CAMERA is mine today, as it always is on Fridays. Out of all three of us, I am the one who has the camera the least. Some might say it's because I film uninteresting things, others because I borderline on having short-term memory loss— meaning I often forget I have the camera and therefore don't end up filming a single thing. The latter is often the culprit. It drives Jasper crazy and might just be the reason that we don't upload anything on Fridays, which isn't a big deal since our weekends are about as exciting as the night shift at a nursing home—minus the demented residents.

A typical Friday night for us usually goes something like this: Lenny hibernates at his house to watch *Desperate House-wives* and ogle Eva Longoria. Meanwhile, I go over to Jasper's house to eat his food and force him to give me a foot massage while we watch endless hours of *Criminal Minds*. This usually results in me spending the night because I'm too paranoid to walk across the street back home at midnight.

So is it even worth filming when I know editing isn't going to get done and our plans are practically set in stone? Nope.

I decide to take the video camera from my backpack and place it on the top shelf of my locker, knowing that I won't film anything today. In mid-replacement of textbooks, the hood of the sweatshirt I'm wearing gets forcefully tugged over my head and smothers my wild curls to my forehead.

"I was wondering where my hoodie went," Jasper's voice teases, and he bumps me out of the way of my own locker to snatch the video camera. "Why do I give you this thing again?"

I pull the hood off my head and attempt to straighten my now fuzzy hair with one hand while the other struggles to hold up my heavy backpack. "Because it's only fair." I poke my tongue out at him and reach for the camera. "Besides, we *never* do anything on Fridays. Unless, of course, you'd like me to film you being thoroughly whipped tonight while you rub my feet." I smirk and swing my backpack over my shoulder, still trying to retrieve the camera from him before I close my locker.

He laughs, dodges my arm, and then sends me a sly smile. "And how do you know that tonight will be boring?" he asks, and wiggles his eyebrows. Laughing, I roll my eyes and slap him on the shoulder when he leans in and makes a noisy kissy face.

Pleased with the scene he's made, he puts the camera back and shuts my locker door for me. Then his eyes glint and he falls against my locker door, leaning into a suggestive pose while attempting a sultry expression.

"You're an idiot," I tell him, and he grins boyishly while placing a hand on his hip.

"Aw, babe," he murmurs with dark, smoldering eyes as he

reaches for one of the tassels hanging from my sweatshirt. "Don't pretend you don't love me."

He's a natural actor, always playing up the drama to make someone laugh. I've become immune to his performances but am entertained, nonetheless. If anything, I've learned to play along.

"You're right," I sigh as I walk away. "I'm truly, madly, deeply in love with you."

Catching up, he throws one of his long arms over my shoulders and tilts his head down to whisper in my ear. "I *knew* it."

"Mhm," I hum, and nudge him off. "Anyway, it's cool if I come over tonight, right?"

"Totally." He nods and returns his arm to rest on my shoulders while we walk. "Mom won't be home until two. No idea how I'm going to occupy myself, otherwise."

My eyes follow the marbled floor, watching as feet zip in and out of my line of sight. "And Lenny's ditching us again?" I ask, even though I obviously already know the answer.

"Eva Longoria is far more intriguing."

"Right," I reason, and shake my head critically. "And *Criminal Minds* is on the agenda?"

He chuckles at this and pulls me to a halt outside his classroom. "It's the only way I can get you to spend the night," he teases with a wink before disappearing inside.

———

Surprisingly, my dad is awake when I drop my school things off at home. The smell of brewing coffee meets me at the door, and I find him leaning against the counter beside the coffeepot when I go to investigate. He's barely awake enough to notice

I've entered the kitchen, because when he finally looks up he seems startled to see me—and he should be. It's not very often I see my dad in anything other than scrubs. But this afternoon he stands before me in an old T-shirt and plaid pajama pants, wild blond hair and five o'clock shadow included.

"Well, you look dashing," I comment while trying not to smile. His eyes follow me to the nearest cupboard, where I pull out a granola bar from the bottom shelf and open it quickly to feed my gurgling stomach.

"Hey, June Bug," he finally says, flinching when the coffee timer goes off. "I had a long night at work."

"Crazy people come to the ER?" I ask, mostly used to the hilarious and sometimes disturbing stories about the people who visit the emergency room late at night. Some people go to the ER for shits and giggles and waste everyone's time, but others come in so messed up they stress my dad out and he can't sleep.

"Always," he laughs softly, and then his face goes grim. "We had a burn victim last night. Burns so bad her skin was charcoal black and flaking off. I can't get her out of my head."

My face distorts and my stomach suddenly wants to deny my granola bar's entry. Some of these stories make my skin crawl. And the worst part is sometimes when we have dinner together as a family, he'll tell us all his ER adventures and completely destroy my appetite, like now.

"What happened to her?"

"Her and a couple of friends thought it would be a smart idea to play with gasoline and lighters in a game of chicken." He looks up from his freshly poured coffee and frowns. "It makes me worry about you, Lenny, and Jas."

I snort. "We're dumb, but not *that* dumb."

"I know," he sighs. "I know we've talked about peer pressure and all of that, but I still worry. People can get hurt if you take games too far."

"We don't play games like that," I remind him gently, and cross my legs under the kitchen table. "We vlog. It's like a video diary. The last dumb thing any of us did for laughs was nothing in comparison. Lenny ate a toxic-looking concoction of peaches, mayo, Jell-O, and pickles."

Dad sips his coffee carefully, eyes tearing up when he burns his lips. "Just be careful?"

"Of course," I say, grinning. He nods and brings his coffee to the table. I watch him pull out the chair beside mine and sit down. "Hey," I ask, and he glances at me, tipping his mug for me to continue. "It's cool if I hang out with Jas tonight, right?"

"Are you spending the night, again?"

"Most likely."

He's silent for a while, lips pursing behind his coffee cup as he stares straight ahead. My eyebrows furrow questioningly, unfamiliar with his hesitation at the request. "You guys aren't having sex, are you?" he asks suddenly, gray eyes sliding over to meet mine narrowly.

I sputter, taken aback at his suggestion and blushing at the idea. Jasper and me? The boy's awkward and lanky, too tall for his own good, with a haircut that never seems to look right. He wears weird graphic T-shirts, openly burps and farts around me, and says and does things without thinking about how stupid he looks—and my dad is implying that I'd have sex with him? I couldn't even *kiss* him yesterday without feeling all sorts of uncomfortable until it was over and I realized it really wasn't that bad. But the point is, the idea of having sex with Jasper is enough for me to scrunch up my nose and squawk, "Jasper? Are you kidding me? *Gross*, Dad!"

After seeing the absolute alarm on my face and hearing my protests, my dad almost chokes on his coffee with laughter. "He's a good-looking guy! I had to make sure," he defends himself with a glimmer of humor twinkling in his eyes. "I wasn't expecting you to be so disgusted."

It's not that Jasper is unattractive; in fact, he's long past the middle-school phase of long skater hair and Pokémon T-shirts. Now his dark hair is well groomed and his face only soiled with blemishes every once in a very great while. To anyone he's considered good-looking, but I've seen him in his darkest hours. I've seen *more* than just his exterior, but his dorky interior as well. I love the guy to death, hell, he's my best friend, but I could never see us being romantically involved. Not now, anyway. Maybe when we were fourteen and I had a little freshman crush on the charming class clown who wanted me to be in on his vlogging project, sure. But not anymore. You learn a lot about a person when you spend time with them. We've grown so comfortable with each other that any romantic feelings would get swallowed up in awkwardness and giggles.

"We're just friends," I insist, and tuck a curl behind my ear. "So it's okay if I go over there, right?"

"Sure." He smiles and turns his eyes down to watch his thumb slide over the rim of his cup. "But, you know. I would be fine with you guys . . . you know . . ."

"Dad!" I shriek, and bury my face in my arms.

"What? I like him. I'd want to have a chat with him first, but I'd be totally okay with—"

"Stop!" I wail, and flip the hood of Jasper's sweatshirt over my head, tightening the tassels to hide my burning cheeks. "You're embarrassing me," I mumble, and hear him roar with laughter, clearly forgetting about his burn patient from last night.

After a few moments of his laughter filling the room and my blush spreading from cheeks to neck, Dad finally slaps me on the back and stands up. "Have fun tonight," he jokes.

I let myself in at Jasper's house and hear the TV's volume turned up well past what could be considered comfortable. Still shivering from the cold autumn air, I remove my boots at the door and pull my hands up inside the sleeves of Jasper's hoodie to warm them up. The hallway light is the only one I see on as I walk down the cutely decorated hallway displaying most of the Lahey family photos.

From the living room entry, I see that I've missed the first five minutes of *Criminal Minds* and that Jasper doesn't even seem to notice, since he's thoroughly engrossed in the show, with his legs taking up most of the couch and eyes reflecting the screen. I quietly walk toward him, feet sinking into the carpeted floor, and tap his feet with my sleeve-covered hands. He moves his legs without even glancing at me and lets me slide right up next to him.

"It's the episode with the creepy cabdriver who kidnaps women because of their scent," he tells me.

"Oh," I say, beaming, "I love this one."

"I know," he says distractedly, and holds out his hands. I pull my icy hands from my sleeves and put them in his warm ones.

His fingers wrap around mine, slowly thawing them out like he always does. "It's cold outside," he comments, and I nod.

"Yeah, well, I stopped over at Lenny's to give him the camera," I tell him.

"You didn't film anything."

"It's his turn," I remind him, and he brings my hands to his lips to breathe on them. He shrugs, eyes still glued to the screen. After a couple of minutes of silent watching, the show turns to commercial and Jasper lets go of my hands and gets up.

Weaving around the low coffee table and stack of newspapers, Jasper mutters, "Be back," and takes off to the kitchen to get snacks. The screen flashes an Allstate commercial, and I bring my feet up to sit cross-legged—a great position for holding a bowl of popcorn—and look around the familiar and cramped living space. Leeann, Jasper's mom, tries to fit everything in here, and the room is simply too small. There's a single couch and a coffee table, an older television set on a short bookshelf, a desk in the corner, her treadmill flat up against the wall. It's a bit snug, and oftentimes one of us will trip over something—like Jasper does when he comes back with a bag of microwave popcorn and two cans of soda.

"Goddammit, Ma," he curses under his breath when he stubs his toe on her weight set beside the coffee table. "Here," he grumbles, and hands me the popcorn and a soda.

Ignoring his grumpiness, I go right in to telling him about this afternoon. "Guess what?" I challenge.

"You're going to give me my sweatshirt back?" he asks, and pulls on the tassels when he's seated himself. I look down at the hoodie I was not actually planning on giving back. I had crashed here on a school night a couple of weeks ago and got toothpaste on the shirt I was originally planning on wearing that next morning. So Jasper tossed me his red Blackhawks hoodie to wear over the mess I'd made on myself. Truthfully, it's one of the most comfortable things I "own," and I don't want to give it back.

"No," I say quickly, and bat his hand away since it was hovering dangerously close to my chest. He slaps me back and then takes his soda and pops it open. "My dad thinks we do the dance with no pants when I'm over here."

Jasper's mouth is full when I say this, and he about spits out his Dr Pepper. Instead he clamps his hand over his mouth and chokes it down, coming up soon after coughing and laughing.

"Did you tell him we do?" he asks with a suggestive look— always the troublemaker.

Despite the grin tugging on my lips, I punch him in the arm. "No!"

He continues to smile but rubs his arm and prepares himself to shoot away when he says, "Should've."

"And why is that?" I ask skeptically, ignoring the fact that our show has come back on.

"It's hilarious that everyone thinks we're together."

"Yeah," I mutter, and stick my hand in the popcorn bag while returning my attention back to the screen. "Except we're not," I say, and lie back onto his shoulder.

Four

Truly, Madly, Deeply

"HEY, GUYS. SO, it's like six o'clock right now and we're supposed to be writing this long, overly thorough paper for English, and this is what we've decided to do instead." I turn the camera to the television screen. We're at Lenny's house, which only happens when he adds to his video-game collection.

Today's culprit just so happens to be the original Legend of Zelda: Ocarina of Time game that Lenny picked up from the game store on our way home from school last Friday. Our reasoning for playing the game at Lenny's is simple. He has every gaming system invented in his lifetime—the Nintendo 64 console being one of his favorites. Also, there's more space in his house to get excited and jump around after defeating bosses.

We all take turns passing the controller around and having our share of playtime, but Lenny mostly hogs it—which is why Jasper and I have been sitting around watching and cheering him on for the past hour.

His parents are used to our antics by now and have busied

themselves in the kitchen with dinner, but his twin sisters, Jade and Ruby, keep making themselves present. Both, despite the number of times we've been over, like sitting before the TV asking questions and getting their wispy blond heads in the way. They like to consider themselves our groupies, and it irritates Lenny to no end.

With my feet propped up on the curve of the L-shaped couch, I've made myself more than comfortable in the spacious and well-decorated living room. Now that I've pointed the camera at the two boys, our audience can take in all the mayhem. Both boys are hunched over and wide-eyed at the screen. Lenny hits buttons frantically on his controller, and Jasper hoots and hollers over and over, "Die, die, die!"

I swivel the camera back around and state quite seriously, "Seems like a better use of our time."

"This version's graphics suck," Jasper notes, seeing that I've turned the camera on. "But nothing beats the original version of Zelda: Ocarina of Time!"

He whoops victoriously, and I shake my head at the camera. "Boys, boys, boys. Single ladies, you aren't missin' much."

"I guess we're vlogging here!" Lenny chimes in, the strain in his voice evident, and he physically jumps out of his seat when Link gets attacked by a temple boss I can't remember the name of. I make a mental note to make a *How to Understand Boys* video on Friday when it's my turn to have the camera—because let's face it, most of our viewers are girls, and this is probably a really low moment for Jasper and Lenny.

"What is that thing?" Ruby asks from her spot in front of the television, her eyes wide in horror at the hideousness of the creature attacking Link.

"It's the monster that lives under your bed," Lenny replies absently, smiling when she shrieks and clutches Jade's arm.

"Don't tell her that!" I scold, and turn the camera off, setting it on the ottoman. Jade shoots up and runs for the kitchen, where the smell of pasta wafts out. Ruby follows her shortly afterward when she realizes that Jade isn't coming back.

"Why?" Lenny counters. "It got them to go away."

I sigh defeatedly, knowing that Lenny's not going to be sorry about sending them away. This is why his babysitting excuses are never believable. Lenny and the twins do not get along well.

After another half hour of Lenny hogging the controller, his parents announce dinner. That gives Jasper and me an excuse to go home. While it's fun for a while, Lenny completely forgets that Jasper and I exist. That's when it's a good time to leave.

It's twice as cold tonight as it was this morning, so Jasper and I run across the frostbitten lawn to stop at his house. He informed me that I'd left my sweatpants there from Friday, so I told him I'd pick them up.

He fumbles with his keys for a minute in front of the house, but then the door is open and we're inside and we're both complaining about windburned ears and red cheeks. He takes my hands right away once the door is closed and breathes on them, rubbing them together to get both of our hands warm again.

"I hate this weather," I groan, sniffling because even a couple of minutes out in the cold has made my nose run.

Jasper nods along but then stops and gives me a mischievous grin. "I don't."

"Uh-huh, and what's there to like?" I retort.

One side of his smile lifts higher than the other, and he

gives my hands one final squeeze before dropping a kiss onto my knuckles and walking away with a wink. My mouth drops open, and I follow his triumphant strut down the hall with my eyes, letting them narrow when he turns to see if I'm coming.

"You know," I say offhandedly while kicking off my boots, "sometimes I swear you're in love with me."

He stands at the end of the hallway and puts a hand on the staircase banister, watching me with a smirk as I come down the hall to join him. "Truly, madly, deeply." He winks again and motions for me to go up the stairs before him. I curtsy and oblige, taking two steps at a time until I'm at the top.

"Truly, madly, deeply," I repeat, and keep eye contact as I walk backward into his bedroom while he tries to force down a large smile.

Lenny's backpack sits heavily against my knee Monday morning while I sit in the backseat of Jasper's car. My feet are propped up on the shared armrest between Jasper and Lenny to avoid the garbage-littered floor of the tiny blue Saturn. I stare out the window, listening to the punk rock songs from one of the boys' CDs and watching my breath pour out of my mouth like smoke while I shiver in the poorly heated vehicle. Like always, we're all groggy and unfit for conversation. Jasper occasionally lifts his hands from the steering wheel at an intersection and moans about how cold his car is. Lenny has his laptop in his lap and is browsing through the comments of our questions video and previous vlog. I have half a mind to pull the video camera from Jasper's backpack and film our drive to school in order to lighten everyone up.

There's suddenly chuckling from the passenger seat, and Lenny flicks my boot to get my attention. "You're not going to like this," he muses while turning in his seat to look at me. "Some of our viewers don't think you and Jas had a big enough kiss."

"Oh, trust me," Jasper snickers. "We did."

My face flushes, and I instinctively kick his seat with more force than necessary. Neither of us bothered to tell Lenny about our kiss Thursday night after he'd left. And, to be fair, he really doesn't have to know. It was a pact between Jasper and me: Be sure no feelings exist before continuing on as friends. Lenny has nothing to do with it, and there is no reason to involve him.

Lenny looks between us confusedly, his lips twitching between excitement and question, but seems to decide it's better not to ask and ignores my exchange with Jasper. "Uh-huh," he says quickly, and carries on. "So I'd be prepared for more camera kisses, if I were you."

I open my mouth to say that we'll be keeping any kind of on-screen kisses to a minimum, but Jasper is quick to reply with, "We're cool with that. It's just kissing, right, June?" His eyes glance at me through the rearview mirror, and I send him a glare.

"I don't think that's the best idea, Jas. . . ."

"But I thought we cleared this up the other night? I thought that's what the experiment was for." Jasper's eyebrows quirk in the mirror, and his low voice turns accusatory.

"Whoa, what experiment?" Lenny asks curiously, eyes darting from Jasper to me in confusion.

"A kissing one, of course," Jasper tells him, and Lenny's eyes grow wide.

"You guys kissed outside of filming?"

"Not romantically," I add in among the chaos, especially since Jasper's way of explaining things is always messy. "Experimentally."

"But why?" Lenny's curiosity has turned to alarm, as if the idea of Jasper and me being in a real relationship is not a good one.

"To sort out feelings—my goodness, Grasshopper," Jasper gasps exasperatedly and turns his attention to Lenny. "Keep up."

"Look, guys, I thought we were friends. Friends don't keep kissing secrets to themselves," Lenny scolds, slamming his laptop shut with an air of finality. "Relationship statuses would be a good thing to know."

"There is *nothing* going on between us," I say, and motion between Jasper and me. "We just wanted to make sure that kissing wouldn't ruin our friendship. We were making sure there were no 'sparks.'"

"But you said yourself that there were no sparks on camera," Lenny says skeptically, eyebrows rising higher than I thought they could ever go up his forehead.

"Wasn't a proper kiss," Jasper sighs, and rolls his eyes as if it were obvious. We now pull into the school parking lot, and Lenny seems to notice because all he does is sigh heavily and shake his head.

After we've parked, though, he finishes. "I'd just like to be updated every once in a while. You guys spend a lot more time together than with me."

Jasper puts a hand on Lenny's shoulder. "That's what the vlogs are for, my man. But I promise to tell you everything."

I groan over Lenny's "Awesome" and kick Jasper's seat again. He just meets my eyes with a cheeky grin and pulls his backpack out from behind his seat.

———————

Allison leans against the locker beside mine, gawking at me with crossed arms and narrowed eyes. "You did *what*?"

I stop shoving books in my bag and put a hand on my hip. "You said you wouldn't freak out," I remind her.

She closes her mouth and shifts. "I'm not freaking out," she says in a less demanding tone, but her hard clench on her textbooks gives her away. "You're the one who should be freaking out. You *kissed* Jasper."

"It wasn't anything serious," I say, and slam my locker door shut. "It was just . . . an experiment."

"June, you had the world's biggest crush on him freshman year."

"So?" I ask. "It's not like that now."

She shakes her head. "Yeah, you'd like to think so, but what happens if those feelings come back—I mean, you've *kissed* him! If those feelings come back and he dates someone else instead, what are you going to do? Date Milo again? I don't think so."

Everyone has a relationship they wish never happened. Milo O'Hara is mine.

Milo wasn't just part of my rebellious phase. He was my rebound after Jasper broke my heart for the first time. I had a desperate crush on him, and I thought he liked me, too, and then out of nowhere he was holding hands with some girl named Bree. I latched onto the first boy who told me Jasper was stupid.

But Milo wasn't good news. He was the boy I hid from my dad until he found a hickey three and a half months into the relationship. He was the boy who got me in trouble. The kind of trouble that lands you in a situation where you have to call your mom at two thirty in the morning asking for a ride home because kids are smoking pot in the basement and getting busy in empty bedrooms while your boyfriend is nowhere to be found.

I was vulnerable and easily pressured into things. Everyone told me to break it off, but I didn't know how. He had a way of changing my mind and manipulating my naïveté. I became someone else to please him, and I liked the attention I received in return. But things got too real as our relationship progressed. When he tried pressuring me into giving everything away, we broke up.

It was Allison's shoulder that I cried on. She had it all figured out before I did. She's intuitive like that. Anyway, there's no way she'd let that happen again. I learned my lesson. Jasper and I are never going to happen, so there's no reason to make a fuss over it.

"Allison, I know better now. Trust me a little, would you?"

She frowns. "I just don't want you to get hurt again."

"Oh, c'mon, it was one time." I shrug and lead the way down the hall. "I'm not letting it happen again."

She just sighs deeply beside me.

"What trend is more disturbing: twerking or 'The Knife Game Song'?" Jasper reads off the question from the comments and then very seriously looks at the camera and replies, "Clearly it's twerking." His eyes seem to glance between Lenny and me for a second, and then he leans into the camera very closely and whispers, "But I only say this because there's a lady in the room."

"You still answered wrong," I tell him with a smack to the arm. "The question should have been, what's more disturbing: thirteen-year-olds shaking their asses or thirteen-year-olds chopping off their fingers?"

Lenny makes a face that suggests he doesn't know whether to laugh or cringe at this, and Jasper's whole face just scrunches up. "Both visuals are pretty bad."

"Clearly chopped-off fingers is worse," I say.

"I don't know." Lenny shakes his head. "I'd rather the twins chop off their fingers than jiggle their butts in front of a camera."

"Are you kidding me?"

"Yeah, now that you put it that way," Jasper ponders aloud, and both boys share matching looks of disgust. I think I can see the Big Brother vibe radiating faintly from Lenny.

"Oh, all right. Next question," I say, and nudge Jasper in the ribs with my elbow.

"Fine then." Jasper shrugs. "This one is for you, anyway."

I turn the computer toward me. Thursdays are always the days where I question the mental stability of most of our viewers, because of the mind-boggling questions they ask us. I'm sure the questions are just for kicks, but sometimes they make me seriously wonder. Despite this, I readjust my position on Jasper's bed and read the next question aloud.

"How do you tell a guy that you're not interested in being more than friends?" After reading it, my brows furrow and I stare blankly at the question for a moment before looking up at the camera.

It's a fairly normal question, but it still causes both boys to snicker. It's hard for me to get my thoughts straight before I answer. I've never had something like this happen before, and I don't want to give this person unhelpful advice.

"Um . . ." I smile a little and brush hair behind my ears. I go for the route I would take in this situation. "I think you just have to be up front about it. Making someone think they have a chance is only going to end up hurting feelings in the end. Stop it before things even get started."

"Cold," Jasper comments. "Not even going to give the poor guy a chance?"

"You can't force feelings," I reply with a shrug.

"Huh," Jasper breathes, and purses his lips at me. "You're kind of a heartbreaker."

"Yeah, okay," I say with a laugh. Lenny snorts and glances between us.

"Next question," Jasper commands, and spins the sticker-covered laptop to Lenny.

Lenny clears his throat and tilts the screen up. "How big is your pe—whoa—uh . . . Wouldn't you like to know?" His cheeks flush pink, and he turns the screen away from himself. His attempt at trying to be smooth has Jasper snickering. I myself have to bite my lip to stop giggles from erupting at the inappropriate question.

"Right," Jasper laughs, and glances at Lenny, who punches him in the arm. The laptop almost slips from Jasper's lap, and I take it away just in case things get heated.

I set the computer on my lap and scroll to the next

comment. My stomach flutters and my teeth clamp down on the inside of my cheeks when I read it. I know Jasper won't have a problem with this, and I shouldn't, either, so I force the nervous flurries away and read the question as confidently as I can.

"Ten-second Jasiper kiss."

And, just like that, Lenny's cheeks lose their flush of embarrassment and a winning smile overcomes his features. I know why, too. As soon as the kiss happens, nobody will remember how awkward he was about his question.

"Oh, time specifications." Lenny beams wickedly and slaps Jasper's shoulder lightly.

"No problem," Jasper replies positively, and scoops the laptop from my lap and places it in Lenny's. "You can count back from ten, if you like," he tells Lenny.

"Fine."

Jasper turns to me and I let a deep breath out my nose.

It's no big deal. It's just a kiss. We've kissed twice before. There's nothing to worry about. I remind myself of these things over and over when Jasper's hand comes behind my neck and brings my face to his. When I feel his lips on mine, I remind myself again that there are no feelings to worry about—maybe to smile and enjoy it. Lenny's at seven and Jas moves his head, bumping my nose and making me want to laugh. It's awkward again, but the tension isn't as high. We just sit there with our lips attached for the whole ten seconds and I, regrettably, think that maybe our viewer could have been a bit more creative with their kissing request.

When the kiss is finally up, Jasper pulls away slowly for dramatic effect and collapses onto Lenny as if swooning. I raise an eyebrow at him and hold down a smirk.

"You guys might as well have a specific segment where you lock lips." Lenny rolls his eyes and slaps at Jasper's cheeks. "Call it Kiss Cam or something."

Five

Maybe We've Had Better Ideas

IT'S NOT UNTIL Friday afternoon that the idea of a "kiss cam" is taken seriously. I promptly dismissed the idea upon its initial suggestion, knowing that things could get out of hand if left up for discussion. The case was closed after that—or so I thought.

Things are starting to go haywire at our chosen lunch table. Lenny brings up the comments from our last vlog and begins coming up with an argument as to why we should do it. Jasper leans over the table to see the evidence himself and quickly tries to rope me into the idea.

"Juniper, it's the absolute worst idea," Allison remarks when it looks as though I'm going to give in.

I know it's a bad idea—a funny and unpredictable idea, but a bad one, nonetheless. I know what she's worried about, but there is no way anything between Jasper and me could develop now. We're *just friends* for a reason. Why ruin a good thing with complications? I figured that out freshman year when he started dating Bree. I decided then and there not to let him get to my head. Everything with him was just friendly, and feelings were never allowed. No complications meant no feelings could get hurt.

And kissing without the complication of feelings? What could be so bad about that?

I had previously thought I would never give my kisses away so easily, but after sifting through the comments, I have to admit our viewers' reactions are worth it. There's something thrilling about having people so invested in you. It's like being persuaded onto a roller coaster you'd never dare to ride otherwise and ending up drowning in your own giggles as you swoop down a near-ninety-degree drop.

Plus, it's fun reading about the excitement people get from a segment where their ship is smashed together by the lips. I'm a crowd-pleaser, to say the least, and it's not even like Jasper and I are doing anything *bad*. Our viewers know that there's nothing actually going on between us—they only *wish* there was. We're being teases, and that's what makes it exciting.

But Allison dropping her two cents into the piggy bank of opinions makes a good dose of reality shoot back into my system, and my excitement deflates like a balloon. She's seen things go terribly wrong between Jasper and me before. Maybe she's right and I can't justify the idea the way I thought I could.

Sighing, I lean away from the computer screen. "She's right. This *is* ridiculous."

"We *all* know kissing between friends never goes well," Allison tacks on.

"We're *not* normal friends," Jasper reminds her. "We live on the Internet, and this kind of thing happens on the Internet all the time."

Allison motions at Jasper accusingly. "Can't you see? He's glamorizing everything in order to get you to play along with his silly game—which, by the way, can only lead to trouble."

Jasper's fingers have been tapping on the table since she started talking, but now he just turns on her with narrowed eyes. "Why are you making me out to be some kind of bad guy? I didn't *do* anything."

"But you *will*," she snaps.

Silence settles over the table. Even Lenny's rapid typing and clicking comes to an abrupt stop while Allison and Jasper stare fiercely across the table. I'm at a loss, not even sure what's happening here. Like I said, Allison and Jasper don't get along well. There's always this tense wall between them. I always thought it was because he pushed her limits with the video camera. Now I know it's because she's bitter about him being reckless with my feelings in the past, and although I'm grateful for her loyalty, I know it's time to prove that Jasper and I are beyond that—because he didn't even know he was responsible in the first place.

"Um, guys," I say hesitantly to break the silence. "You can put your claws away. I honestly think that maybe the 'kiss cam' is taking things a bit far, but I don't see any harm in doing it as long as when I say *that's enough* it stops, because I can easily seeing this going too far."

Jasper's eyes lower from Allison's startled ones, and he swallows. "You want to make Kiss Cam a thing?" he asks me.

I glance at Lenny's laptop and think about all the views and the excited comments. "I guess so." Then I look between Lenny and Jasper and feel the tension still radiating from Allison and decide to lighten the mood. "But only if *you two* contribute a little something as well—don't pretend you didn't see the Jasper and Lenny ship sitting on the edge of their seats in anticipation for some of that action as well."

Lenny's eyes widen, and he leans away from Jasper, who grins hugely and wiggles his eyebrows at him. "*No*," Lenny squawks.

"Oh, come on, Leonard. Give me some sugar." Jasper leans in with a coy smile and flirty wink, and Lenny falls out of his seat and scowls. Allison snorts beside me and shakes her head.

"You *know* that's *not my name*. Stop being *weird*." He dodges Jasper's reach, and Jasper leans back, face red with laughter. Lenny's face turns pink and he slams his laptop shut.

"*Fangirls*," he curses, and stalks off.

"Fangirls, indeed," I repeat through a giggle.

Jasper turns back to me, still half chuckling, and runs a hand through his chaotic hair. "But actually. You want to do it—Kiss Cam?"

"Pull that on camera, and it's a deal," I barter with a sly smile.

Jasper looks over his shoulder at a flustered Lenny hovering semi-close to the table until he knows it's all right to come back. "For that reaction? Let's do it."

Nodding, I say, "Let the shipping begin."

Allison sighs heavily beside me but doesn't say anything. When Lenny rejoins the group and I tell him my decision, we spend the rest of the lunch period joking about ships and discuss making an announcement video after school. Allison, though, sits silently beside me, playing with her food in a disapproving sulk.

———

I'm still confused about the whole ordeal between Jasper and Allison even after lunch period is over. So later in history during a partner discussion of a Vietnam War document, I seize the chance to ask Allison what all the fuss was about during lunch—besides the obvious.

Without trying to sound desperate for an answer, I go ahead and ask, "What happened with you and Jasper before?" Allison's sharp jaw becomes sharper when her mouth snaps shut and clenches as though I've brought up something frustrating. "Jasper Lahey is a coward—but you didn't hear that from me," she replies, and then purses her lips and straightens the document on her desk like she's going to ignore me now and go back to her points.

"Jas is the least cowardly person I know," I state smoothly, and it's true. Despite what other people might think of our vlog, he walks around with his camera and films things anyway. He doesn't embarrass easily, or at all for that matter, and owns up to all his problems. It's out of spite that she calls him a coward.

"I wouldn't be so sure," she retorts, and clears her throat to continue with the Vietnam discussion before time runs out. I watch her carefully after that. What I thought was anger seems to be exasperation, but exasperation about *what* I intend to find out.

———

Jasper is reading in bed when I arrive back at his house later that night after the Kiss Cam announcement video. I wanted to stop back home and see my parents before they left for work or went to sleep but ended up alone again within the hour.

It's a short walk across the street, and my hands aren't too cold, but the moment I sit down beside him he drops his book onto his chest and holds out his hands. After setting down my laptop, I give him my hands to warm up. He holds mine in his and uses his palms to press against my fingers.

"You *really* sure about Kiss Cam?" he asks after a moment. He's slouched farther down than me against his headboard, and his messy dark hair falls into his eyes when he looks up.

"Yep," I reply, but he sits up quickly and drops my hands. His book tumbles off his chest and falls into his lap to reveal the graphics on his Superman T-shirt.

"I didn't mean to pressure you into the idea or anything, earlier," he tells me hastily, and his eyes scan my face. "It's just that it's never been a big deal to me—kissing—unless there are emotions there. You can really feel those, you know? I just thought we wouldn't have to worry about anything unless one of us started to feel something for the other person. Then we could decide what to do from there."

"Jasper," I cut in, and set a hand on his shoulder. "It's cool. I totally agree with you. It's not a big deal. I mean, it's you after all. I trust you more than anyone."

He laughs at this and nudges me. "Good."

"And speaking of trust," I say, and he stops reaching for his book and glances up. My mind goes back to this afternoon with the episode between Allison and Jasper. It seemed like she knows something about him that I don't. He wouldn't lie to me now. He couldn't. I've just decided to do this Kiss Cam with him. I told him I trust him. Besides, since when does Allison rank higher than me?

"We're best friends," I clarify, and he nods, his eyes twinkling with humor. "You tell me everything?" His brows furrow in confusion, but he nods nonetheless. *"Everything?"*

"What's this about?" he asks, his voice sounding concerned and his eyes narrowing.

I feel guilty for questioning him with little evidence, and my hands become restless in my lap. "It's just," I start, and then pause to sigh and shrug. "You and Allison today."

He stops me there by putting one of his large hands over my mouth. "She assumes too many things."

I pry his fingers off my cheeks and hold his hand in mine. "What does she assume, exactly?"

"*Things*," he says again more fiercely, and then opens his book and leans back against his headboard without explaining himself.

I know it's pointless to argue and pressure Jasper to explain what he means by "things," so I just sigh and open my laptop to answer comments on VlogIt.

In the lull it takes for my computer to warm up, I glance over at Jasper. Just as my eyes slide over, I barely miss seeing his flutter back down to his page as though he was already staring back.

It's a normal thing for me to look up and see that he's been watching me, but it's not so normal that he quickly averts his eyes to make it seem like he wasn't. Maybe I'd made him uncomfortable by mentioning his dispute with Allison. He could have been glaring for all I know.

Six

Virgin Panties and Lacy Bras

IT'S WHEN MY arm flings across Jasper's mattress and hits him that I realize I've once again fallen asleep at his house. Jasper groans sleepily and rolls away from me, taking the blanket with him and leaving me cold and in a state of partial awareness. My eyes flutter open after a moment or two of gradual waking, and I turn my head to see him cocooned in his giant orange comforter with nothing but a mop of dark hair sticking out the top. I breathe out a slight chuckle and sit up.

The room is still cloaked in darkness, with only a thin glow of sunlight peeking through his heavy curtains. My laptop is still open beside me, screen black and inactive. I notice my sweatpants have rolled up my legs during sleep, and I quickly kick them down while sliding my computer onto my lap.

Lenny uploaded the Kiss Cam announcement onto VlogIt last night, and I'm eager to see the response. My computer hums when my fingers tap across the touchpad and then plays out a little tune while my desktop flashes onto the screen, a picture of Lenny, Jasper, and me at a meet-up with some of our viewers as my background. Jasper sighs beside me and brings his blanket up to cover his fuzzy head. I shake my head and bring up VlogIt to check on the video.

It's late into the morning, about eleven o'clock, and according to VlogIt Lenny had uploaded the video at around two in the morning. Already there are thousands of views and a couple hundred comments.

sammyforever12: Will there be separate videos or will they appear in your daily videos?

I read the comment and purse my lips. Lenny, Jasper, and I had briefly discussed this but hadn't made concrete plans. I have to skip answering the comment until I know for sure. However, I'm sure that the segments will be called Kiss Cam and that they will appear randomly in our daily videos. I have to clear some things with the boys first. So I continue to scroll.

_noonecares: Forget Jasper, guys. Leniper needs a turn! Like for a Lenny and June kiss!

I shake my head vigorously in response. Kissing one of them is enough—and Lenny would *never* allow that to happen. His crush on Eva Longoria prevents him from becoming anyone else's. Every time someone brings up Leniper, Lenny makes a point of telling me: "June, I love you. But no way." I continue to scroll.

green_fizzle_pop: Don't mind me, just leaving this kissing request here. I say you two should fight and end with a superhot kiss. Have you read the fanfics lately? They clearly need some guidance. . . .

My eyes grow wide and I choke down an explosive laugh. Is this person suggesting we inspire some fanfiction? Is this what the Kiss Cam has already come to? My face is warm with a blush, and I bite down hard on my lip to stop the goofy smile from spreading across my cheeks.

Acting out something like that for a fanfiction writer to create a story around is both embarrassing and intriguing. It's almost shameful that I'd want to read whatever they'd come up with. My curiosity is starting to become dangerous. I resort to replying to her.

WereVloggingHere: Alas, a creative request—but for the purpose of better fanfiction? Ah, I should've known this would happen! Is it terrible that I'd like to read whatever the writer comes up with? The result of Kiss Cam shall be very interesting, indeed.—June

I hit enter and the comment pops up beneath the girl's. It's only seconds later that she excitedly replies:

green_fizzle_pop: Ohmygosh, you actually replied to my comment!!! After two years of following you guys, it finally pays off! And YES. You'd be the coolest people EVER. There's not a lot of fanfiction surrounding you guys, and those who do write it need a little boost. I

want you guys together SO much, even if it's only in
fanfiction—GOOD fanfiction. LOVE YOU GUYS.

I giggle at her comment, unable to believe what I'm reading. I'd
never read Jasiper fanfiction before. In fact, I didn't even know
that people actually wrote it. I just knew that people who shipped
us screen-capped moments where Jasper and I looked at each
other or touched each other. Now I know we actually have
fanfiction.

Would it be terrible if we actually encouraged love stories
about us? It's harmless. I'd read fanfiction about other people,
because, what can I say, I'm an Internet junkie. I know people
have the potential to create very risqué stories about us like they
do about others, but it's not like we have to read them. If they
want to believe something, they can go right ahead. We like
keeping our viewers happy, and there's no point trying to stop
the inevitable.

Even though this person makes me laugh and gives me
things to think about, I can't bring myself to reply to her again
and instead continue to scroll through the messages.

I must be laughing too much or typing too loudly, because
shortly after the fanfiction comment, Jasper kicks off his blanket
and sits up in bed. Turning my head, I see him give me an
annoyed look. But it's hard to feel bad when his hair is sticking
up on one side and pressed snugly to his head on the other.
There's also the fact that his shirt is askew and his eyes are tired
with sleep, making him look rather pathetic.

"Why're you so *loud* in the morning?" he whines, and flings
himself facedown beside me, burying his nose deep into the
mattress. His voice is muffled when he adds, "Jus' wanna shleep."

"It's nearly afternoon," I tell him unsympathetically, and pat the top of his head. "You were going to sleep the day away."

He turns his head and looks up at me through his eyelashes. "That was the idea, June."

"Terrible idea," I tell him flatly, and turn back to my computer.

"What're you doing, anyway?" he asks while my fingers tap quickly across my keyboard.

"I'm on VlogIt."

He sits up and crawls behind me to look at the screen. His breath is at my neck, blowing a curl across my ear, and I think about moving out of his way until his chin comes to rest on my shoulder.

He hums after reading a few comments and then rolls out of bed. "I think we have a sailing ship, what d'you think?" There's humor in his voice, as if he's almost proud of it.

I watch him stride across his room, yanking open dresser drawers and pulling things from his closet. "I'm going to shower. Be back in ten."

He leaves after that and I sit on his mattress, staring after him. There are moments in a friendship when you realize the other person has stopped caring about leaving you alone to entertain yourself. He used to be worried about doing that. He also used to wake up the moment he knew that I was awake, but that rarely happens anymore. Also, he doesn't make me breakfast like he did in the good ole days. Lenny jokes about us turning into an "old married couple." There's probably a lot of truth to that statement.

I hear the water turn on in the bathroom and decide to go get breakfast while he's away. The whole house is dimly lit, so I flick curtains open on my way to the kitchen. The kitchen is a bit dirty and cramped. Dishes are piled up in the sink, the countertop has patches of scattered crumbs covering its surface. When I see this, I decide that cereal isn't a good idea and open a cupboard in search of Pop-Tarts. I have to dig a little, but find a box in the back of the cupboard. Jasper's not a fan of them, but it's a quick option for me when I'm over. Usually, I bring some over and they get tucked away.

I tear at the shiny packaging, making quite a bit of noise on my way back up the stairs. I stop trying to open it, though, when I pass Leeann's room. This time I notice her door is closed, whereas it's usually left wide open. I figure she's home after a long night and try to be as quiet as possible on my way back to Jasper's room.

Back inside his room, I rip the packaging off and stuff half the pastry in my mouth while bouncing back onto his bed. Shortly after, Jasper comes into the room dripping and shirtless.

"You know," I say around a mouthful of Pop-Tart, my eyes dropping down to his bare chest. "I think people are right about us."

"How'd you mean?" he asks, and throws his T-shirt over his shoulder with one hand while the other roughs up his damp hair with a towel.

I raise an eyebrow and let my eyes flick between his face and his naked chest multiple times. Even his girlfriends are never with him long enough to view him half-naked. It's not that bare chests are unusual on guys, it's just unusual on Jasper. He's scrawny, so he feels insecure about being shirtless in public. But he'll walk around me when he's shirtless after a shower. When we were younger, I used to feel special about being close enough friends with him that he'd trust me even though he was uncomfortable about it.

"Oh," he says with a smile. "Really? June, I've seen you in your underwear about a hundred times, but this is what you use as evidence? Reevaluate that, because I think most of those rumors online are due to *you*." He laughs and pokes out his tongue.

"You've never seen me in my underwear," I tell him matter-of-factly. "We have the No Peeking Rule."

"Right, because I totally follow that." He winks.

My mouth drops open, and I set the pastry I'm eating onto his bed. "You do *too*," I insist.

He shifts his weight onto one hip and tosses the towel into his hamper. "You're changing in front of a guy and you think he's not going to peek?" he laughs, and pulls his shirt over his head. "Yeah, I don't think so."

I stare at him in disgust, totally appalled that he's broken a rule we'd shook on. "Then the rumors are *your* fault!"

"I don't tell anyone about your virgin panties and lacy bras—which, by the way, are totally ironic to wear at the same time."

"Wow," I say with a scowl.

"I think we're even," he states indifferently, and plucks his deodorant off his dresser. "You see me shirtless—which is a big deal for me—and I can take tiny looks while you change in front of me—which is a big deal for you. You don't tell anyone about how unimpressive my body is, and I don't brag to anyone that I get to see you in your underwear, like, all the time."

"I could slap you right now," I warn him, while my face reddens and my stomach knots in embarrassment.

"The fact is," he continues, ignoring my warning altogether, "the rumors only exist because we're friends with the opposite sex. It has nothing to do with who's seen who practically naked. You've seen me in my underwear, so what?"

"I'm a girl," I grit out, anger hinting in my voice.

"Great," he says, sounding bored, and pauses while he applies deodorant. "We also kiss on our vlog. It's all irrelevant to our friendship."

My jaw clenches and I close my eyes to take a breath. "Keep talking, Jas, and I'm seriously going to slap you."

He doesn't say anything, and my ears ring with the silence. I can't even wrap my head around what's just happened. Maybe it's not as big of a deal as I'm making it out to be, but then again it is. We're best friends. I've already agreed to kiss him in a vlog, which was a huge decision and highly out of character for me. Now he tells me he's been peeking at me while I change? We had the No Peeking Rule for a reason. He shook on it. What else has he agreed to where he hasn't held up his end?

"June," he finally says, and my eyes snap open, body turning rigid. "I didn't mean for that to make you upset."

"Well, it did," I hiss, and slam my laptop shut. "I know you don't have boundaries like normal people—trust me, I get that. But when we shake on something like the No Peeking Rule, I expect that I should be able to trust you, especially since you're my friend."

His face turns apologetic, eyes softening when they meet mine. "Sometimes I forget that we still have boundaries."

"What is that even supposed to mean?" I ask exasperatedly.

He shrugs and scratches at his jaw a little uncomfortably. "We share food, sleep in the same bed—I mean, you practically live here. We're going to be kissing all the time now. Do you want me to continue?"

"Some boundaries are necessary when you're friends with the opposite sex, otherwise . . ." I stop and drop my eyes from his. It's the thing I'm afraid of with Jasper but never want to openly admit. I'm afraid of us being more than friends. I'm afraid I'd lose him.

He lets out a breath and runs a hand through his hair. I keep my eyes on my feet while he comes to sit beside me. He smells like Old Spice and toothpaste, and something that's distinctly Jasper. It's a comforting, familiar smell that makes me melt into his side and rest my head on his shoulder.

"I get it," he says quietly. "Sorry."

"I'm still mad at you."

He rests his head on mine and throws an arm over my shoulder to squeeze me closer. "I would be concerned if you weren't. I obviously crossed a line."

I nod into his arm. "Yeah, you did."

"I won't do it again," he promises. "It was by accident the first time, anyway. After that it kind of became a game to see if I'd get caught."

I send my fist into his arm and he winces. "Why am I friends with you again?"

He chuckles. "Because I didn't let you have a choice."

I smile at this because it's true.

Seven

Rescue Breath

IT'S ANOTHER FREEZING morning in the backseat of Jasper's car. The heat is turned all the way up, but the only thing his car spits out is cold air. My hands are tucked under my thighs to keep them warm, and my jacket is pulled up past my lips so that my breath warms my neck and chest. Jasper is quietly maneuvering his way around traffic with his gloved hands tight on the steering wheel. Lenny bops his head along to the heavy drumbeat of the mix tape he brought along to play in the car.

Like every other morning, we're all too sleepy to talk. However, it seems every other stoplight, Lenny and Jasper will make eye contact and share silent smiles. Then Lenny will swallow down laughter and the moment is gone.

I let out a loud breath and tuck myself into a tighter ball, allowing my head to swivel over and my eyes to follow the many cars that hurry past Jasper's at above-speed-limit speeds. Again, out of the corner of my eye I see Lenny and Jasper share matching grins. I'm too tired for games but am quickly getting annoyed. I wonder if they're giggling about something I've done. Choosing to ignore them for the remainder of the drive proves to be difficult.

Once parked and minutes from being late, I open the door swiftly and start a quick stride across the parking lot. Jasper's and Lenny's voices follow me, giggles and hushed whispers about things they refuse to include me in. It's early and they're acting ridiculous and I don't have time for it, so I enter the school alone and make my way to class.

Jasper and Lenny hung out yesterday, and now they seem to have some inside joke I don't understand. Their secretiveness is making me irritable, especially since I have a feeling it's about me. A part of me thinks it's about the No Peeking Rule. It's the same part that makes me blush every time the thought crosses my mind.

Jasper has an unusual way of making me flustered today. It's a new, impish side to him that's making me irritated. It's as if he's doing this stuff to get a reaction from me.

———

Sometimes you need to confide in another girl. So I decided to confide in Allison. She's one of my closest girlfriends—or rather, one of my *only* girlfriends. She's smart, quick-tongued, and most often mysterious. She can keep a secret, and that's why I choose to keep her close.

Allison stares at me blankly from her desk. "He . . . peeked?" she asks with narrowed eyes after I relate to her what happened this weekend with Jasper.

I nod. "That's totally weird, right? It's not just me overreacting?"

The bell rings for class to start, and the students around us take their seats. The chime barely makes an impression on us and we lean in closer, lowering our voices so that we can still talk somewhat undetected during attendance.

"Uh, yeah," she states easily, and then shakes her head. "June, this whole thing just doesn't feel right. . . ."

I wave her off. "I know, I *know*—"

"And that should have definitely been a red flag. . . ."

"Yep."

"So tell me again *why* you're still going through with Kiss Cam?" Her brows are furrowed together and confused, and there's something else twinkling in her eye that I just can't place.

Our history teacher calls out my name and I raise my hand absently while my body leans in closer to Allison, trying to decide how to justify myself.

The whole No Peeking Rule episode between Jasper and me has been bugging me even after he apologized. I needed to talk to someone who wasn't Lenny and wasn't my parents. There was something about the way he worded it. How he wouldn't go "bragging" about seeing me in my underwear—as if he liked the view. I admit that looking back on the moment makes me uncomfortable. Especially since he's my best friend and *especially* because of the Kiss Cam. To me it's beginning to feel as though one wrong turn and Jasper and I could end up together. It scares me because I don't want to ultimately end up losing him.

"I guess I'm just banking on my decision to say 'stop,'" I admit. "We're not far enough in yet. We've just *started*, and VlogIt is excited." I pause. "And, I don't know . . . I kind of like kissing him?"

Allison searches my face for a moment, and it looks as though she's gearing up to say something, but then she bites her lip and stops. Instead, she reaches into her backpack and begins pulling out her history stuff. I wait, but the only thing she says is "here" when her name is called for attendance.

"Allison?" I whisper.

She glances at me and frowns. After a few pensive taps of her pencil, she turns back toward me. "Promise me something," she orders quietly.

I blink a couple of times, puzzled. "Okay?"

"Try to remember what it was like a couple years ago when things start getting too real with him."

Then she turns her attention to our teacher, and I'm left to sink back in my seat to think about everything that could go wrong. I hate it so much I think about all the good things that came out of VlogIt instead, and forget about the promise.

By the end of the day I'm tired of riddles and secretive giggles. With Jasper and Lenny running about with jokes only they understand, I feel really out of the loop. Not to mention, Allison is either playing mother hen or is keeping something from me, too. Either way, I feel a little run-down by the end of the school day.

Back in our neighborhood, we all fall in through Jasper's front door, Lenny tackling me while Jasper runs into the kitchen to grab after-school snacks, like my Pop-Tarts, Lenny's favorite potato chips, and a couple of cans of Dr Pepper and Hawaiian Punch.

I push Lenny off me, cursing at him while he laughs and yanks at me again as we enter the living room.

"Would you *stop*," I groan. "What is *wrong* with you two today? You both are acting bizarre. What's taking Jasper so long?"

I barely finish my sentence when there's a loud clattering in the kitchen followed by a giant *thud*. Everything becomes silent: no cursing from Jasper, nothing indicating that whatever fell was getting picked up, just the sound of a rolling pop can. Lenny and I glance at each other, wide-eyed, and hurry in to see what happened.

Rounding the corner, we find Jasper out cold on the floor and our snacks strewn around the kitchen.

"Oh my God," I gasp, dodging miscellaneous snacks as I jump across the room to crouch beside Jasper.

"What happened?"

"How am I supposed to know?" I ask irritably, trembling a little as I try to shake Jasper awake.

"Did he faint?"

I glare at him from across the room. *"Don't just stand there, Lenny!"*

"Well, is he breathing?" he asks, bouncing across the room to kneel down beside me.

I place my finger under his nose and watch his chest. Nothing. My eyes widen in panic, and I frantically grab for his wrist.

Somewhat relieved, but still shaking, I announce, "He's still got a pulse."

"You're the only one who knows anything about CPR, June," Lenny reminds me urgently.

"Then call 911! God, Lenny!" I practically scream as I tip his chin up.

Swallowing nervously, I pinch his nose closed and steady his head.

"I haven't done this in real life before. . . ."

"June!"

With my heart pounding hard in my chest, I squeeze my eyes shut and seal my lips over Jasper's for the first rescue breath. Except things don't go how I remember from Red Cross CPR training, because a dummy doesn't suddenly grab the back of your head and stick their tongue in your mouth. My hands slip on the kitchen floor, and I fall on top of Jasper, who is clearly perfectly conscious.

Next thing I know, Lenny's throaty, boisterous laugh is filling the kitchen, Jasper is holding me in place while delivering fierce kisses, and I'm frozen still with glowing red cheeks.

It takes me a moment to realize what's going on—too long, because just as quickly as it began, Jasper is releasing his grip on me.

I fly off him and he sits up, red in the face and grinning slyly. He quickly turns to face the spice shelf behind me.

"Kiss Cam!" Jasper yells, and a giggle-ridden Lenny sprints across the room to take the camera off the shelf and point it directly at me.

"I hate you guys!" I screech, and surge at Lenny. All this time they had me thinking that something was wrong—but no, they had been planning the first Kiss Cam. They had been slinking around all day, sneaking glances at me, sharing matching smiles, and getting me all wound up for a Kiss Cam!

I slap every part of Lenny I can reach that he's not shielding with the camera. "We got you so good!" he mumbles through a fit of laughter.

Then I turn to Jasper, who is curled up in a ball on the floor, laughing his lungs out, and shove him.

I scoot back and stand up. "That was the *worst*! I seriously thought you would *die* on me, Jas! You guys, I feel so *sick* right now. *Oh my God*," I ramble, my hands shaking more furiously than before. I feel like I can barely speak, but I'm laughing, too. Laughing because I'm embarrassed and that was so *ridiculous*. "Who's idea was this?"

Jasper coughs and stands. "Now," he muses, "I believe the username was ChloeAnne."

I wipe Jasper's spit off my lips with the back of my hand. "What was the request?"

"Reenact the lifeguard scene from *The Sandlot*."

"Worst," I tell him seriously, inwardly noting that it was one of the most terrifying experiences of my life.

Lenny shakes his head enthusiastically and lowers the camera. "Best."

Jasper strides across the room and I take a step back. "Hey," he says in an unnecessary whisper, and I send him a dirty look while he tries to stop laughing. "Hey," he says again, louder. He sighs and reaches for my face. I pull away.

"You have a little spit right there." He points to the corner of my lips and I wipe it away quickly, still scowling at him.

"I hate you two," I repeat. The adrenaline and embarrassment has faded so that my nervous laughter has completely disappeared. "Seriously, that *wasn't* funny."

Lenny glances between the two of us, trying to decide if I'm really mad.

"So, guess what," I decide in a high voice. "*I* get to plan the next Kiss Cam. You'll see exactly how unfair this feels."

Lenny's eyebrows rise up his forehead. "Are you kidding?"

I turn to him. "Oh, c'mon. I need you," I say sensibly.

There's no way I could pull off what Jasper did without Lenny. I'm mad at Lenny, don't get me wrong, but I can tell by the goofy grin on Jasper's face and the panic on Lenny's that this was *Jasper's* idea. And *he's* the one who should pay.

I turn to Jasper. "But *you*, on the other hand. *You* are in for some serious payback."

Jasper lifts his chin and narrows his eyes thoughtfully. "Fine, do what you want. But I *dare* you to top that."

"Fine," I say.

"Fine," he repeats.

We look at each other for a moment, and slow smiles start creeping up our cheeks. The kind of smiles that bring a challenge.

Two can play at that game.

Lenny looks between us excitedly; I can see his head swivel in my peripheral vision.

I have a little something in mind, something a certain viewer in particular would be incredibly excited to see unfold.

Eight

Kiss Me

ALLISON GIVES ME a disapproving look across the lunch table on Tuesday as Lenny and Jasper chug down milk carton after milk carton while I record them, shaking my head with silent giggles.

"I saw the Kiss Cam," she whispers to me, and my finger slips on the camera, jogging the footage.

"Yeah?" I say nervously, hoping the ruckus the boys are making drowns our conversation out. She looks at me pointedly and then wiggles her eyebrows.

Allison's still convinced that the Kiss Cam is a bad idea and makes a point of being as concerned as possible. But she's also been teasing me about it—and I usually end up a little embarrassed.

"Mm-hmm," she hums. "So, what? You have to plan some revenge, or how does that work?" She doesn't sound particularly interested, but her questioning is enough to seem supportive, nonetheless.

"I told Jasper I'd get revenge," I mutter low enough that the camera can't catch it. "Lenny and I are trying to finish the planning for Thursday."

"Nothing too crazy, I hope," she comments. "Would hate for Jasper to take it the wrong way."

I send her an annoyed look. "You *know* it's not like that," I remind her.

"Yeah, yeah," she says.

Jasper glances over to me then, and I catch his eye. He gives me two thumbs-up, and I look over to Lenny, who pushes an empty milk carton away like he's going to be sick.

"Winner!" he gloats victoriously. I shake my head and turn the camera toward me.

"Now, if you guys don't mind, it looks like Lenny might throw up on me again, so get out of my way, I'm vlogging anywhere but here!" With that, I shut off the camera and hand it back to Jasper, who is dishing out some pretty vicious smack talk.

Allison lightly kicks me under the table to recapture my attention. "Remember what I said earlier."

"Lenny and I have got this," I assure her.

"Okay, then," she replies.

———

It seems like an average Thursday. VlogIt is pulled up on Jasper's laptop, and it sits waiting on his bed between Lenny and me while Jasper is busy messing with the lighting. My stomach is fluttering with nervousness and even a bit of excitement.

Lenny clears his throat next to me, and I turn my head enough to meet his eye with a faint smile. He can't hide it, though, and his lips spread into a large, easy grin. Tonight is the night I'm getting my revenge.

"Today's theme," Jasper tells us as though we've forgotten (and how could we?), "is yes-or-no questions. It should go relatively quickly, seeing as there will be no elaboration to our answers unless completely necessary."

It's hard to hold down the laugh that is threatening to burst. Yesterday Lenny anonymously sent a yes-or-no question to our own channel that is meant deliberately for elaboration. And if this all works out according to plan, my Kiss Cam will be a surprising success.

"All right," Jasper says, talking mostly to himself while he gets comfortable between Lenny and me and begins to scroll through the comments under WereVloggingHere. "Let's get started."

With that, he hits record and sits back on his mattress. We all smile at the camera and repeat our well-rehearsed opening bit.

"I'm Jas."

"I'm Lenny."

"I'm June."

"And we're vlogging here!"

"Last week we told you guys to send us yes-or-no questions," Lenny announces to the camera, using many hand motions while he speaks in order to distract himself from becoming tense with anticipation. "We are going to answer as many of these as possible in the next ten minutes, explaining only when necessary."

"Our top comment is anonymous today," Jasper tells the camera, and his finger swipes down on the touchpad to read it out loud. I lick my lips in anticipation and stare straight ahead past the camera, eyes finding the fan art taped to his wall. "It asks: Jas, have you ever seen June naked?"

Lenny can't contain it any longer and rolls backward onto the orange-covered mattress in a fit of laughter. My knuckles come to rest between my lips to cover my smile. I know the only way that this will be convincing is if I can actually get flustered.

"No," Jasper says simply, but I jump in before he can read the next comment.

"But he has seen me in my underwear. So, close enough."

Jasper's cheeks actually flush and his fingers pause over his keyboard, face lowering to look at me in utter disbelief. Then the look vanishes and is replaced with a cool smile. "That didn't actually require an explanation." He winks.

I have a hard time keeping eye contact because of the sheer ridiculousness. "Well, I thought we were going to be completely honest."

"Yeah, but you weren't naked, so it doesn't apply to the question," he grinds out through a smile, and the blush on his cheeks seems to darken.

"Well, the definition of 'naked' is different for everyone," I say, and turn to him with crossed arms and a glare. I try to think about the emotions I was feeling this weekend when I found out he peeked while I changed. Slowly, I can feel new embarrassment and fresh anger surface. I had felt completely exposed. Lenny looks at us through his fingers, laughter subsiding unsurely when he sees my attitude shift.

Jasper looks back at Lenny in alarm and then leans in close to whisper, "What are you doing?"

"What am I doing?" I ask in shock, and shove his shoulder

back. "What were you even thinking when you thought it'd be a good idea to peek at me when I changed?"

"I told you that was an accident!"

"Right," I scoff, and roll my eyes. "You just happened to accidentally look over your shoulder and stare at me."

"My eyes were roaming! I saw you in the reflection of my mirror." His voice is wavering and defensive, eyes shining with what looks like guilt.

I shake my head, lips curling inward angrily. "And then suddenly it was a game."

Jasper stands up and I stand up, too, mimicking his actions in order to get a reaction. I catch a glimpse of Lenny from the corner of my eye, quietly lifting the camera up to follow us. I remember then why we're fighting. I need to find a place. I need that moment.

"I told you I was sorry! I thought we settled this! I had no idea you were still upset."

"That's because you think you know everything," I snap, eyes meeting his coldly. Adrenaline is releasing into my system, and my stomach is knotting. I can feel myself letting go of any control I have ever had around Jasper. I know we're not typical friends. I know he doesn't have boundaries. But for now I'm forgetting all of that. Right now it's all about getting the reaction I want.

Jasper's mouth drops open so wide I think he forgot how to speak. Not only has his face turned a blazing red that spreads from the tips of his ears down to his neck, but he appears to be quite petrified by me. It's as though he's forgotten how to function.

"You could have saved us a lot of trouble if you'd just done it earlier," I tell him.

He stutters, trips over his words, stares at me as though I've come completely undone, but then, as he always manages to do, he snaps out of it and seems to become another person entirely—and now he's reached a level of embarrassment that brings about rage.

"Done what?" he seethes with an unusual amount of sarcasm.

I've been looking for an opportunity, and I know this is it. So with a mischievous smile dancing on my lips, I breathe, "Kiss me."

He stops, frown deepening. "What?"

I step forward and grab the back of his head, closing the small gap that is between us. He's taller, so I have to stand on my toes and press my body to his, but he bends to meet me halfway. When our lips meet, it's angry and heated and nothing like any of our other kisses felt. He cradles my neck in his hands and kisses me with so much force that for a moment I forget my basic motor skills. My hands fall from his hair to his shirt, where it's easier for me to cling.

His body presses to mine in a way that makes my body want to sink to the ground. I've never been kissed so firmly or held quite as tightly.

For a moment I forget why we're kissing so hard I can't breathe and pulling at each other this frantically. But then his hand sweeps down to the hem of my shirt like he's forgotten about the camera and Lenny, and I remember why.

We've gone too far, and I can only imagine the discomfort I'm putting Lenny through. So I hesitantly pull away. Jasper's body is shaking, but not in a way you can see, rather in a way you can feel only when you're this close to him. My eyes flutter open faster than his and I pull back completely, unclenching my fingers from his shirt.

His eyes stay closed, and I swear his breathing catches when I say loud enough for Lenny and the camera to hear, "Kiss Cam."

Then his eyes snap open, and I don't see anything except my own reflection.

Nine
Hot and Bothered

THE BLANK LOOK in his eyes vanishes with a flutter of his eyelashes, and his kiss-swollen lips slowly form a smile. It's as though the fogginess, the sweet oblivion of the moment, has been lifted, and he turns to Lenny and the camera quickly.

"Wow," he says hoarsely, and runs his fingers through his chaotic hair. "I wasn't expecting that."

It's an obvious statement made in the early moments of a daze. I can tell he's being careful by the way his voice holds back its normal amount of dramatic flair. Even his eyes stay far too concentrated on the lens of the camera.

Lenny's eyebrows are raised high on his forehead, almost disappearing into his hairline, and he looks over the video camera to meet my gaze. I can tell he senses the shift in mood, too, a certain kind of controlled tension.

There's a moment of silence between us all. Jasper's hand dropped from my neck to my waist before, and now completely falls away from me. Then he clears his throat and sits down on his bed. For a moment he looks between Lenny and me and then finally says something.

"Aren't we going to finish the questions?"

His voice sounds normal again and is laced with the kind of humor that suggests Lenny and I are acting odd.

With a final glance at Lenny and a shrug Jasper pretends not to notice, I wipe my mouth and sit down on Jasper's right side again. Lenny grins at us and mentally shakes off the awkward before marching forward and putting the camera back on the tripod. Then he takes his place on Jasper's left.

Jasper's got his laptop back on his thighs and scrolls down to the next question. When he looks back up at the camera he smiles largely. "Next question: Do you sing in the shower?"

After we finish recording the remainder of the questions video, Lenny takes the footage and goes home to edit. He doesn't leave in a hurry this time, though. He keeps looking at me curiously, scrunching his eyebrows and glancing between Jasper and me. He wants to know what happened during that kiss—which wasn't supposed to be as long and frantic as it turned out to be. I almost want to tell him to throw the segment out entirely, but for Jasper's sake and my own, I decide not to say anything. All I can do is shrug.

When he leaves, however, I begin to get a sinking feeling in the pit of my stomach.

Lenny leaves Jasper and me sitting on the couch in Jasper's living room, watching the evening news on low volume and twiddling our thumbs.

"So," I say after a few minutes of inattentive television

watching. He turns his head a little toward me.

"Yes?" he asks with curious humor.

I let out a breath, ready to explain and defend everything that happened earlier, because the kiss wasn't supposed to get that heated. "That Kiss Cam wasn't my idea. It was a request we got awhile back—"

"I even *read* that request," Jasper interrupts with a quiet laugh and a shake of his head. "I didn't think you had the guts to ever do it."

I snort and turn my body to his, tucking my leg underneath so that we're the same height. "What about *you*?"

He gasps and blinks a few times. "I would've gotten slapped!"

My eyes narrow as I think over the possibility. Finally, my lips purse and I slouch back. "Fine," I agree.

It returns back to silence, a kind of guilty one this time, and Jasper's fingers tap against his lap as though he's thinking. He wants to say something, I can feel it. So I sink further into the cushions and wait several more minutes.

"It was a good kiss," he says suddenly, eyes trained on the television and body rigid like he's afraid of what I'll say. "A *really* good kiss," he repeats thoughtfully with furrowed eyebrows— this time more toward himself.

My eyes watch him steadily. He scratches his jaw, dragging his nails across his skin slowly, seeming to ponder what he's said.

"Is that so?" I ask, letting my tone become teasing. He senses me poking fun at him and turns his face to me with a brilliantly devilish smile. One might have thought he'd gotten away with something.

"Oh, yes," he declares exaggeratedly. "Say, wanna make out?"

Giggling, I shove him away when he begins to lean in with puckered lips and fluttering eyelashes. "Stop!" I shriek when he ducks under my arm and slides up closer beside me with a mischievous glint in his eyes.

He climbs over and throws one leg onto the other side of my lap so that he straddles me. I cover my face with my hands, blushing so badly I don't want him to see. Despite me shaking my head and calling him out for being ridiculous, he tries to pull my hands away from my face.

"Are you blushing?" he laughs while wrestling me.

"No!" I deny quickly, and try sinking into the couch. I can feel my face ablaze and my body shakes with laughter and desperation. My mind keeps thinking up ways to get myself out of the situation I'm in. I could let him win and wiggle away. With enough force I could push him off. He's only kidding with me, but I can't help but feel anxious at the idea of defeat. What is he even up to? I feel horribly guilty that my mind even considers this match ending in a ferocious, needy kiss.

"Juniper," he gasps breathlessly with giddy exertion "you're totally blushing!" He finally manages to pull my hands away from my face and giggles boyishly when he sees the crimson stain across my cheeks.

"You're embarrassing me," I say helplessly, and attempt to pull my hands from his.

"Payback," he says simply, and squeezes my hands.

"For what?"

He thinks for a second and I notice that playful gleam return to his ever-sparkling eyes. He locks his gaze with mine and leans forward ever so slightly, but my breathing stutters and I flinch back anyway. An airy laugh escapes when he lets out a breath, but he doesn't let my gaze leave his. Slowly, he continues to inch forward, but not toward my face. He lowers his face to my shoulder and turns his head so that his nose brushes against my neck. The goose bumps appear before I can stop them, and he chuckles again. For a moment his breath just blows against my skin, and I can't stop the shivers or the nervousness that paralyzes my body.

"For what?" I repeat shakily. My mind is drifting into dangerous territory, and this time Lenny won't be here to stop us from getting too carried away with this game.

His mouth latches onto my skin then, leaving a kiss burning into my collarbone. I let out a shaky breath that causes me to flush in embarrassment. But he doesn't stop, and I don't want him to. He starts leading a trail of kisses up the column of my throat. My hands clench and unclench in his until he releases them, and they immediately go to grab the front of his T-shirt. He moves himself closer to me on my lap, keeping his face close to mine until he's settled and then drops another light, open-mouth kiss to my jaw. It's horrible how badly I want him to just kiss my lips and be done with it. I can't even deny how much it aches to be this way. My mind seems drowned in want and guilty pleasure. It's unfortunate that the kiss I want so badly is from Jasper.

Then Jasper pulls my hands off his shirt and simply rolls off my lap. My body tingles with the loss of his body heat and unfulfilled wishes. I'm completely thrown off, admittedly angry that he's pulled away so suddenly and for no reason at all. I was *urging* him on.

I look sideways at him, my hands still halfway suspended in the place where he'd removed them from his shirt. He sees the confusion, the furious blush that sets my whole face and neck on fire.

He raises an eyebrow in a suggestive way and kicks his feet up onto the coffee table. "For leaving me hot and bothered," he finally answers with a cheeky grin.

I've never wanted to punch him more in my life.

"Well, at least I actually *kissed* you," I groan moodily, and resituate myself on the cushions. He just shakes his head and lets out a small chuckle.

———

Jasper got me on the next Kiss Cam. Lenny and I came over to Jasper's house after school on Friday—which should have been suspicious because Lenny never comes over Fridays. Anyway, I was caught off guard when Jasper appeared out of nowhere and planted one on me.

The Kiss Cam request: Smack Cam meets Kiss Cam.

I got him back, though, the following Wednesday. I *really* got him. I set up the camera by myself—no Lenny needed—and got him the moment we walked in the front door.

Kiss Cam request: Wall-slamming.

I'm still surprised I was strong enough to tug him back and push him in place.

Things are different but the same with us after those Kiss Cams. There's an edgy uncertainty to each of our actions, skepticism toward every move the other makes. It's a game to see who can push the other over the edge. While it's friendly, there's something extra that we put into each of our kisses—as if we're somehow trying to trick the other into thinking there's something more.

Lenny helps Jasper and me set each other up and cheerleads us into doing more and more outrageous stunts. And, at this point, Allison just smiles and shakes her head, like she wants to tell me something but she can't.

Ten

Twelve Days of Kissmas

THE AISLE I walk down smells like artificial pine trees and that musty smell decorations get when they've been stored away all year. "Jingle Bells" plays on an endless loop, red and silver bulbs shine under the fluorescent lights of the superstore, and giant plastic snowmen fall into my path every couple of steps.

It's that odd time of the year, when every store in town—at the exact same time—stocks up for the holiday. This year's date of choice ends up being a Saturday. It was just last Thursday that turkey and cranberry sauce were on sale and Jasper and his mom were helping my family make Thanksgiving dinner.

It was the day after the wall-slamming Kiss Cam, and Jasper kept giving me suggestive looks across the table that I had to pretend weren't making my stomach knot. There is no way my dad would be finding out about Kiss Cam. That would only give him the wrong idea, and the next thing I knew he'd be giving me condoms for Christmas.

Anyway, I have this sneaking suspicion that Jasper will be getting me back very soon. For right now, though, I can walk through this giant superstore with Allison, Lenny, and Jasper and be completely relaxed.

"Hey—hey, guys . . . Look!" Lenny's voice is a pathetic sort of excited, and I have to smile to myself before I even turn around and see he's got a red bulb stuck to his nose and an antler headband atop his head. Jasper has the video camera in hand and turns it on him.

"Sweet!" Jasper chuckles. "Where'd you find those?" Lenny takes a few steps back and shows him the bucket of red noses and headbands. Jasper trots over and begins digging through the box, showing the camera elf ears and jingle bells. They start trying on different looks for the vlog.

They're completely enthralled, and I shake my head in disbelief. My eyes have already gone back to looking up at the wreaths and Christmas lights on the top shelf. I don't even remember why we came down this aisle. Maybe Jasper dragged us over.

"What's the big Christmas special going to be this year?" Allison's rich voice turns scratchy this time of year from the cold, and I almost don't recognize it's her speaking until I glance sideways and find semi-interest in her face.

Every Christmas on VlogIt the boys and I find something grand to do. Three years ago, we opened fan-mail Christmas gifts on camera. The year after that, we reenacted a modern-day Nativity story. Last year, we live-streamed a Christmas-special questions video, since Christmas landed on a Thursday. This year is yet to be decided. However, we asked our subscribers what they wanted to see, and I have yet to check the comments.

I shrug. "Not sure yet."

"Well, didn't you give your viewers options?" Allison wonders while she reaches for various Christmas decorations and inspects them.

I shove my hands in my coat pockets and look back at the boys. "Usually, if someone makes a good suggestion it'll get a couple hundred likes. That's how we narrow it down."

"Are you nervous for what it might end up being?" Allison asks curiously, and I know she's being genuine by the softness of her usually sharp features.

"I trust the viewers," I tell her. She nods, but doesn't quite meet my eyes.

There's a loud crash behind us, and we both swivel around to find that the boys have managed to knock down a dancing Santa Claus from a couple of shelves up. Before I know what's happening, Jasper's ordering us to run, and we're being pushed out of the aisle and dragged to a new part of the store. I pretend not to notice the way Allison smiles at me when Jasper grabs my hand.

Later that evening, I lay back against Jasper's pillows with my computer open in my lap. It's my turn to narrow down the options for the Christmas special video. This job is the worst, because you have to sift through hundreds of top comments and pull out the ones with the most likes. I've already been working on it for a half hour and have a list of ten options. I should be less surprised that most of the suggestions are different Christmas special Kiss Cams.

Lenny sits at my feet with his computer open as well. He's

been spending more and more time with Jasper and me since Kiss Cam started, and my theory is that he's here for paranoia purposes only. However, he's editing our shopping vlog right now with headphones on, so I don't think he's up to any funny business.

I'm not quite sure what Jasper is doing. His computer is open, too, and I think he might be replying to comments and e-mails. He's annoying when he does this, because he laughs out loud and types exaggeratedly. Even his facial expressions fluctuate, as though he's having an animated conversation.

I look up at them. Both have their eyebrows scrunched in concentration—each for different reasons. Bored, I sigh as I scroll through another page of comments. Most of the comments are different variations of one another. Some tell us how much they love our vlog, others say they want to marry Lenny or Jas or me, but most of them go like this:

> Christmas Kiss Cam! (Wouldn't be opposed to some Leniper or Jenny action, too, you know! Wink, wink.)

> Mistletoe Kiss!

> Jasiper Comes Out for Christmas!

They all tell Jasper and me to attach our lips to each other or finally reveal our secret love affair. I'm quite amused that some people's biggest Christmas wish is to see Jasper and me as a couple, but also bored with cheesy requests. I feel a little bad when we can't fulfill the Leniper requests, but also grateful that Lenny would never let that happen.

And as I scroll through, it reminds me that Jasper and Lenny owe me an onscreen Jenny moment. I make a mental note of that for later.

Our Kiss Cams aren't simply there to be boring. Jasper and I try to make them as ridiculous and surprising as possible. If our Christmas special is going to feature Jasper and me locking lips, then our viewers better come up with something more creative than a smooch under some mistletoe.

It's not until thirty-five pages into our top comments that I finally find something worth a second glance—and it's worth a second glance for more than one reason. Not only is it ingenious and perfectly festive, but it has three hundred plus likes.

Christmas Special Request: Twelve Days of Kissmas

There's not a second of hesitation. I reach over and tug on Jasper's sweater a couple of times to get his attention. He lacks excitement when he turns to me, but I don't care if I've interrupted him reading a hilarious e-mail from one of his VlogIt friends.

"Can I help you, Juniper, dear?" he asks in mild amusement once he notices how eager I am.

"I think I found our Christmas special." His eyes widen a little at this, and he sits up as though he's going to peek over at my screen. I turn my screen away from him, though, and hug it close to my chest. "Guess," I order.

"What kind of special is it?" he wonders. "I need to be able to narrow it down."

"Kiss Cam," I tell him, and that's all he needs to hear, because he shoots an answer back instantly.

"Mistletoe."

I shake my head, lips turning up into a toothy grin. He purses his lips, thinks for a second, and then shrugs helplessly. "I have no idea."

Lenny looks at us and pulls off his headphones. "What's going on?"

"Juniper thinks she's found us a Christmas special," Jasper fills him in.

They both look to me expectantly.

"Think puns," I say, leaning forward a bit and waiting to see if they'll catch on, but they only continue to look at me blankly. "Twelve Days of Kissmas."

Lenny's face lights up, and he nods enthusiastically.

It takes Jasper a moment to register, but when he does, he bolts straight up and smiles at me, eyes going wide in amazement. "That's brilliant!"

"Isn't it?" I agree eagerly, and swing my laptop around to show them. They crowd around to read the full request.

Jasper tilts his head from side to side as though trying to decide what he thinks of the request before saying, "It's not really a Kiss Cam, though. I mean, we're both going to know about them."

"Who ever said the kisses had to be a surprise?" I ask. I thought the same thing when I read the request. We *could* have staged a kiss together. It was never in the rules that a Kiss Cam had to be a surprise. We've just been making it a competition.

He seems to agree with me and nods slowly after a few seconds. "It—uh—you wouldn't find it weird if we actually planned them?"

"Nothing changes," I say, completely brushing off his worries. I don't see any reason for him to be uneasy about it.

"Except that it's a conscious decision to kiss each other

instead of *stealing* kisses from each other." He bites his lip after he says this, and I don't really understand what he's getting at. In fact, I find this to be the better option. We'll know what to expect. It'll be a little like our first kiss on camera.

"It's not a big deal," I laugh, but his brows furrow. "Seriously, it's probably better that we both know."

"She's right," Lenny says. "It would be way easier for me, too."

I nod and gesture at Lenny. "See?"

"Yeah," he says, and his eyes seem to reflect some internal calculations. "Yeah, you're right."

"One condition, though," Lenny pipes up. "*I* get to plan this Kissmas thing. I've had it up to *here* with taking orders from you two."

"Deal," I say easily, and Jasper follows suit.

"Awesome," Lenny says, and rubs his hands together like a mad scientist in the lab contemplating the purpose of his freaky monster creation. "Your fate is in *my* hands now."

Jasper shoves him. "Oh, get back to editing, Leonard."

"That is *not* my name!"

———

"Oh." Allison's eyebrows shoot up her forehead when I tell her about the Twelve Days of Kissmas on Monday morning. She flips her dark hair over her shoulder and leans forward on her desk with her head in her hands. "How *festive*."

"It's kind of fitting, isn't it?" I wonder aloud while we talk quietly in the last few minutes of class. I get a nervous flutter in my stomach just thinking about it.

"Uh-huh, because best friends usually go around playing an aggressive game of tonsil hockey around this time of year," she points out with a puckered smile. I catch a flash of amusement in her tone, but also that same guarded indifference to the idea of Jasper and me kissing for VlogIt.

I scrunch my nose up and reach across the aisle to nudge her. "Jealous?"

"Oh, I can't be," she teases. "He's definitely the Han Solo to your Princess Leia. The Ron to your Hermione. The Peeta to your Katniss—whatever."

My face flushes, and I shake my head. "You think you're real funny."

"I'm *just* sayin' . . ."

I glance at the clock, so close yet so far from releasing me from this teasing match. I will the hands to move faster.

"Don't you ever get the feeling that maybe *something* is up between you two?" she asks as she fiddles with the scarf she's wearing. "I mean, just *really* think about it. You have to be getting some weird vibes, right?"

I set my chin in my hand and shake my head. "It's all in good fun, Allison. We've been through this. If something started to feel off, don't you think I'd have called it off by now?"

"Not if you like him," she retorts, and her lips twitch into a small, suggestive smile.

I feel my face heat for what feels like the hundredth time and clasp my hands under the desk. My stomach always begins to knot at that suggestion. It's *not* like that, everybody knows it. And I really don't like thinking about repeating the past with Jasper. But what if Jasper felt something for me? Allison always seems to be hinting at *something*.

But I just can't let that happen. No matter what, I am going to make sure Jasper and I stay just friends. Nobody will get hurt that way, and I don't have to worry about losing my best friend in the aftermath.

"There are no feelings between Jasper and me," I assure her.

"Okay," she sings, but she sounds unconvinced.

The bell rings then, and I push myself from my desk and hurry out without waiting for her. I just can't have her putting any more silly ideas about Jasper in my head. That is dangerous, *dangerous* territory.

Eleven

Voluntary Tasting

ALLISON'S SUGGESTION ABOUT feelings really starts to get to me as the day goes on, and I fumble with my locker, unable to open it the more flustered I get.

I do like Jasper, but *only* as a friend. And we love each other, of course—like *family*. I know this. My parents know this. My friends know this. Hundreds of people online know this. It's about as obvious as stating that the grass is green.

However, we're not *into* each other *like that*, and there's no way we ever could be, because I like the way we are *now*. And, hey, when you've got a good thing going, why change it?

Years ago, when I first met Jasper, we were about as insignificant in each other's lives as silent letters are in the English language. That all changed when we realized that Lenny had a cookie-cutter life with parents who were home by four o'clock and who wanted him home by nine every night. Leeann was rarely home, and my parents' odd work hours kept me from seeing them. That's when Jasper and I started to seek each other out. While Lenny went home for the night, Jasper and I bonded over strange things like his secret love for oldies music and my dislike of the color yellow.

Our friendship with each other put to shame the relationship we had with Lenny. We've all become tighter knit since VlogIt, of course, but no matter what, there will always be those long nights teaching Jasper how to braid hair and him trying to show me how to effectively read a comic book that make us closer. We've invested a lot of time into each other.

That's really all there is, though—invested time. It's a family union between Jasper and me, not a romantic one. Our love is merely platonic—nothing close to the magical sparks of a budding romance.

So, we kiss . . . a lot these days. Does that really matter in the grand scheme of things? There are no sparks, no shivers of pleasure—at least not on my end. My trembles are the result of nervousness, the shakiness of my breath is inexperience, and the added heat created out of competitiveness.

Allison knows nothing about Jasper. He's loud and passionate and extremely unpredictable. He is both easy and hard to read at the same time. There are no boundaries in his mind, no lines that can't be crossed. If he truly loves me the way she suggests he might, then I would feel it in his kisses, hear it in his voice. But I don't.

I feel weak just thinking about Jasper and me together. The awkwardness that would replace the effortlessness. The way his passion would compete with my demure nature. We'd be somewhat of a chaotic couple—always fighting, always searching for the fluidness that used to come without the pressure of commitment. I would want one thing;

he'd fight with me for the other.

Some people just work better as friends, and I think we found that out a long time ago. That's why my freshman crush faded into nothing but curiosity.

The flush of panicky nervousness that surged through me minutes earlier now settles into cool composure. My fingers steady on the dial of my locker, and I'm able to open it with relative ease. I even laugh a little in spite of myself.

Kiss Cam really is taking us for a whirl.

———

That evening, I recline back against Jasper's legs while he plays with my hair. Lenny sits on the floor with me, hiding in the curve of his living room's massive couch. He's got his computer in his lap and throws out suggestions for the Twelve Days of Kissmas—which happens in about two weeks. Until then, he figures we should hold off on the regular Kiss Cams. We're spoiling our viewers, anyway.

"On the first day of Kissmas, my true love gave to me a hickey for the Jasiper Team."

Jasper laughs at this and twirls one of my blond curls around his finger. "Wait, who's giving who the hickey?"

"Good question." I nod, raising my eyebrows a little at his point. After thinking the stanza over in my head again, I tack on, "A bit oddly phrased, but kudos to using the Christmas rhyme."

Lenny shrugs and goes back to scrolling down the list, eyes reflecting the bright screen. Jasper continues to run his fingers through my curls, ruffling them up and pulling them straight. I rest my head back against his knees and look up at him. From this angle his nose seems large and his eyes small underneath thick eyelashes. He removes his hands from my head and sticks his tongue out at me. I mimic him and then turn back to Lenny.

"Mistletoe kisses . . ."

Jasper bumps me with his knee. "Looks like we're gonna have to invest in some mistletoe." I elbow him back and shake my head.

"Snowball-fight kiss . . ."

Jasper jostles me with his knees again and I slap at his shins, rolling my eyes at his immaturity.

"Oh, look, try on different festive lip balms and guess the flavor off the other's lips."

This time Jasper shakes my shoulders so hard I almost get whiplash. I know what he's thinking—and it's not good. Is that even an ethical thing to do as best friends? I mean, sure, I guess Kiss Cams aren't. But, this . . . Well, this is voluntary tasting. And *that's* where I draw the line.

He's still shaking me, making the idea bounce around in my head without rest. Finally, I snap, "Would you knock it off?"

He doesn't let up, so I pull out of his hold and crawl over to sit on the other side of Lenny. Lenny turns to look at me with a goofy half grin as Jasper leans back with a pout.

"That one's a good one," Lenny says impishly, and I cover my face with my hands, groaning at the idea.

"I say that one's definitely a possibility," Jasper adds in a teasing manner, and I know he's leaning forward again, waiting for a reaction.

"We have *two* weeks before Christmas."

"Then we're already behind," Jasper exclaims, and bounces

across the couch to get behind Lenny and me. Lenny nods thoughtfully.

Making an exaggerated motion, I turn around to look at Jasper. "That idea is disgusting."

"Are you kidding, babe?" Jasper scoffs. "That's totally hot."

My eyelids droop along with the rest of my face as I stare at him, completely unamused. For a moment there is nothing but the soft whirring of Lenny's computer and the muffled voices of Jade and Ruby upstairs. Jasper stares back at me challengingly, waiting for a smile to peek up through my weighted-down expression. I just find a point on his face, like the light splatter of freckles across his nose, and let out a deep breath.

"You're despicable."

"Me?" he gasps in horror. "Despicable?"

"No class . . . whatsoever," I deadpan.

Lenny, for whatever reason, finds this absolutely hilarious and throws his head back in laughter.

"But slamming me against my front door and shoving your tongue down my throat was classy?" Jasper asks with a devilish twinkle in his eyes. His hair is in such disarray I can practically complete the image with a pair of horns.

Lenny laughs even harder, stuttering out, "Oh, *burn*."

The expressionless composure I was able to act out earlier wavers when my skin tingles with heat and my mouth drops open.

"I did not *shove* my tongue down your throat!" I claim feebly, feeling mortified when the statement only causes Lenny's face to redden more with cackling humor.

"Oh, you did, and it was great. Now, back to the matter at hand . . ."

"I hate you."

Jasper puts a finger to my lips and quietly shushes me through a large smile. "Hush, good-lookin', you didn't let me finish."

I swat his hand away and narrow my eyes at him in warning. Lenny's laughter has subsided to soft chuckles, and he looks between Jasper and me in interest. I think he may have moved the laptop away from us for safekeeping and now crosses his legs to make himself comfortable.

"The viewers call the shots—"

"Obviously."

"*Shhh*," he insists, and dives forward to clamp a hand over my mouth. "Help me out, Lenny?"

Lenny looks genuinely confused for a second. Even though Jasper raises his eyebrows and nods for him to finish his train of thought, Lenny shakes his head helplessly.

Sighing, Jasper turns back to me, meeting my eyes. "Look, would you rather act out Christmas Jasiper fanfiction or test lip balm?"

"Who said anything about Jasiper fanfiction?" I mumble under his hand, and he rolls his eyes.

"As *if* that's not going to turn up," he sighs dramatically. From the corner of my eye I see Lenny give a contemplative shrug to Jasper's statement, and I know that Jasper's going to win this one.

"Ugh," I groan, and pull Jasper's bony hand off my face. "*Fine*. But *you* can have fun finding festive lip balm."

Jasper grins victoriously and runs a hand through his unruly hair as though he simultaneously can and can't believe I gave in. "Oh, trust me," he says once his hand has run its course and hangs limply from his neck. "I will."

When I get home later that night, I'm greeted at the door with giant green Rubbermaid containers and multiple mostly damaged cardboard boxes. On the inside of the door, I'm startled to find a Christmas wreath hanging festively and almost tangling with my hair. When I remove my shoes, I find that our regular welcome mat has been replaced with an Elves Welcome red-and-green one. Looking around, I see tinsel and bows everywhere.

Overwhelmed by everything—including a funny, sweet smell in the air—I look around helplessly for the source of this nonsense. All of a sudden, my mother's head pokes out from the living room and I remember that it's her day off. Just a glimpse of her answers all my questions.

She's 110 percent into the holiday spirit. Her light-brown hair is swept back in a red scrunchie and she's got this ridiculous striped sweater on. She's even bothered to apply some bright red lipstick.

This is a fantastic example of my festive mother. It doesn't matter what holiday it is—she's gonna get with the season.

Valentine's Day, for example. For the rest of us, it's a painful holiday complete with frilly pink ribbon and heart cutouts; but to her it's the perfect opportunity to wear pink and buy flowers for the house and leave a little handwritten note on my dresser telling me how much I mean to her. Really, you don't know how to celebrate a holiday until you've met my mother.

"Guess what I did today?" she sings to me from her post behind the decked-out living room entryway.

"Taxes?"

But she doesn't even wait to hear what I've said. "I pulled out all the Christmas stuff—can you believe how much we have? Oh, and your father is getting a tree next week. Isn't that exciting? For now we're just going to have to spruce this place up with the rest of it." She nods to the boxes behind me.

I barely have enough time to process what she's rambled on about before she's talking again. "Why are you standing in the doorway, June? It's drafty over there. Come over here. ABC is already airing all the classics."

I trudge across the fairy-light-lit hall to meet her in the living room. Before I get there, however, she bustles over to turn off "Deck the Halls," which has been playing on her iPod dock. Then she whirls around to turn up the volume on the television.

Now I can place the odd smell I sensed in the hallway. While my eyes check out her decorating job, I notice that both sofa side tables have lit cinnamon-apple candles on them, releasing rich, homey aromas.

"C'mere, let's watch together," she urges, and takes my hand in her dainty one, dragging me to the sofa.

"Mom."

"Look, it's *Rudolph*. We haven't seen that one in a while," she comments as she settles in, pulling the throw blanket down from behind us.

"Mom."

"Are you comfortable?"

"Mom," I sigh apologetically, because she looks so determined to spend time with me. "I have school tomorrow."

She looks surprised for a moment, her blue eyes confused, and then her posture softens and she sinks down into the cushions. "Oh."

This is how it always goes. Whenever she has a day off she makes these huge plans, forgetting that *I* don't share the same schedule. The disappointment in her eyes makes my stomach sink, because really, I don't *have* to go to bed now. She's just overwhelming when she's in these moods—and that's not a real reason not to spend time with her. So, I compromise.

"*One* movie," I say.

When she hears this, she smiles a brilliant smile and wraps an arm around my shoulders. "That's my girl," she says proudly, and then presses her forehead to the side of my head. "If only Jas didn't steal you away all the time!"

My cheeks flush and I squirm away. "Mom," I sigh, "he's not stealing me away."

She leans back and holds me at arm's length. Turning my head, I consider her motherly gaze and warm smile. "Oh, honey, he's tryin'."

I just shake my head while she chuckles and pulls me close to cuddle. "Baby, you are truly blessed to live in a dreamland."

Even though she holds me tightly and I can't see her face, I can imagine her red-lipped, all-knowing smirk.

"Maybe you're the one in a dreamland," I scoff.

"Maybe," she agrees, "but then I wouldn't be the only one."

Twelve

Ride Me Like Rudolph

IT TURNS OUT that I was wrong about having two weeks until the Christmas special. You see, when your Christmas special is called "Twelve Days of Kissmas," that means you should probably start twelve days prior to Christmas to really capture the spirit of it all. So when next Monday rolls around and Jasper announces that Kissmas starts *today* over lunch, I almost do a spit-take all over his face.

Apparently, Lenny did a video announcing what the Christmas special would be. And since I didn't even bother to check VlogIt to see if any new videos went up over the weekend, I have zero time to prepare. I don't even know when Jasper had time to pick up festive-flavored lip balms—because I guess that's what we're doing tonight.

All of a sudden, Christmas is just around the corner and Kissmas is right after school.

"If we're testing lip balms tonight, then what are we doing every night after that until Christmas?" I ask in a half panic, trying to piece together when all this planning took place.

Jasper's eyes hood in a way that seems completely unamused, and Lenny just shakes his head and spoons chili into his mouth like he's not going to get involved.

"You're kidding, right?" I meet Jasper's glare across the table and shrug hopelessly. There is no way I could be any more confused in this situation. He sighs long and hard in the most dramatic way he can muster.

"We discussed it over lunch last week—or was that the *one* time your headphones were *actually* playing music?"

I wince slightly, remembering last Wednesday. I have a habit of putting my headphones over my ears even though my iPod isn't playing any music. That's how I *avoid* conversations—so, really, why did he even think trying to talk to me was a good idea? Tuesday night I had downloaded a new album and decided to listen to it at lunch the following afternoon. Any nods I gave him last week were dismissive, not decisive.

He pushes his tray away and buries his head in his arms across the table, groaning.

"I have a list," Lenny says suddenly, and I nod to him gratefully. "I'll make you a copy and give it to you tonight so there's no need to be a *drama queen*." He looks at Jasper as he says this and then shakes his head again. "Jeez, like getting her back on track was *that* hard, man."

"Not the point," Jasper mumbles back sharply, and lifts his head to look at me again. "You can't blame me for any decisions I thought we *all* made last Wednesday."

At this, Allison—who has been sitting beside me silently, eating her lunch and absorbing the conversation—now jabs me in the side with her elbow. I glance at her quickly, giving her a short glare before returning my gaze to Jasper. I didn't need a jab in the side to know that that sentence could mean trouble.

"What are you talking about?"

Jasper shrugs. "I've gotta admit, there's some things on that list I thought you'd never agree to—but then again, we're tasting lip balm off each other's lips tonight, so, I mean, what's worse than that?"

Allison lets her elbow brush against my side again, gently this time, as though trying not to annoy me but also trying to get me to notice what she does. My front teeth find my bottom lip momentarily, trying to bite down any dramatics.

"I don't know, Jas," I say steadily, "what *is* worse than that?"

Jasper makes a face, staring past me as though trying to remember, and then starts listing. "The classic mistletoe kiss on Christmas, eating two ends of a peppermint stick until our lips meet in the middle, watch a Christmas movie and kiss every time they say 'Christmas' ... Oh! and seeing if we can give the other person a hickey shaped as a Christmas tree."

"*Great*," I say, thinking that that is a *lot* of kissing. But, really, what did I expect to come from this? It *is* called Kissmas, after all—and Jasper isn't exactly a bad kisser. Plus, the requests could have been *way* worse.

I was expecting some intense kissing from the way he was describing it. But he makes everything seem dramatic.

Jasper finds the sarcasm in my reply and rants, "At least they don't want you to ride me like Rudolph—goodness, Juniper, they're *mellow* requests."

Allison gasps "Oh, God" at his remark and hides her blushing cheeks behind her hands. Lenny, though, just starts giggling. I stutter at first, but end up managing, "I'm not saying they aren't."

"Great," Jasper says quickly, and gives me a large, stretched-out grin. "Then can we kiss and make up?"

I stand up and shake my head. "*Too* cheeky," I mutter, and walk away to take care of my lunch tray, barely catching the way his smile turns into a ridiculous-looking pout.

"Don't worry," Allison's voice trails after me, teasing Jasper. "You'll be getting plenty of lip action later."

My head whips backward across my shoulder, jaw slack. Never in a hundred years did I ever think she would say something like that.

———

Later, at Jasper's house, Lenny presents me with the full list of Kissmas kisses and I decide that, really, they aren't bad at all and I should make the most of it. After all, I get to casually kiss my best friend without things getting weird. How many people can say that?

When Jasper presents the lip balms to me shortly after my arrival, I'm startled to find that there are twelve of them—which I guess he found clever, since there's twelve days of us kissing until Christmas—and he's picked out the six that he's going to put on his lips for me to guess and six for him.

He puts my set into my hands and then goes across the room to explain the editing process for the video to Lenny. I go to sit down on Jasper's vibrant bedding and spread the balms out in front of me. After checking the cute holiday-esque labels, I've discovered that he's given me the flavors hot chocolate, gingerbread, pumpkin spice, eggnog, sugar cookie, and sugar plum. Where he got these flavors of lip balms, I haven't the slightest idea. I am curious, though, about the flavors he's chosen.

After a few minutes of Lenny tripping over electrical cords and Jasper almost dropping both the camera and his laptop in an attempt to set up the camera with his hands full, Jasper finally settles down beside me, while Lenny makes himself comfortable on the other side of the room at Jasper's desk. He's decided to stay out of the Christmas special unless the moment presents itself. He likes his place as director—thinks it's an esteemed position, or whatever. I think he likes it because there's less of a chance of getting nailed by a cannon in a ship war.

Jasper's got his six lip balms clutched between both hands so that he doesn't drop them, and nods for me to hit record. Leaning forward—being careful that my lip balms don't roll off the edge of the bed—I hit the record button, and the little red light flashes next to the lens. When I settle back next to him, Jasper introduces the Christmas special.

I listen to him wish the audience a "Very Merry Kissmas" and proceed to tell them what today's kiss(es) will entail. He explains that we each have six different flavors of lip balm and that we'll take turns guessing which flavors the other is wearing by tasting it off the other's lips. Then he announces which flavors he has that I will be guessing: peppermint, apple cider, cinnamon sugar, chocolate truffle, apple cinnamon, and toasted marshmallow. He lets me tell the camera which ones I have, and then we start.

He decides he'd like the honor of putting on the first lip balm flavor and closes his eyes, shuffling the tubes around in his hands for a second before he picks one out of the bunch and dumps the others next to him on the bed. His eyes snap open and he smiles at the camera as he pops the cap off and begins applying the balm heavily to his lips.

"This tastes really good," he tells me after he's taken a practice swipe over his lips with his tongue.

"Does it?" I ask a bit cheekily. He nods and leans forward, and I realize that now I have to kiss him.

I don't make a big deal about it. I simply lean forward and capture his slick lips with my own, trying to get as much of the balm onto my lips with a few lingering pecks. Pulling away, I lick my lips and try to guess what the sweet taste is. It's unusual, more of a vanillalike taste than anything I would have expected from his list.

"Is it the marshmallow one?"

He nods and lifts up the tube. "Toasted marshmallow, actually. Good job."

"Thank you," I say around a light laugh.

Then it's my turn, and I pick up the flavor that's closest to my fingers when I go to choose from the pile next to my thigh. I remove the cap and begin to apply it, not even bothering to look down at the flavor. Jasper watches the applicator slide across my lips, winking at me when my tongue flicks out to check if there's enough. I have to laugh, even if it's slightly awkward giggles.

"Ready?" I ask.

He leans forward without reply and sucks at my bottom lip for a moment before pulling away. His eyes crinkle in thought as he tries to decipher the flavor and then mutters, "Hold on," and dives forward again, pulling my face closer to his and using his tongue to lick the balm off.

I almost choke—because *what* is he doing?

He pulls back a second time and thinks, lips pursing in some sort of confusion. I raise an eyebrow at him and he explains, "I can't tell if that's gingerbread or pumpkin spice."

"It's probably gingerbread!" Lenny calls from the other side of the room.

I look down at the label for the first time. There's a little gingerbread house with snowflakes covering the rest of the packaging. In bold little words along the bottom it reads GINGERBREAD, and I show him.

"And how exactly would you know that?" Jasper calls back to Lenny challengingly.

"'Cause you'll *know* when it's pumpkin spice. Haven't you ever had a latte? You just *know*, man."

Jasper stares at him dumbfounded, shaking his head and scratching his chin like he doesn't even want to know what Lenny is talking about. Then he looks at me and I shrug.

"It's true," I tell him with a hint of humor. "You'll just *know*, man." Jasper shakes his head and I turn back to Lenny. "If you had your own channel on VlogIt," I say, "your username would be TypicalWhiteGirl. I just *know* that's what it'd be."

"Yeah," he agrees, smiling. "I'm not ashamed. Pumpkin spice lattes run through my veins this time of year."

I laugh at this, and Jasper swats the tube out of my hand while rolling his eyes. "I'm surrounded by idiots," he murmurs to the camera in despair while shaking his head.

Pretending to look offended, I watch him pretend the whole thing never happened and pick out a new flavor.

It goes on like this for a while. Both of us continue to try new flavors on and guess what they are, and the kisses become more absurd each time. Where my kisses seem more practical and cute, his are just flat-out ridiculous.

He holds my face close, kisses me, licks his own lips, and then repeats. At one point he attacks me, pushing me backward onto the mattress, claiming how much he loves the taste of the hot chocolate one. Later, he manages to get me so caught up in the moment with the way he brushes his thumb across my jaw and teases my mouth with his tongue each time he gets the opportunity to slip it between my lips in an open-mouth kiss that Lenny has to yell, "Oy! Break it up!" to snap me out of it. I think if it weren't for him this would have been boring, because in the end we're almost completely reduced to giddy laughter.

When all is said (or rather kissed) and done, Jasper ends the video and Lenny begins to mull over all the footage he has to merge with today's vlog.

Lenny swivels away from Jasper's desk, singing to us, "And on the first day of Kissmas, Jasiper gave their team a make-out session they'll never believe."

Thirteen

Kinky

KISSMAS GOES ON to be our best Christmas vlog yet. Viewers rave about the ingenuity, commenters sign up to join the Jasiper ship, and our Christmas special makes the front page of the VlogIt website—and it's only the fourth day.

After kissing lip balms off each other's mouths, we treated a peppermint stick like spaghetti noodles (a bad idea that hurt our teeth and made our mouths sting from the mint—we gave up before our lips even touched), and watched *How the Grinch Stole Christmas!* and kissed every time the word "Christmas" was said (fourteen times, to be exact). So today, the fourth day of Kissmas, we're giving each other hickeys—shaped like Christmas trees.

I have a few concerns about the fourth day of Kissmas, and they go something like this:

1. The most appropriate place to make a hickey (that isn't totally lame) is on one's neck.

2. My dad has saved his vacation time for Christmas, and he's off starting tomorrow.

3. There's a possibility he could see it.

4. Wearing scarves and turtlenecks every day is pretty fishy.

5. Concealer melts off.

There's only one way of putting this: I'm screwed.

I was hoping I could get away with wearing ugly Christmas sweaters with turtlenecks underneath—because 'tis the season, but I have one turtleneck, and since I don't get off school until next Tuesday I've concluded it'd look pretty suspicious—hence numbers two through four on my list. My other option was concealer, but I've found from having two past boyfriends and observant parents that concealer is useless.

Pros of having busy parents:

1. You get free rein of the house 99.9 percent of the time.

2. You can get away with being around friends all day long.

Cons of having busy parents:

1. Since they don't see you daily, they try to make up for things by being snoopy, asking questions, and staring at you for extended periods of time.

With that in mind, I tried to convince Jasper that hickeys weren't going to happen, but he blew me off, saying, "You already agreed,

Juniper. No take-backs." Even explaining the situation didn't help. In fact, it made him more excited about the video. It was as though the idea of me doing the walk of shame and trying to hide the bruise was going to be the best part of the fourth day of Kissmas.

———————

If I thought what we did looked like shooting amateur porn before, I really hadn't taken into consideration the possibility of shooting a hickey-giving video. The lights have never seemed so bright, Jasper's bed so sexual, and the camera so cheap. What is about to take place on said bed under lights bright enough to make me sweat and before a video camera that will broadcast those events to the entire VlogIt community is anything but innocent. Lips and tongue and shiny, bruised skin . . . I can see it now—a screen cap of our video used as a porn site ad.

Maybe I'm being dramatic, maybe I'm nervous, and maybe Lenny isn't looking at me from Jasper's desk with all-knowing eyes and a toothy grin. The lucky idiot gets to cop out after introducing the fourth day of Kissmas and saying something witty we can tag on at the end of the video. I hold his eye for a moment from the safety of Jasper's doorway and shake my head at him.

Lucky idiot.

He simply winks at me and then raises his eyebrows.

Jasper appears behind me, having left his room to freshen up or something as I came up the stairs. As he slides past me to enter his room, I notice he's changed his shirt. He wears a simple button-up with the first few buttons undone to expose the entirety of his long neck. He takes my hands once he's facing me and breathes on them, doing what he always does when I've been out in the cold. My hands are already thawed, but he keeps his lips on my fingers, blowing steadily on them and looking at me with big brown eyes. I meet his eyes with the same amount of flirtation—jokingly, of course—and greet him with a sassy smile. His lips tug up into a smile as well, and he drops my hands.

As he's walking away, he calls over his shoulder, "I hope you don't plan on wearing that for the video."

Even though I know what I'm wearing, I glance down at my sweatshirt and then back up at his undone buttons and realize what he's getting at. I actually don't plan on wearing the sweatshirt. I was going to throw it off before the video. However, as I look at Jasper sitting on his bed with part of his chest peeking out of his shirt and I envision myself next to him in a spaghetti-strap tank top sucking on his neck, I start to get some *thoughts*.

If any more skin gets flashed, I'm positive we could consider this whole thing to be borderline dirty. But Jasper's already made it clear that there's no way I'm getting out of this, so to answer him, I tug off the sweatshirt and toss it aside, receiving a cheeky smile in return.

"I value our friendship," he whispers to me when I've seated myself beside him in front of the camera. I know he's trying to crack an innocent joke, but all I can think about is the time he straddled me in his living room and pressed his lips along the side of my neck, making me crazy in anticipation for those lips to be on mine. It's a dangerous thought, so I distract myself by ordering Lenny to do the introduction, which he does excitedly—enjoying the way I squirm. He's been on Jasper's side since this thing started, and I just don't get why.

While Lenny talks, Jasper straightens the collar on his shirt, running his hand along the inside to pull the fabric off his neck. Feeling self-conscious myself, I pull the top of my tank top up, ensuring that it covers any and all cleavage. Jasper might be my friend, but he's ogled me in my underwear, and I don't trust his mouth being around so much exposed skin.

I really shouldn't be so worried about a little *hickey*, but it's Jasper, after all. For the sake of dramatic flair, he'll do anything. That's not skepticism, that's truth.

"We're like vampires," Jasper whispers under Lenny's voice.

My eyebrows pull together, and I give him a worried face. "What does that even mean?"

"I would demonstrate," he says around a naughty grin, "but Lenny is still introducing the video, so that would be rude."

"If you bite my neck," I warn, lifting a finger to shove it at his chest, "I will bite you back *harder*."

"Kinky," he mumbles with a smug grin.

I'm about to say something back, to warn him that I'm not playing games since this request leaves a visible mark I'll have to explain to my parents, but Lenny's final words drown me out.

"And on the fourth day of Kissmas, Jasiper gave their team matching hickeys—fangirls now scream!"

Lenny stands up and pauses briefly before the camera to adjust his jeans (giving him more to edit out) and turns to Jasper and me with a wrinkled nose. "Have *fun*," he coos, and walks away, saluting us at the door. "Lenny out."

Jasper's taken over the talking, but I can't hear much over the pounding of my heartbeat in my ears. It's silly that I'm being so uptight about this, but Lenny—my rock, the one who pulls

Jasper and me apart when we go too far—is *gone* and I have to pull myself together. It's just *hickeys*. It's just a bruise that I have no good way of covering up.

What if my dad sees? Or my mom? Well, I don't want to have to think about explaining myself. Long story short, I wouldn't be sleeping over at Jasper's anymore.

In short, Jasper really shouldn't be leaning toward me now, and he definitely shouldn't be pressing his lips to the side of my neck, at the bottom where my sweatshirt can probably cover the mark—so maybe it's not so bad. He's being careful.

Despite my best efforts, I have to stifle a groan when he starts sucking my skin between his teeth. My face heats, and I feel his smile against my neck. The camera is right in front of us, I have to remember that, I have to keep my eyes on that little red light. I know I can't do this in silence; just imagine how awkward our viewers would feel. Besides, it's too easy to get lost in whatever Jasper is doing with his mouth, so I start rambling. I start talking to the audience, hoping it'll distract me and keep Jasper in his place. There won't be any funny business tonight.

Things like, "Doesn't this make you guys feel weird? Aren't you guys like twelve?" and "Warning, do not try this at home unless you want to be thoroughly embarrassed by your parents," and "We're just friends, I swear," tumble out of my mouth before I can stop them. Every time Jasper moves his mouth or starts using teeth and tongue, something silly comes out of my mouth. It's like word vomit during a school presentation. Your hands shake and your head is foggy and all of a sudden you have no idea what you're saying or why you're saying it. The worst part is that Jasper actually cracks up here and there. He catches on quickly to what I'm doing and starts getting more creative to see what other ridiculous things he can get me to say.

It's only a couple of minutes, but it feels like hours when Jasper actually leans back to admire his handiwork. I sweep my hair to the unbruised side of my neck and lean into the lens to show the viewers and see what it looks like for myself. To say I'm actually disappointed that his turned out so well is an understatement. It didn't feel like it was going to turn out as a Christmas tree, that's for sure. But now it's there, and Jasper was careful about the placement—even though he made me think he wouldn't be—and it wasn't as bad as I anticipated. So I swallow down the nervous flutters that have been building since this morning. The worst part is over, and now it's his turn.

I thought Jasper would be more laid-back about the whole thing, but I guess he's determined to be difficult. When I start at the top of his neck, under his jaw where it will be more visible, he squawks his disapproval, saying he shouldn't have been so nice. Then, as I start to mark his skin, he goes on and on about how I'm such a "naughty girl" who deserves to be on the "naughty list," and that's what wins him a sharp bite, making him jump away and gape at me in horror.

"You are getting *coal* for Christmas, Juniper!" he shrieks.

I'm always saying how theatrical Jasper can be, but I can feel the mischievous inkling spreading through me now that I see how much control I have over the situation. Feeling particularly sassy now that my torture has ended and he's putting on a show, I flash him a wicked grin and lean toward him with wide eyes. "Really," I wonder, maybe a little too flirtatiously. "I thought I was getting mistletoe."

He sees the challenge in my eyes and smiles proudly. "And *I'm* the troublemaker?"

I laugh and pull him back by his shirt collar. "Settle down and let me finish. You brought this on yourself."

He snorts at this but allows me to finish. I'm not sure if it was worth it, though, because the hickey ends up looking like a snowman instead of a Christmas tree. Not to mention he decides it's okay to be totally obnoxious halfway through by moaning and embarrassing both himself and me. At first I thought the little sigh was an accident, like mine was at the beginning of the video, but no, justice was not served. He just got louder and louder. After a while I had to quit because things were starting to sound a bit too raunchy. At least the viewers will laugh.

Luckily, I don't have to face either parent all night. I've also discovered that as long as I wear a hoodie, the hickey isn't visible. The bulkiness obscures it almost completely—and if I wear my hair down, it's like it doesn't even exist.

Jasper dropped the camera off at Lenny's and walked me home. He also reminded me that tomorrow we order eggnog milk shakes and attempt to tie the stem of the cherry on top in our mouths. He thinks he's already victorious but I'm researching the art of cherry knotting.

Four days down, eight kisses to go.

Fourteen
Condoms for Christmas

THE LAST DAY of school before winter break is a Tuesday. Over lunch Lenny gives all of us candy canes and bunches of jingle bells to hang on our backpacks—making us the most annoyingly festive people in school. Allison and I exchange small gifts in history. She pulls a forest-green scarf from her backpack and wraps it around my neck, saying how much it complements my hair color. I give her a water gun—which had to be done discreetly because guns are not allowed in school, even if they only spray water—and tell her it's for spraying Jasper when he's bad. She shoots Jasper at least twenty times before the final bell rings.

At the end of the day, people elbow one another to get to their lockers and leave. Random caroling bounces from group to group, making "Deck the Halls" get permanently stuck in my head. The festivities are upon us all, and the excitement of winter break is so heavy in the air I could reach out and touch it.

Jasper meets me at my locker. A hat fit for Kris Kringle falls down over his eyebrows, and the white pom-pom at the end rests on his shoulder. "Why, happy winter break, Juniper," he laughs, eyes gleaming with holiday elation.

"With that hat you look just like Saint Nick." I wink at him, and he gasps when he realizes I've quoted *How the Grinch Stole Christmas!*, the movie we previously locked lips to for Kissmas.

"Now, I thought you never wanted to talk about that again," he teases, and grabs the video camera I've ignored all day from the top shelf of my locker. "We had so many camera moments today, June. What a waste."

I roll my eyes and swing my backpack over my shoulder. "Nobody cares what we got for Christmas, Jas. They only care about how many times you manage to stick your tongue down my throat."

He chuckles despite himself and rolls the camera between his hands. Not even a little blush. I'm disappointed. Have we reached the point of no return with this? Have we done it so much we can talk about it out loud like we're discussing homework? He doesn't seem to notice my furrowed brows but replies, "Very true, but we do run a *vlog*, after all."

"Ah, yes," I sigh. "I forget how we got Internet famous in the first place. Yeah, we totally don't deserve the hype."

Jasper shrugs. "They think we're funny—and hot."

"Neither of which is true."

Jasper makes a noise of disagreement so loudly I can hear it over the slam of my locker door. He uses pushing up the fuzzy white brim of his hat as an excuse to flex his hardly there muscles and then purses his lips, making a face he thinks is absolutely smoldering but actually looks ridiculous. "I don't know what you're talking about," he says between pouty lips. "I'm a total babe."

I cross my arms and raise an eyebrow, shaking my head in a silent *no, Jasper . . . no.* He simply wiggles his now visible eyebrows and stares intensely at me behind squinted lids.

"What are you doing?"

Lenny steps around me, his blond hair also tucked beneath a Santa cap. The rest of him is bundled up in something I'm sure his mother made him throw on before he left the house. A bubble vest over his ugly red Christmas sweater, a knitted scarf that looks like it might have pink in it, and bulky gloves. I can't tell which one of them looks more ridiculous.

Jasper still holds his flexed-arm, squinty-eyed, pouty-lipped pose but looks to Lenny instead and replies in a theatrically deep voice, "Being a chick magnet. What the hell are you wearing?"

"I regret letting my mom drive me to school, okay," Lenny says defensively, and then makes a pinched face and tacks on, "Quit looking at me like that. It's creepy."

"It's smokin'."

"No." Lenny shakes his head urgently and grabs my sleeve. "Because I love you, June, and we've been friends for ages, I've got some advice I want you to take very seriously because I'm afraid you're on the receiving end of some creepy seduction tactic."

I giggle at the tone of his voice, which sounds like he's trying really hard to be serious but a laugh is trying to intervene. Still, I turn to him, alarmed, and ask, "What is it?"

He leans in close to my head and whispers directly into my ear, "Run, run far away from this guy."

With that, he tugs hard on my sleeve and we both take off down the nearly deserted hallway toward the student parking exit. Jasper calls after us and Lenny pulls me closer, dodging stragglers while shouting, "Sorry! Pardon me! Coming through!"

I can barely run because I'm laughing hard and my legs feel like they're made of nothing. Once, I hear Jasper's hysterical, high-pitched laugh when he's managed to catch up. He tries grabbing for my waist, but Lenny reaches back and swats him off.

People are throwing us looks of complete disgust, beyond annoyed with our antics. Someone spews a mouthful of profanity at us when my backpack brushes up against him in our mad rush to get outside. I hear Jasper mutter a quick apology, but then Lenny and I are at the door and slamming our bodies at it, shivering when the cold air hits our skin.

The ground is covered in a thin layer of crunchy snow, and I know patches of ice are hiding underneath it. I pull back on Lenny a little and we slow down, but still rush across the parking lot to Jasper's car, knowing that he never locks it and we could break in and lock him out long enough to adjust things—which he hates. We're almost there, his tiny blue junker is sitting patiently, begging us to attack, and Jasper is screaming something like, "You idiots can *walk* home!"

Then Lenny slips on a thin sheet of ice that cracks under his weight, I trip over him, and Jasper lands on top of me in a series of stumbles and cuss words. My whole body stings, and I think I hear several bones in my body crunch under Jasper's weight. Dizzy, I groan and lift my head, seeing Jasper has fallen sideways across my torso and my legs are tangled with Lenny's.

"You guys suck so much! I hate you—oh my God, I bit my tongue! Kissmas can't happen without this tongue! You've killed the magic, you jerks! You broke the moneymaker!" Jasper carries on, slowly pulling himself up.

Lenny just mumbles something incoherent about his ankle and covers his face with his hands. All of us flinch when someone's horn blares at us. We're fallen soldiers smack-dab in the middle of the battlefield. Slowly, we move out of their way. They blare their horn the entire time we're picking ourselves up, and even though he's limping, Lenny flips them the bird.

"That was *not* a good idea," I moan while we're piling into Jasper's car. Once seated, I pull a banged-up elbow close to my body and feel around the sore part, hissing when all I feel is throbbing and stinging.

"You're *so* gonna get it tonight for Kissmas," Jasper threatens, starting his car with a flick of his wrist.

Lenny groans beside him and pulls his right foot into his lap. He then proceeds to remove his wet shoe and sock to poke at his hurt ankle. This makes Jasper swat at him, grumbling something about smelly feet and no sympathy.

"You're broken," I shoot back. "I'm not getting *anything*."

"Maybe I'll make you kiss it better," he snaps, and lifts his eyes, making eye contact with me in his rearview mirror. I glare back at him and shake my head.

We sit like this for a couple of minutes, all groaning over one thing or another. It's not until we're too far to turn back that Lenny realizes he lost his Santa cap sometime during our wild escape, making him sink into an even fouler mood. He doesn't realize, however, that Jasper stole it as payback for plotting against him. After Jasper drops Lenny off at his house, he pulls a red-and-white hat from under his legs and dangles it before me.

"Think I should tell him?"

"You kicked him when he was down," I say flatly, body stiff

both from our fall and his cramped car. "Don't give it back to him and I'll give you a reason to complain about your barely damaged tongue."

He seems intrigued by this and drops the hat in the passenger seat before completely twisting around to look at me. His eyes twinkle and his lips quirk upward. "And what is it you would do?"

"Don't you worry about it," I say simply, and run a hand through my curls.

"Kiss me better, and I'll go and give his hat back," Jasper offers, chin lifting as he awaits my response.

I tilt my head a little in confusion and raise an eyebrow at him. "I'm already kissing you later."

"No, like right now," he says.

I try to laugh, but it comes out as a startled gasp, like I've lost the ability to make normal-sounding noises. He just looks at me with the same waiting expression. "Aren't you sick of kissing already?"

He laughs—a proper chuckle—and shakes his head. "June, I will never get bored of kissing."

"Maybe it *is* weird that we do this," I say after a pause.

"C'mon," he begs, and reaches over to brace himself on the passenger seat while he wiggles closer to me. "It's not weird unless you're feeling—"

"I'm not," I interrupt quickly, feeling the need to clear that up before he gets any ideas.

"Well then, what's the big deal?"

My arms are crossed in my lap, legs crammed up against the back of the passenger seat, and he's practically stretched across the middle of his car, lower lip jutting out pleadingly. It looks like a truly desperate situation.

"It's not a big deal," I say carefully, and his face lights up. "I just think that it's excessive." The pout returns.

"Lenny's waiting . . ."

"Jas—"

"Is one measly peck too much to ask?"

I groan, knowing Lenny will find some way to make me feel guilty for not winning back his hat because I didn't feel like giving Jasper a little peck on the lips. He'd shake his head and joke about how our friendship wasn't worth saving for one little kiss—how unfortunate for me. He'd hold off giving me my Christmas gift or something of the sort. He'd never let me forget.

Jasper's muttering a chorus of pleases, so I finally just roll my eyes and lean forward to shut him up. My lips catch his on an intake of breath between words, and I make sure it's short enough that he can't savor anything. However, just as I'm starting to lean back, the hand bracing him on the passenger seat breaks away and braces itself on the back of my head instead to keep me stationary. Startled, I try to pull away, but he laughs and keeps pressing repeated kisses all over my lips— whether I kiss him back is completely irrelevant.

"All—better," he says around two final lingering kisses and then grabs the Santa cap and bolts from the car to Lenny's front door.

I'm too dizzy to say anything back.

———

When Lenny sees me later that night, he's got his hat back—and he's also limping, but he told us not to worry about it. I guess he twisted it, but it doesn't look bad. Anyway, before we start the ninth day of Kissmas, he hugs me to his side and plants a kiss on my cheek.

"Thank you," he sings into my ear. "How about we try that again when it's not icy outside?"

I think about all the kisses Jasper stole a few hours back and understand Lenny's desire for revenge.

"Deal," I whisper back, bumping my fist against his.

My dad is waiting with drive-through fast food when I get home later that night. I know because the moment I walk through the door I can smell burgers and hear him breaking my mother's No Eating in the Living Room rule. I quickly pull off my boots and hang up Jasper's Santa cap (which I'd removed during Kissmas and hid under my hoodie—winning a little revenge for Lenny) and jog into the newly claimed man cave.

Since my dad started his vacation, he's been doing nothing but sitting on his butt in front of the television watching ESPN and munching on whatever he can find. Yesterday, I witnessed him eat an entire bag of potato chips as soon as my mom left for work. For the first time in my life, I was the one who had to play bad cop and remind him of Mom's No Eating in the Living Room rule and call him out for acting like one of his heart-attack patients. He didn't look the least bit guilty. In fact, the satisfaction on his face reminded me of a toddler who smiles at you the whole while they're being scolded for drawing on the wall or eating cookies before dinner.

When I enter the room, I find him ripping the wrapping off a cheeseburger, with his feet propped up on the coffee table. The television is flashing football highlights while an annoying voice makes comments. I can tell he's been in the same spot most of the day when I notice the ratty nightshirt and sweatpants combination he's wearing.

When he sees me he pauses for a moment, long enough for ketchup to drip from his burger to his lap, and then, as if I'd barged in at an inconvenient time, he sighs, "I wasn't expecting you."

I raise an eyebrow.

"There's no school tomorrow."

I shrug and lean against the entryway. Sure, I would usually sleep over at Jasper's, but I wasn't going to let that happen tonight after Kissmas. That idea just screams trouble.

"I thought we'd hang out since I never see you," I tell him. It's only partly true. I'd rather sleep over at Jasper's like I usually do, but after all that kissing, it didn't feel appropriate. Plus, when I thought about sleeping over, I felt guilty knowing my dad would be all alone.

His lips purse a little, eyes narrowing as he considers this, and then he shrugs and pats the cushion beside him. When I seat myself, he pulls another burger from the bag beside his feet on the coffee table and turns the volume on the television down. I can feel his eyes on me while I unwrap the burger. It's something I'm used to, because my parents always look at me for long periods of time—like they're trying to soak me in or something—but then he pushes some of my curls away from my face and I freeze. Jasper's hickey is on the side of my neck that's facing him.

"Have you been kissing somebody?"

I turn my face toward him, which probably doesn't help, and try my best to make a face that suggests I have no idea what he's talking about.

He chuckles and points to my lips. "This is how I found out about your last boyfriend, remember? Kiss-swollen lips and"—he pushes the neckline of my hoodie down and pokes at the bruise there—"hickeys."

I can feel the blood rushing to my cheeks and my face warming, but I don't know how to stop it. I feel dumb, like I can't come up with a coherent sentence without stuttering. The embarrassment numbs my entire body. Still, I attempt to defend myself somehow by saying, "I wore some tinsel as a scarf today, and it irritated my neck."

He looks skeptical and then moves his finger back up to point at my lips. "Explain that."

"My lips get chapped in the winter."

It doesn't look like he's buying a single thing. Instead, it looks like he wants to laugh at the pathetic excuses I'm trying to get him to believe. He's silent for a moment, eyes moving around the room as if searching for something. Then I watch him glance back down at my neck, shake his head and then turn back toward the television.

"Tell Jasper to stop eating your neck and come over to dinner sometime."

At this point, I've gone ahead and taken a bite of my burger. Upon hearing that sentence, however, I promptly spit it into a napkin and start coughing up the pickle I inhaled when he said it.

"What?" I sputter, and dive for his soda to stop the coughing.

"Tell Jasper to stop eating your neck—"

Slamming his cup down, I look over my shoulder and snap, "I heard you the first time!"

He scratches his stubbly chin, trying to hide a smile. "I know it's Jasper."

"I'm *not* dating *Jasper*!"

He grins. "I work in a hospital, June Bug. I know when someone is bullshitting me."

"I'm not—" I stop and bury my face in my hands to allow myself a deep breath. How could he have possibly noticed my lips are a little red from kissing? I'd kissed Jasper over twenty minutes ago in a game we invented called Kiss Pong, where we threw candy cane Hershey's Kisses across his kitchen table into each other's mouths. Every time we were successful, we locked lips. To be honest, it was kind of fun—but that's not the point.

"Why are you so embarrassed?"

"I'm not dating Jas," I repeat, face still buried in my hands.

"So you're just kissing him, then?"

When I don't answer, he lets out a long sigh and leans forward to try and pry me out of my huddle.

"What's up?" he asks as soon as I'm sitting up again. I can't look at him, though. My cheeks will only turn a brighter shade of red. I was hoping I wouldn't have to explain all this to him. My dignity is at stake here.

"We—uh—it's a long story," I admit.

"I've got more than enough time."

So I reluctantly go on to tell him about Jasiper, the fans, the dare, the invention of Kiss Cam, and finally Kissmas. He stops to ask questions about things he doesn't understand, like "shipping" and why we would agree to do something as dumb as kiss each other. He thinks it's creepy that people want to watch us do that. I explain it to him the only way I can: Spider-Man and Gwen Stacy. He has a soft spot for his childhood hero,

Spider-Man, and thinks Gwen Stacy is hot—so he gets the idea of shipping right away. I leave out all the details about the kinds of kisses that happen—but I don't think he wants to know about those anyway.

When I've spilled all my guts to him, he runs his hand over his face and then through his unkempt hair, groaning a little. He doesn't look mad or disgusted by my choices. Instead, he looks tired.

"It doesn't make sense," he says after a moment. I blink in confusion, having thought he understood everything completely.

"What aren't you getting?"

"Isn't there some . . ." He stops, and his hands do some weird motions. His face looks strained, but finally he just spits it out. "Isn't there some . . . tension?"

"Uh . . ." I don't know what kind of tension he's referring to, but by the look on his face I can guess he means sexual tension. "Oh my *God*, Dad! I am *not* having this conversation with you!"

"Well, what?" he asks, scratching the back of his head. "Do I need to buy you condoms for Christmas? Do you *like* him?"

"Dad!" I'm horrified. The blush is burning down my neck, and I'm hiding my face in my hands again.

"C'mon," he groans, and I can tell he's equally as uncomfortable. "If we're going to be talking about boys, then I need to ask."

"We're not talking about boys. We're talking about Jasper," I grind out.

"Who, if you haven't noticed from waking up next to him for years, has a penis."

"Oh my God." I feel like sinking into the cushions of the couch

and disappearing forever. All these years I'd tried to avoid noticing what the male body does overnight. I do not need it being brought up by my dad.

"Look, I know you're a smart girl and I trust you, but what you're doing with Jasper is not smart, June. I'm not talking about sex here. I'm talking about this no-strings-attached kissing show. Do you know how many friends-with-benefits relationships actually work out? Close to none. And, to be completely honest with you, it doesn't make me feel good about you doing all this with him and then being open to other relationships. It's dirty."

"It's *just* kissing."

He must sense the frustration in my voice, because what he says next is gentler. "Somebody is going to get hurt—and he would be one hell of a friend to lose."

I don't say anything after that. I know he's right, because I've thought about the exact same things. But Jasper promised me something in the beginning. When I start to get uncomfortable, we stop. And, well, should I be uncomfortable?

When Allison suggested we might have feelings for each other, I *did* have a moment of panic. And it's no secret I'm not opposed to kissing Jasper all the time—which *is* weird, right? But it shouldn't be, because we have this all figured out, Jasper and I. So, really, it's nothing to worry about.

Well, except for the fact that everything seemed far too sincere in the back of his car when I "kissed him better." Was it a possibility? Were there feelings developing? Did we need to stop?

The more I think about it, the more uncomfortable I get with this whole thing. Perhaps we are well into dangerous territory and I've been ignoring it for the sake of Kissmas. But we can't just call it off now. We *have* to finish it. Maybe after Kissmas . . .

But will it be easy to break off Kiss Cam when it's now a segment in our videos? What would our viewers think? They'd know something is up and start rumors. And then there's Jasper. Would he be offended? He *has* to understand, right?

At this point it seems that either way one of us is going to get hurt—but I don't know how to stop it.

Fifteen

The Faults in Our Kissing Arrangement

THE TALK WITH my dad gives me a lot to think about, but Kissmas makes it hard to decide what to do. After mulling over the problem for a while, I've decided that my dad is right. I know I already had time to think about Kiss Cam before we started it. I also know that things shouldn't be weird unless feelings are involved—that's what Jasper and I discussed—however, I can't ignore the fact that my dad is right. This whole thing is *dirty*. How can I kiss Jasper and then turn around and flirt with the attractive boy who sits behind me in calculus? What does that say about me? What does it say about Jasper?

A part of me wants to think like Jasper and not care about what is considered "normal" and what is considered "abnormal." Like him, I'd just like to go with the flow. But I know that one of us has to be responsible—and since I know he never will, that leaves me. I have to be the one to end this arrangement, because it's just not right for friends to behave this way. We've gone too far.

The problem is I'm conflicted, even though I know my decision is right. How will we be able to drop Kiss Cam when Kissmas has made it so popular? What are our viewers going to say when we suddenly end the segment we've put so much emphasis on and know they enjoy? How is Jasper going to react when I tell him I can't go through with this anymore? Is he going to respect that I'm no longer comfortable with it, or is he somehow going to convince me that the segment needs to stay?

I know he doesn't want Kiss Cam to end. He gets all giddy every time he gets an e-mail about it, reads a comment about our ship, or starts filming the next day of Kissmas. He thinks it's some sort of fun challenge. It's a game to him. He's not going to understand.

I get nervous every time I consider all the conflicts that could arise the moment I put Kiss Cam on the chopping block. I feel even worse when Jasper kisses me over the next three days, because he doesn't know how Kissmas is going to end.

But it was the deal from the beginning. When I say stop, we stop.

———

Waking up Christmas morning still gives me the same warm feeling that it did when I was younger. The only difference is instead of waking up at seven in the morning to jump on my parents' bed, I wake up at ten in the morning and bang on my parents' door before heading to the bathroom to try and make myself semi-presentable. If you have parents like mine, you know how crucial it is to tidy up a bit before opening gifts, because even if you get a pair of socks, you're taking a picture. Twenty years from now I'm not going to care about that pair of socks, but for the sake of "memories," I have to go through with the whole process—even if I have to fake a smile.

My parents make it downstairs before I do, and my mom goes ahead and turns on all the Christmas lights. She's also taken time to light all her cinnamon-apple candles, which is going to make the house smell sweet before we finish exchanging gifts.

After my dad gets the camera, we all sit down in front of the tree my mom and I decorated a couple of weeks back. I watch my dad's face light up when he opens the gift from my mother, I watch her gush over some diamond earrings, and my parents capture my face after I open every single present they got me. There is hugging and more picture taking that makes my cheeks hurt. My mom starts laughing so hard she cries when my dad tries to set up his new tent in the living room but can't even get it to stand upright. I *do* end up getting a new pair of fuzzy socks, so I slide down the hall in them until I lose my balance and fall down.

My mom makes homemade cinnamon rolls later in the morning, and I go back to my bedroom to change. Every year my family and Jasper's go over to Lenny's house for a big meal. It gives Lenny, Jasper, and me an opportunity to chill out and exchange gifts while our parents socialize with one another.

Usually, I just throw my hair up and go in my sweatpants, but I can't this time. While our parents are catching up over sugar cookies and Mrs. Davis's homemade white hot chocolate, Lenny, Jasper, and I are going to sneak off to film the final day of Kissmas. If I'm getting kissed—especially on camera—I need to do better than pulling on a sweatshirt so I don't have to wear a bra. So I dab on a little makeup, and dress in a white sweater and dark jeans. The effort I put in doesn't go unnoticed by my dad, either, because when I meet him and my mom downstairs I receive a raised eyebrow once he's taken in my appearance. The suspicion stops at him, though, because my mom sighs in relief upon seeing me—praising God I've matured enough to realize that my appearance is a direct reflection on how she's raised me.

We walk across the street to Lenny's house, just kitty-corner from ours. His parents welcome us at the door with Jade and Ruby at their sides. Both girls shove their way through the door to hug my legs, and my mom hands her cinnamon rolls over to Lenny's mom.

Then we're inside and Lenny's sisters are trying to show me everything they got for Christmas and Lenny, decked out in flannel pajamas, is trying to pull them off me. I'm too overwhelmed by food and Leeann's hugs and the Davises' perfectly decorated house to even notice Jasper's absence. When everything final settles down, though, I realize he missed the food. After being served some of Mrs. Davis's white hot chocolate and sitting through Jade and Ruby's gift presentation, I'm able to sneak off with Lenny—leaving his entirely blond family with mine and Leeann.

"He ate before you came and locked himself in my room so Jade and Ruby couldn't bother him while he was setting up," Lenny explains to me as he drags me up the winding staircase behind the kitchen. I've been wondering where Jasper has been hiding, and Lenny didn't want to explain it to me in the middle of our families, lest they notice his disappearance, too.

"I'm just surprised he got away with it," I say breathlessly at the landing. "Leeann's always bragging about him."

"She's got herself to celebrate this year," he replies. "You know, with her promotion and all. She's too excited to talk about our vlog."

"Thank God. My dad knows about Kiss Cam, and I don't think he needs a reason to bring it up," I tell him.

Lenny stops just in front of his bedroom and yanks my arm back. "He knows *what?*"

I glance at his door, knowing Jasper's just behind it. "He saw right through me," I whisper. "Hickey and all."

"Shit," he mutters.

"Yeah." I sigh. "We talked and it got me thinking—but I think I need to tell you and Jas at the same time."

"Uh-oh." He searches my face, trying to guess what I could be talking about.

"Yep," I sigh again, and take a final stride toward his bedroom door and open it.

Lenny and I step in to find Jasper is wearing that stupid Santa cap he'd stolen back from me and standing underneath some perfectly hung mistletoe.

"Merry Christmas," he greets us, opening his arms dramatically to display the busy Christmas tree pattern on his sweater.

I smile, "Merry Christmas."

He flashes his pearly whites and places his hands on his hips. "Are you *ready* for this?"

Lenny closes the door behind us and then comes to stand by my side. I toss him a side glance and then nod at Jasper. "I am," I say. "But I've got some news first."

Jasper shrugs. "What news?"

The smile I wear falters, and my heart begins pounding for no real reason at all. "Well, my dad knows about Kiss Cam now—"

Jasper's smile vanishes. "Is he downstairs *right at this very moment*? Is he going to *kill me*?"

I snort at the absurdity of the idea of my dad wanting to kill Jasper for kissing me. My dad likes Jasper way too much, so that pretty much guarantees that will never happen.

"No." I laugh, and then collect myself, knotting my fingers together behind my back. "It's just, you know, weird that he knows. And it kind of got me thinking that we shouldn't do Kiss Cam anymore."

Jasper's posture sinks and Lenny moans pathetically, *"Aw, June. No."*

I shrug defeatedly. "I know, guys. But I think maybe this should be our finale, you know? After this, I don't think continuing while my dad knows is a good idea. I've got a crazy guilty conscience just being up here right now. Besides, I miss the good ole days when it was just the three of us making stupid daily videos. Unscripted, no pressure, just fun. I think Lenny's really gotten the short end of the stick here." I gesture at Lenny, and he wraps an arm around me, but I can't tell what Jasper is thinking. His expression is vacant.

I hope that it makes them understand why Kiss Cam needs to stop. The popularity on VlogIt isn't worth it. My guilty conscience is eating me alive. Plus, we're a broken group. Lenny gets pushed to the side, and it turns into the June and Jas show. We're vloggers, not some reality TV stars. We need to face the facts. We need to see the repercussions.

"Okay," Jasper finally says, and the light returns to his eyes. He just needed a moment to process. "You say enough is enough, then that's what it is."

"Really?" I say, my voice hopeful. Lenny squeezes my shoulder.

"Anything for you, Juniper, dear." Jasper winks. "Just kiss me good. It's Christmas, after all."

I realize Jasper is my best friend, sure, but he's also a great kisser. He's gawky, yes, but he knows how to make me blush. He's not the hottest guy I've shared a kiss with, but his suggestiveness and unfailing wit make him hard to ignore. He's disgusting, but he's charming. He's difficult, but he's passionate. Right now, I'm going to forget the fact that he's my gawky best friend who's disgusting and difficult and allow myself to drink up the other side of him.

Lenny picks up the camera, and I march up to Jasper and wipe off his goofy grin with a kiss that makes my toes curl and his fingers tangle in my hair. It's a final kiss, and we give it everything. It leaves a lighthearted feeling dancing amid the heat. Every messed-up best-friend fantasy I'd been blushing over for the past couple of weeks runs through my mind, so I kiss them away. I leave them on his lips, sealed with a kiss. And then it's done.

"On the twelfth day of Kissmas Jasiper leaves their ship, a final kiss they'll never forget," Lenny sings.

———

New Year's Eve my parents are back at work, so I do what I've always done: bring my lonely self to Jasper's.

After the last kiss we shared under the mistletoe on

Christmas, we've pretty much returned to normal. Since we aren't kissing every day anymore, the whole idea of Kiss Cam feels like something from the past. And even though we all know it's a very recent thing, we don't treat it that way.

But I have to admit. I do miss having to be on my toes, ready for Jasper to swoop out of nowhere and kiss me in the way I've grown so used to. It sort of feels like something is missing, but I figure it's normal—all part of adjusting.

The viewers figured out Lenny's riddle from the last Kissmas video, which in combination with our weeklong kissing hiatus, has turned them berserk. Although some cheeky viewers speculate that Jasiper kisses may be over, but perhaps there is hope for Leniper or Jenny.

And I did try to get some Jenny action. But to no avail. With Kiss Cam off the table, Lenny was having *none* of it.

Now Jasper's feet are propped up on the coffee table in his cramped living room. He's popped popcorn and pulled out the Pop-Tarts and Dr Pepper for us while we watch the ball drop in Times Square. The room is dark except for the glow of the television. People's New Year's resolutions are sliding along the bottom of the screen, and there's fifteen minutes to midnight.

I'm a bit suspicious of him. He's having the worst problem sitting still and just *won't* stop glancing in my direction. At one point I actually catch his eye and frown in confusion, but he just gives me his usual impish grin and piles some more popcorn gracelessly into his mouth.

"Oh, hey!" Jasper jumps up suddenly from his spot beside me and dashes out of the room. "I forgot to give you something on Christmas!"

I turn my head from the final performance of the night, eyes following Jasper out of the room. I'm curious, yes, but not curious enough to wait with my heart beating rapidly for his return. Instead, I just roll my eyes and sink back into the couch, turning the volume on the television up even though I don't know who this performer is or what his song is called.

After a minute, Jasper jogs back into the room and tosses a small package at me. I catch it and wait for him to sit down before examining the neatly wrapped box in my hand. It looks too small to be interesting, so I reach across the couch for my jacket and slip it in my pocket.

"Thanks," I say. "I'll open it when I get home."

He looks a little disappointed and readjusts himself next to me a couple of times. Again, his restlessness is noted, and I give him a weird look.

"You okay?" I ask with a slight laugh.

He adjusts himself again, and then scratches his jaw, eyes staying trained on the television and not meeting mine.

"Uh, no," he admits, and then runs an anxious hand through his hair and turns to me, having changed his mind. "Actually, yes. I'm great, actually. And I was just wondering if you were great."

My eyebrows pinch together, and I can't help a nervous laugh from tumbling out. "Yeah, Jas. Everything is good."

It suddenly feels very tense. I can sense something not right with this whole situation, and my stomach does somersaults while goose bumps rise on the back of my neck. I can't place the weird vibe I'm getting, and a part of me thinks I don't want to.

"Good, good." He nods and pinches his lips between his fingers to think. I lean away from him slightly—scared for what he might say next. Finally, he takes his hand away from his mouth and props it up on the back of the couch as he attempts to make eye contact with me. But he seems to have a hard time maintaining it.

"Jas . . . ," I say carefully.

"So, listen."

My eyebrows hike up my forehead, and my heart does a couple of nervous flutters. "Okay . . ."

His voice is a little shaky. "So, I've been thinking that maybe I haven't been the most honest person lately."

Suddenly, it clicks and I freeze. Goose bumps pop up along my arms and my breath hitches in my throat. My body is in paralysis but my mind is racing. I swallow hard and manage to ask the question, "Really?"

"Really." He pauses, and I know he's just as tongue-tied as me. "When we were kissing, it wasn't supposed to mean anything, right?"

I nod, but mechanically, mind foggy and world unfocused.

"Well, I would be lying if I said I didn't feel something." Far away, the countdown to the New Year has begun. "And I think you do, too."

I bite my lip and shake my head and he reaches out to stop me.

A little desperately he swoops back in and claims, "There is no way that was one-sided. You have to know . . ."

"Jas . . ."

Thirty, twenty-nine, twenty-eight, twenty-seven . . .

"If you're afraid that things will change—they don't have to. Nothing has to change," he continues, more urgently now, and shaky. "We can still be us, exactly the same except when someone asks if we're a couple, I can say yes. Because, June, to me you're more than just my friend."

Fourteen, thirteen, twelve . . .

"Jas—"

"And I want to start my New Year *with* you."

He's finally able to look me in the eye just as the blinking ball in Times Square has reached the end. *One* is still ringing in my ears. I meet his eyes for less than a second before he kisses me into the New Year. Those eyes are soft brown and his cheeks are flushed and then his lips are warm on mine and it's a real kiss. No camera, no bet, no experiment, no revenge, no blackmail.

He's confident and gentle. The first press of his lips on mine is sweet, but my stunned unresponsiveness makes the second urgent. After that, he's all I can feel. One hand is on the back of my neck, the other pulls my body flush against his. I can feel how strong his feelings are for me with every kiss.

I was too late. Everyone was right. He's in love with me and I'm not in love with him and it's the most horrible feeling I've ever experienced. I let Kiss Cam continue and he thinks I let it continue because I love him, too, and I didn't know how to say it. He thinks we've been hiding our feelings, but the only feeling I can admit to having is lust—and it's not a good enough reason to let this relationship happen.

My hands slide up his chest to push him back, but I end up pulling him closer when his tongue dips into my mouth and his true kissing skills are revealed. My brows furrow at how weak I am, and I become frustrated. I feel even more pathetic when he pries my mouth open again and I release a shaky breath between kisses, trying desperately to stop him, but not knowing how to get my body to stop wanting him.

There's pressure building up in my chest, and the sinking feeling continues to spread. I'm shaking with fear when I realize it. I can't push back because I know it's all over when I do.

Jasper finally surfaces to catch his breath. Breath uneven, he leans his forehead on mine, and that's when I let a tear leak out of the corner of my eye. There has to be a rational one, one who has to think about what's best for a relationship.

"Jas," I choke out.

His eyes flutter open and he pulls away from me, eyebrows knitting together worriedly.

"June, what—?"

"We can't."

"What are you talking about?" His voice is sharp, so different from the gentle tone used seconds ago that I flinch.

"We can't do this," I repeat, and meet his eyes with a halfhearted shrug. "You're my best friend and we have this vlog and—Jas—think about Lenny for a second, huh? Think about the kind of pressure our relationship would go through with it being public to the world. We've seen vlogging couples fall apart and viewers take sides—and it's just messy, okay? And Lenny. Since Kiss Cam, people have forgotten he's even a part of WereVloggingHere. What happens if we break up? I—I can't imagine what I would do without you."

His jaw is clenching and he stops looking at me when I mention the vlog. I'm getting desperate. I need him to understand. "You promised, Jas," I say tensely. "You promised not to do this to us. You said there was nothing, and there was something."

"I thought—"

I press my lips together and shake my head.

He slaps his hands against his knees and makes a strangled noise that sounds a little like he's letting out a deep breath and a little like a laugh. Then he leans backward against the couch cushions and buries his face in his hands.

"Jas," I say hurriedly, "I don't want this to change things. I just want to be like we were."

There's a moment of silence between us where the only thing I hear is my heartbeat and the fuzzy noise of the host's voice on the television.

"Me too," he says after what feels like forever. "But I'm going to need a little time."

He walks me to the door a little while later when the tense atmosphere turns awkward and neither of us wants to look at each other. Before I step outside, I turn around to look at him for probably the last time for a while. He smiles at me, but it's not the Jasper smile I'm used to. He's broken and I'm the reason.

He said he wants space, to keep some distance between us while he sorts himself out. After that, he told me we could be like we were before Kiss Cam. It's a silver lining, I suppose. Until then, I guess we're just going to have to respect new boundaries—boundaries we've never had before.

"I didn't want this to happen," I say outside his doorstep, hugging myself against the wind.

"It doesn't have to," he says almost hopefully. But that hopefulness fades when I look at my feet and swallow guiltily. I can't leave him like this, so I start reaching for straws.

Before he closes the door, I step forward and say, "I love you, you know."

"Yeah," he says, and sweeps the door past him until it's almost closed, "but not the way I love you."

After that, I walk back home and lie on the couch and spend my first day of the New Year alone.

Sixteen

For the First Time

AFTER SPENDING NEW Year's alone, I didn't expect to see anyone for the rest of break. Then midafternoon rolls around the following day and someone is banging on my front door, forcing me to sprint from my bedroom to the entrance before the noise wakes up my dad. A part of me pulls open the door to stop the ruckus from continuing; the other part is hoping to see Jasper standing there.

When I open the door, my stomach sinks even though I knew I was getting my hopes up by expecting Jasper. I'm surprised, though, to find Lenny on my front steps, hands now shoved into his pockets and blond hair ruffled by chilly gusts of wind.

"Hi," he says after a moment of silent consideration.

"Hi," I say back, still wary as to why he's on my welcome mat. It's not that it's unusual for Lenny and me to hang out alone, but it's not an everyday thing, either. And, well, I'm certain Jasper would have gone to Lenny after what happened on New Year's Eve.

"I was just with Jasper," he says slowly, eyes steady on my face. I swallow hard and nod, my eyes dropping to look somewhere besides his.

So he did see Jasper. They probably talked about me—about that night—and now Lenny is here to make me feel terrible all over again. I spent New Year's alone thinking about how simply I had rejected Jasper, how accepting he was of it, and how empty I feel—empty because I have this awful feeling that we'll never be the same again. Empty because it feels like I've lost my best friend, even though he insists after some time he'll be fine. But I know better. His confession, the way he kissed me, how he couldn't even look at me when he pointed out how different our loves are for each other. When his feelings for me fade, he'll be left with a skeleton of our relationship. When we attempt to fill it back out, he won't see what he saw before. I'm afraid he won't want me. That he'll have learned to live without me. He'll only remember the pain I caused him and he won't want to risk it again. That's Jasper. He did it with his dad and he'll do it to me, too.

"Can I come in?"

I'm surprised by the request, which sounds cordial, and lift my head to scan his face and see if I heard him right. I was under the impression that Lenny would be angry with me after hearing Jasper's side of the story.

"Please?" His voice is sincere, and when I meet his eyes, they're soft. I know he's not here to tell me off.

I let him in and lead him into the living room. Our Christmas decorations are still up, and I see his eyes roam around the room, taking in all the lights and bows. I'm glad I decided to get properly dressed this morning.

He sits down in the same spot my dad spent all of winter break, but he balances on the edge of the cushion like he's hesitant to make himself too comfortable. I sit down next to him in the same fashion.

"Is he okay?" I ask in a small voice, ashamed to have to ask this about my best friend. I never wanted to hurt him. I didn't realize his feelings for me were so great.

"He's . . ." Lenny stops and shrugs. "He's confused."

"Oh no," I mutter, and bury my face in my hands, anchoring my elbows on my knees.

"He thought he read the signs right. . . ."

"I thought we were just joking around, you know?" I interject. "He made me think we were just messing around, and he lied. He lied, and now I don't know if we're going to be okay." I drag my hands down my face, cheeks burning with frustration.

If he would have just *talked* to me about it. If he hadn't been so rash, maybe, just maybe we could have figured this out. We wouldn't be in this mess. But no, Jasper doesn't think like that. He schemes and he's unrealistic. Maybe he thought Kiss Cam would spur something inside of me. He was wrong. His idea to bring us closer only tore us apart. I hate to be angry at him when we're both hurting, but I can't ignore that we're in this mess because he lied.

"He's not mad," Lenny says gently, and places a cautious hand on my back. "He doesn't hate you. He's in love with you—"

"Stop," I say, eyes squeezing closed. I can't hear that. Not Jasper.

His hand slides off my back and he's silent for a moment. I don't know if I'm being too sensitive or hostile, but it makes my stomach flutter uncomfortably when I hear those words. All I can remember is the look on his face before he closed the door in mine. It's a punch to the gut. I wish I could fix it. I fix everything. But I don't know if I can fix this. I can't fix someone's feelings. I can't hear those words.

"I was rooting for you guys," Lenny murmurs a moment later.

I sigh and my teeth grit together. "You and everyone else." I absently trace shapes into the couch cushion and try to make sense of everything that has happened. It makes my insides crawl and my brain go fuzzy. "It just . . . It wouldn't work."

"Why do you do that?"

"Do what?" I ask defensively. Heat builds up under my skin, but I force myself to breathe around it, to keep my face stony. Every part of me seems to be in disagreement.

"Try to convince yourself of things that aren't true."

"I'm *not*—"

"You are," he argues. "And you know how I can tell? You use me as an excuse. You use your friendship. But those are *positive* things, June. I support you guys, and strong friendships make relationships stronger, okay, that's fact. So stop using it as an excuse because you're scared and it's new."

"It's more *complicated* than that," I groan. "Allison would understand."

"Well, I want to understand, too. My best friend is brokenhearted and I want to know why." Lenny is hardly ever serious. He's a giant mush-ball of giggles and jokes, and to see him so strong of will is terrifying—and it makes me realize how weak of a fight I'm presenting.

I run my hands through my hair and release a low sigh. "He's too valuable of a friend to me," I reiterate. "I can't risk a messy breakup, okay? I don't want to feel that kind of hurt."

Lenny doesn't say anything back, and I assume it's because he knows that each turn is a dead end with me. I'm stubborn about this. He can't possibly understand. I don't want him to undermine me or convince me of things I'm not even sure are real.

But I melt. I have to know what he really thinks while he's being completely honest with me.

"Do *you* think Jasper and I are going to be okay?" I ask softly.

He breathes an airy chuckle out through a smile and wraps an arm around my shoulder, drawing me close to his side. "There really isn't a Jasper without a Juniper, is there?"

I cling to that thread of hope and nod to myself before resting my head on his shoulder.

———

The rest of break is quiet and lonely. I find myself spending a large amount of time locked away in my room, turning pages of magazines, answering e-mails (which ends up being somewhat difficult, since most of them concern Jasper and me and our kissing escapades), and watching some of my distant Internet friends' vlogs on VlogIt.

It brings me back six years into the past, when being alone was my entire life. I guess I never fully realized how much Jasper changed everything by pulling me out of my hammock and daring me to eat Mentos and Coke. What if Lenny hadn't stepped in? What if I'd walked away? What if Jasper hadn't taken an interest in me in the first place?

I don't like what I see. I don't want to give him up. He changed things, he fell in love, and six years later I walked away anyway.

I guess I sound desperate, but the thing is I've stumbled upon our own channel while watching my friend Danna's. Jasper's posted a New Year's resolution video with Lenny. My absence is practically unheard of. So this distance thing is serious. Does this mean he doesn't want me in the vlogs until he's sorted out?

I never watch the videos, because I hate seeing how I look and sound on tape, but there has always been a little bit of curiosity. Why do our viewers love us? What is it that brings them back, keeps them entertained?

I remember when WereVloggingHere was invited to a meet-and-greet. Our viewers told us that we are their friends, people they wish they knew, funny, interesting. I think about all the comments under our videos, informing the other viewers of a Jasiper moment, maybe even a Leniper or Jenny moment. Comments that ask us for advice. My mind wanders to the many e-mails I've received, flattering or otherwise. People who want to know us. They see something in the three of us: Jasper, Lenny, and me.

They see something in Jasper and me, not just our viewers, but the people in our lives, as well. I think about my relationship with Jasper, Kiss Cam, what Lenny has said, what my parents have noticed. Suddenly, I have the urge to watch the videos. I want to see what everyone else sees.

And that's it. I scroll through our channel's archive and watch us from the beginning.

I watch my hopeless affection for him bloom freshman year, his fingers constantly wrapped up in my curls that summer, Lenny's sly looks at the camera when Jasper and I banter, late night giggling into the camera at his house, my absence during periods of time when he had a girlfriend. I watch previous

Valentine's Day dances, snowman building in the dead of night in three feet of snow, the belly-flop contest from last year, and our first Kiss Cam. I watch all the Kiss Cams and Kissmas, too. I even read the comments. New and old.

I watch until it's late into the next morning and sunlight is filtering in through my curtains. Until the only thing I see when I blink are the words of our viewers.

Em_Bee: You two need to open your eyes and realize you are meant for each other. #Jasiper4Ever

leabasil: The sexual tension between Jas and June . . .

thatCRgirl: So, I just started watching WereVloggingHere. Are Jas and June together?

writingspaz: I met them at the meet-and-greet and they were so funny! P.S. Jas and June are closet lovers. ;)

ocean_: Kiss Cam confirms Jasiper is REAL.

I want us to be together so badly after watching the vlogs that I regret staying up all night to see them. I shouldn't have watched them. I screwed up. I let him slip out of my reach.

I want us to be like what they see, what I see, in the vlogs. The little family that we are, best friends, maybe soul mates. There *is* something there, and I've been too stubborn to let myself realize it. And maybe it's not too late.

———

It's back to school again on Monday, and Jasper picks me up like he always has. Lenny is already seated comfortably in the front seat, his backpack and Jasper's in a pile beside me. After settling in by pushing my knees against Lenny's seat and tucking my backpack under my legs, I slam the door and let the silence settle in around us. The buzzing awkwardness is new between Jasper and me, and he immediately fills in the gaps by flicking the radio on and turning it up high enough that I can take a hint. He doesn't want to talk to me. I avoid looking in the rearview mirror as much as possible. Lenny escapes the tension the whole ride to school by pulling his laptop out and messing with some editing software.

Jasper doesn't wait up for either of us after we're parked. My fingers and the tips of my ears are cold thanks to his slow-working heater, so I throw my backpack over my shoulder, push my hands into my pockets, and make a mad dash to the school entrance alone.

Lunch turns out to be worse than being trapped in a car with him for fifteen minutes. Jasper and I have always sat across from each other. So when I show up to our table and he's sitting there, already picking at his food, I hesitate. I don't want to change seating arrangements, but I don't know if he would mind. School isn't the best place to confront all the things that happened over break.

Allison brushes past me and takes her place, giving me a frown when I don't immediately sit down beside her. I don't want her to get involved because I know she'll push a finger into my chest and taunt "I told you so," so I send her a reassuring smile and sit down across from Jasper. He lifts his eyes from his tray then, and meets my gaze.

He looks unsure of himself, like he doesn't know if looking at me is okay. I don't want the awkwardness to ensue. I want to fix things—let him know that I was wrong before. So instead of looking away, I lock my eyes with his brown ones and smile, softly at first but then wider when his eyes smile back.

"You're awful quiet," Allison notes, and Jasper's eyes leave mine to look at her instead.

She's right. The bounciness isn't entirely there, the camera hasn't been out when I've been around, and he hasn't said a word to me all day. I know why, though, and Allison doesn't need to be involved. So when Jasper's eyes flick back to mine, I shake my head subtly.

"I—uh—" He looks back to her, rubbing his fingers across his chin and then dragging his nails down the side of his neck. His eyes are searching for an excuse until finally he clears his throat. "I'm just really tired. Still getting into the swing of things."

Lenny arrives then and immediately picks up a conversation with Jasper, their chatter helping to distract from the initial awkwardness. Allison engages me in a conversation of our own. I half listen into Jasper and Lenny's conversation, where Jasper sounds only a fraction as excited as usual. I glance at them occasionally and notice Jasper duck his head as he listens to Lenny. Then, like he's done a costume change behind a curtain, his head lifts up and there's a smile stretched across his face. Soon his clear, humor-filled voice is lost among those around us.

I can't get over it. Even in the midst of my discussion with Allison, I keep my eyes trained on Jasper, watching the laughs tumble out and his eyes gleam. I don't get why he can't do that with me. Why can't he do a costume change and pretend? I made a mistake, and he's making it hard to confront him.

Jasper realizes I'm watching him sometime later and licks his lips when he catches my eye. It's a slow movement. His eyes drop and his lips disappear behind teeth and tongue, a nervous habit.

He's nervous.

That's when I understand. He took off his mask on New Year's Eve. I've seen the face behind it. The magic and wonder are gone. He needs a new mask. He needs a new outlet. Until then, he's vulnerable. Until then, he can't hide. For the first time ever, I can see right through him.

Seventeen

Half a Heart

THINGS DON'T CHANGE as quickly as I'd like them to. I didn't expect Jasper to let the tension between us continue. It's not like him to drag things out. But every morning I get into his car and it's the same thing. He turns the radio up loud, keeps his eyes on the road, and removes himself from conversation. During lunch he doesn't meet my eyes unless Allison probes him. When Lenny pulls me into conversation, I can tell Jasper tries to keep the pep in his voice when we share a few words, but mostly he keeps his comments directed at Lenny. I see him across the hall at our lockers and he seems to be his normal self. However, the moment I cross into his line of sight he grows rigid. It's discouraging, and plucking up the courage to talk to him has never been this hard.

I know he's still vlogging. He wouldn't stop just because of what happened between us. It's always been *his* thing, anyway. But it's upsetting to be separated from his world like this, and it hasn't gone unnoticed by our viewers. My e-mails are piling up, most of them questioning my absence. If they're coming to me for answers, I know he hasn't attempted to discuss or acknowledge my disappearance. He's cut me off.

It's a frustrating balance of avoidance and calculated attempts to be his regular animated self with me, and I never know what I'm going to get. He said he needed space, not *this*.

By the end of the week, I'm so tired of walking on eggshells and our growing distance that I know I need to say something before our awkward interactions become the new norm. I have to let him know that there's a possibility I made a mistake—that maybe it's okay if we *do* try to be something real.

I decide to take action on Friday when there's no sign of Jasper trying to change the way things have been going. He can't keep avoiding me, and I can't keep chickening out. Because I *have* been chickening out, and that's because I'm afraid he'll be angry at me for putting us both through this. But I don't know that for sure. And if Jasper was serious about his feelings for me, then maybe I still have a chance to mend what I broke.

When the final bell rings, I go back to my locker to pick up my coat and get rid of books I won't need over the weekend. With my backpack resting on my feet, I plunge one arm into the sleeve of my coat and look over my shoulder to see if I can find Jasper among the other students. My fingers are fumbling with my zipper when I see him across the hall, leaning against the door of his locker. The zipper comes to a halt halfway up my torso when I realize that he's not alone.

I can't make out who it is, but the girl is my height with short, gold-colored hair. She's twisting from side to side as she talks to him, hugging a textbook close to her chest. Something she's said makes him lift his chin and deliver a flirty half grin. I'm curious now and pick up my backpack in preparation to get closer to the scene. But just as I'm closing my locker door, I notice her scribble something onto the corner of some notebook paper and rip it off to hand it to him. He takes it and holds it tightly between his fingers as he watches her walk away.

If this had happened weeks earlier, I would have walked over and snatched the scrap of paper from his hands to discover it's a phone number. He would have wrestled me for it, and I would have teased him and asked him a ton of immature questions regarding the budding relationship. But that was then, and this is now. Seeing him smile so brightly at that other girl when he's done nothing but give me forced smiles makes my insides burn.

It hardly seems fair. I know I don't deserve those charming smiles, but to see something that was *mine* directed at someone else leaves an uncomfortable feeling boiling under my skin. It makes me second-guess everything that happened between us.

It's a sense of urgency that breaks me from my stunned reverie and pushes me in his direction. We've all been meeting by his car at the end of the day. After that it's a silent ride home, and he drops me off first. This time, however, I'm changing the pattern. I have to say something, and I have to do it quick.

I catch him before he makes it to the student parking exit and tug him back by the sleeve before he pushes the door open. "Hey," I say.

He swivels quite dramatically and stumbles out of my grasp, which is so Jasper-like that I can't help but roll my eyes.

"I—uh—June . . . hi." I smile softly at him, thinking about how strange it is to see him this way with me. His confidence has been shattered, that's for sure. I myself feel my throat tighten when he says my name. We haven't had a private discussion since that night. I don't plan to do it here, but I figure I'll give him a brief notice.

Ignoring the way his body recoils from me, I give him the news. "We need to talk. Today, Jas."

His eyes meet mine nervously, like he's afraid I'll further hurt his pride or humiliate him in some way. I can't believe he'd think that of me, but at the same time I understand why.

"Like, *talk* talk or . . . acknowledge each other, or . . ." He trails off.

"I have no problem acknowledging you," I say a bit aggressively. Then, upon seeing his jaw clench, I add in a gentler tone, "That's part of what we need to talk about."

"Fine," he says coolly, and lets his weight fall onto the door, pushing it open.

He lets me walk out before him and then we walk separately to his car, finding Lenny ready to go in the passenger seat.

———

Jasper parks in his driveway and pulls the key out of the ignition, cutting off the radio. The silence doesn't have time to settle, Jasper makes sure of that.

Grabbing hold of the passenger seat headrest to help him twist around, he looks me dead in the eye and asks, "Are we doing this here or in the house?"

I wasn't expecting him to be so forward, seeing as he's been beating around the bush for the past week. However, I ignore the brashness, since I don't want to lose momentum. He probably figured it will be easier for both of us if we do this quick and to the point. I can't argue with that approach.

"Your car's heater works like shit, Jas. My hands are freezing."

"Fine, we'll do this inside." It's a snappy response that begins and ends with him opening and slamming his car door. There's an edge to his voice and I don't know where it came from, but I intend to put an end to all this as soon as possible.

I follow him out and jog across the lawn to keep up with him. When we step through the entry, he barely gives me time to shut the door. He grabs my hands from the doorknob and brings them to his lips, letting his massive hands fold over mine and trap the heat. My heart jumps into my throat, startled by the action, but melting as well. This is our thing.

His eyes meet mine for a moment, and then he drops my hands like they're burning his and turns away. My face flushes with embarrassment. He must have seen my mouth drop open or my eyebrows stitch together. Maybe he felt my pulse quicken. Perhaps he let go suddenly because he thought he saw a glimpse of something that could make the rejection sting even worse. My hands clench and I force myself to take a breath.

He quickly pulls off his jacket, and a chain around his neck gets caught in the zipper. In a panic, he quickly unhooks it and throws the jacket away while hiding whatever is around his neck under his shirt.

"What was that?" I ask, knowing full well how Jasper feels about wearing jewelry—and it's not good.

He looks back at me with flushed cheeks and furrowed brows that quickly disappear when he notices the confusion on my face.

"It's . . . nothing," he says quietly, and shakes his head. "I'm sorry about New Year's."

"I'm sorry, too," I reply just as quietly. "That's actually

what we need to talk about—"

"Look," he interrupts, "I know what you're going to say." He turns his body completely toward mine, and we stand across from each other in the narrow hallway, looking like we're about to duel.

"You don't, actually—"

"I do," he insists with a forced smile. "And that's okay, because I'm over it and I'm moving on."

"What?" For a moment, I swear my heart stops beating.

He reaches into his pocket and pulls out the piece of paper that girl handed to him after school. "This is a phone number from a girl named Elaina. She wants me to text her, and I'm willing. We have a class together, and she's a great girl. If things go well, I might just take her to the Winter Semiformal next month."

"Elaina?"

"Yeah, you see, it fixes everything," he explains. "I can be with Elaina and we can go back to normal, just like you want."

It feels a little like sleepwalking off a cliff. For a moment you're wandering, trying to make sense of everything, and then all of a sudden—you've hit free fall.

I can feel the buildup in my chest before I can register what's happening with me. I feel hollow, like I've lost everything. Like I just lost the race by a nanosecond—I even watched it happen. I watched them flirt, watched her hand him her number, and watched everything I thought I could save disappear.

And all I can do is stare blankly ahead and say, "Oh."

"Yeah," he replies a bit sheepishly. "So don't worry about us. I'm better now."

I nod without fully realizing what I'm doing, and then I'm

saying what I know I'm supposed to say. "I'm happy for you. I missed you."

"I missed you, too," he repeats back with a boyish half grin, and strides back toward me to give me a short hug. "So we're good?"

I pull out of his arms and brush hair behind my ears. "Yeah, yeah, we're good," I tell him without meeting his eyes. "Glad we worked that out."

Everything is numb, and I realize I'm still completely bundled up in my winter clothing and glance back at the door. "Well, I'll see you tomorrow, then."

"All right." He plasters on a smile that I can't decide whether is real or fake, and I leave.

Then I'm suddenly in my bedroom, collapsing onto my mattress with a tight chest and cold hands. I have no recollection of walking across the street, or fumbling with the key, or checking to see if my parents were home.

I run my hands over my face and through my hair and let out deep breaths.

Forget it. Move on. Forget it. Move on, I repeat over and over.

I slide out of my jacket and hang it up, and when I do, I notice one pocket is heavier than the other. Frowning, I stick my hand in and discover Jasper's Christmas gift to me still wrapped up in festive paper.

Sniffling, I rip open the package and slide the lid off the box, and when I realize what's inside, and what he tried to hide earlier, I curse myself and toss the trinket into my nightstand drawer.

I jump into bed and pull the covers over me and try deep breaths again, but they're useless, and the name Elaina is permanently etched in my head, and a half-heart necklace weighs so heavily in the drawer beside me I'm afraid the second floor will collapse.

So many what-ifs run through my mind, and I'm so overwhelmed that I let myself cry.

Eighteen
Verbal Smack-Downs

SOMETIME DURING THE following week, like all of Jasper's romantic interests, Elaina has lunch with us. Not knowing her, I sit quietly throughout the lunch period and listen to her talk to Jasper and Allison.

I didn't really get a good look at her before, but while she's chatting with the group, I eye her up. Before I only saw that she was my height with short, straight, gold-colored hair. Now I know that she's got small green eyes and a small pointed nose. Her lips are round and pouty—also small. Everything about her is soft and delicate, making her cute. Even her smile is slight and shy—but maybe that was just her trying to be coy.

Allison revealed to me in our last chat that Elaina shares an English class with her and Jasper, meaning that Elaina recognizes her face and tries including her in conversation. But from what I gather from Allison's simple answers and tendency to redirect the questions to Jasper, she doesn't like Elaina very much.

I can see why that is, too. Allison is extremely opinionated and blunt, and so is Elaina. From the way Elaina talks, I can tell that they hold the exact opposite views on nearly everything. Allison is conservative and doesn't beat around the bush unless she's harboring one of her secrets. She gives it to you exactly how it is and brings up an argument based off past experiences. When Elaina speaks, she has no filter. She says exactly what's on her mind and argues her opinion, even if it's the *wrong* opinion.

While this leads to playful banter between her and Jasper, it has Allison clenching her fork and forcibly swallowing verbal smack-downs. She's being polite for Jasper's sake, but I know she'll be ranting all the way to history. Something a part of me can't wait to hear.

I can see why Jasper might like Elaina, though. She speaks so freely it makes for exciting conversation. She's unconventionally pretty, accidentally flirty, and funny when you get her going. I thought she'd be quiet and small and dainty, but if anything, she makes up for being tiny with her big personality. Jasper can barely keep up with her, and I can tell by the way he looks at her when she laughs that moving on won't take long at all.

I can't help but smile softly at him when he gives her one of those looks of admiration. I wonder if he ever looked at *me* like that.

———

"I *knew* something was up," Allison says as we climb the stairs to history.

"What are you talking about?" I ask tiredly, dragging my feet as we go.

She scrunches up her eyebrows and crosses her arms. "Don't give me that, June," she scolds. "You and Jasper have been weird. Not to mention he's suddenly all cozy with that Elaina girl from our English class. They always get vocal during class debates, but now it's just downright embarrassing. It's like they're arguing their points as an excuse to flirt." She shakes her head dismissively and then thoughtfully adds, "He does this every single time."

"I have no idea what you're trying to get at," I say, "but Jasper and I are fine."

"As if," she scoffs. "All of you are hiding something from me. Well, I want in. I *deserve* to be in. What happened over winter break?"

"*Nothing*," I say firmly. I would tell her, but I'm afraid if I talk about it, I'll fall apart in front of her and she'll remind me how she predicted something like this would happen. And if I'm being honest, I don't want to hear that right now.

I stop before the classroom doorway, allowing her to walk in first. She does and walks across the rapidly filling room to sink into her seat with a frustrated sigh. Leave it to Allison to try to uncover secrets that have been buried away for their own good.

It's not that I don't trust Allison, because I do—obviously. You can tell her anything and she won't tell a soul. Instead, she'll keep it to herself and use it to give you advice and pick your brain.

She loves to know everything. It gives her this kind of rush. Whether it be school knowledge, world knowledge, or political knowledge, she will take it in and talk about what she knows all day long. But secrets, those are different. She treats secrets like jewels, the most valuable of information. Once she has them, she's not giving them away. What she will do, however, is discuss the secret with you whenever she can. It's like taking that jewel, polishing it, and turning it into some kind of ornament to increase the value.

Sighing, I slide into the desk beside hers and drop my backpack to the floor.

"I guess it's just a coincidence, then, that Jasper is doing the ole Distract Myself with a New Girl thing that he always does when he can't stand *it* anymore?" she asks in a high voice that's trying not to be demanding, but ends up coming out as accusatory. She doesn't look at me when she says it, but busies herself with getting her history folder from her backpack, her nearly black hair falling in front of her face.

It's the word *it* that make my fists clench in my lap. What does *it* even mean? Is she implying that the relationship Jasper and I share becomes too much for him, so he puts the pent-up energy into some other girl? Or is she simply stating that *I* become too much?

"Allison," I warn, feeling the heat rise in my chest.

"What, like it's not obvious? Every time you two start getting too touchy and warm, he runs to another girl so he can put some space between you—not because he hates you, because c'mon, this is Jasper we're talking about, but because he knows you're not into him like that. He's been running away for years. And now he's doing it again. So, what happened, June?"

My heart races as she talks, and I can feel my eyebrows furrowing together, eyes growing wide in anticipation of her next words. Could it be true? Has he been in love with me longer than I thought—and how long? Freshman year? I had the biggest crush on him then. Surely he would have known—sensed it at least—yet he still went after another girl? Could he possibly be that afraid of rejection? Would I have said yes to him then? If it's true, why did he keep that secret for so long—and how could Allison possibly know all this? But then it dawns on me that this is all Allison speculation. That even if it is true, it's too late. I've killed my chances now.

So after a moment of white-hot excitement, the flame dies down inside me and I resign myself to a faint orange glow.

I decide I have to fill in some information for her. So I quickly relate to her everything that's happened since New Year's Eve before the bell rings.

"Whoa," she says under the shrill ring of the bell. She looks down at her desk and taps her fingers across the surface for a moment. "You're going to hate me for saying this—but I knew things would happen like this. But this is just what you guys do. When one of you starts to feel something for the other, you pour those feelings into someone else. He did it with Bree. You did it with Milo. Now he's doing it again with Elaina. It's textbook Jasiper."

I smile a little at her last comment but slump back into my chair in a defeated posture. "Maybe it's not meant to be."

She shakes her head. "No, I think it means you are. You're never apart for too long because you miss each other too much. I've seen it happen a hundred times with Jasper. You've just got to wait, June."

"What if this was it?"

She reaches across the aisle and places a warm hand on my shoulder. "You and Jasper? Not possible. Like I said, just wait. Be patient with him. You care about him, and he cares about you.

If you want it, it's worth it. Do you want it?"

I think about everything Jasper and I have ever been through, how everybody we know sees something special in the two of us, and I nod. "Yeah, I want it."

"Then be patient. He'll come back." With one final squeeze, she pulls away, and I'm pulled back to a world where Jasiper doesn't matter and American history does. I figure, it's time I really took her advice.

I'm not too surprised when Jasper brings Lenny and me straight to his house after school on Thursday. Since he's been including me again, I'd been hoping to do the Q&A video with them tonight.

When we're inside removing our jackets and shoes, I notice Jasper turn toward me, ready to grab my hands, but then he stops himself and shoves his hands in his pockets instead. I was willing to let him warm my hands because they're freezing, but seeing him stop reminds me of our new boundaries. Warming my hands, something he's always done, is now off-limits.

I try not to let the disappointment reflect across my face when I pull my hands away and bring them to my own lips instead. His eyes catch mine for a moment, seeing me take over, and he quickly turns away, mumbling something to Lenny about being hungry.

Lenny must have noticed the exchange and looks back at me when Jasper begins to make his way down the hall. "You okay?" he mouths.

I give him a reassuring smile and nod.

Patience, I remind myself. *Patience.*

Nineteen

Another Obstacle

JASPER TOPS OFF his gas tank on the way home from school almost a week later. While he busies himself with the gas pump, I try not to inhale the gasoline fumes that somehow waft in. Lenny sits in front of me, laptop pulled out and fingers banging vigorously over the keyboard.

My head rests back on the seat, and I tilt it to the left to watch Jasper as he bounces around to keep warm while the numbers grow on the pump. I can see my breath now that he's turned his car off, not that it was doing much to warm us up in the first place, but for some reason it seems twice as chilly when we're standing still.

He met me at my locker for the first time today in what has felt like forever. Usually he would have slung an arm around my shoulder, or ruffled my hair, or jostled me around. You could tell, though, that it'd been a little while since we messed around with each other like that. When he came by, he leaned against the locker next to mine and announced himself with a cheery,

"Hello, Juniper." It was familiar and different all at the same time. I, of course, responded just as cheerfully, but I still think he noticed the hesitation. Things were starting to go back to normal, which was exciting, but at the same time, I wished things could be different with us. I wished I hadn't been so stubborn.

"So what do you think of her?"

Startled, I snap my head forward, in case I was caught staring, and look at the back of Lenny's head a bit guiltily. "Sorry, what?"

"Elaina," he says, and pushes the sun visor down so that he can look at me in the mirror. "What do you think of her?"

Lenny doesn't know what Allison knows. He doesn't know how I feel about Jasper now. And I figure it's not the right time or place to let him know. So I shrug and tilt my head from side to side thoughtfully. "She seems all right from what I've seen." My fingers are restless in my lap. "She's like the other girls he's dated."

"Allison doesn't like her." Lenny smirks. "Did you see her face when Elaina dissed a teacher she likes? I think she saw red."

I breathe out an airy laugh. "You didn't have to hear the rant she went on about Elaina after lunch. So, what about you? What do you think of Elaina?"

"Like you said." He shrugs. "She's the type that he dates. You know, chatty, smells good . . . liberal. She's got Jasper written all over her."

I nod and the driver's door pops open, letting in a blast of cold air followed by Jasper. Sinking back in my seat, I adjust my knees and tuck myself into a tighter ball, letting my head fall back against the seat. Lenny's eyes flit back up to the mirror briefly, and then he folds the sun visor back up, allowing my eyes to fall back on Jasper without worry.

I watch him while he drives and make a mental checklist, ticking off areas where I meet the requirements of being datable according to his standards. I never thought I measured up to his past girlfriends. All of them have been charismatic and playful and lovely on all accounts. I never once had a problem with them. I would get annoyed when they'd order Jasper around when his plans involved me, but it was easy to see where they were coming from. I was a threat to them.

Maybe they were threatened by me because they saw something that I don't see in myself. It's possible that I tick many things on his list, but line me up next to Elaina and I'm sure she ticks more.

Jasper glances up into the rearview mirror and notices me staring. I give him a quick smile and turn my head to look out the window. I want to tell him everything, but I know I can't.

After a short gathering at Jasper's with Lenny, I go straight to my bedroom. My laptop is open on my bed, but the screen black. I had been answering e-mails before Jasper picked me up this morning, and I guess I forgot to turn my computer off. It doesn't matter now, because I push the screen down and shove it to the foot of my bed after I sit down.

I hadn't given the trinket much thought, just tossed it away and buried my face in my pillows.

Pulling my nightstand drawer open, I'm greeted with odds and ends I don't need but don't want to get rid of, either. At the top of the pile there's a letter we received from VlogIt a few years ago, inviting us to a meet-and-greet. I kept the pay stub of my first paycheck. Old friendship bracelets from middle school are littering the bottom. My fingers feel around for a while, coming across paper clips and developed pictures I had forgotten about, until finally I feel the uneven edge of a broken heart.

I pull the simple silver pendant from the drawer and hold it up so that I can see it reflect the setting sun from the partially covered windows in my bedroom.

I don't know why I wanted to see it so bad, and even as I'm holding it before my eyes I don't understand what possessed me to dig it up. Sighing, I drag a hand over my face and lower the necklace into my lap.

I wonder what he's done with his since the last time I saw it, when he was frantically slipping it back under his shirt. They were for us, and now I don't know if *us* is going to happen. So what do you do with something like that? Do I keep it tucked away in my drawer as a token of sentiment? Do I rid myself of the evidence?

I don't think he's gotten rid of his. Like me, I think he's keeping it stashed somewhere. It would feel wrong not to keep it. I mean, it's from Jasper, after all.

Running a hand through my hair, I lift the necklace back up and purse my lips, deciding that it's best to keep it stashed as before. Like the other things in my nightstand drawer, it's not necessary to keep, but I don't have the heart to get rid of it, either. It's just one of those things you carry with you. You carry it with you because maybe one day it'll matter again.

When I arrive at school the following morning, there's a note taped to my locker alongside a rose. I stare at it in confusion for a second and glance down the hall in both directions. Students march up and down the tiled floor, but nobody looks particularly suspicious, so I flip the top open to examine the messy handwriting.

> Winter Semiformal? Let me know yes or no. I'm always an option.
> —Milo

I swallow and glance over my shoulder to check the hall again, because Milo is the kind of person who would love to see the look on my face right after reading the invitation. When I confirm that he's not in fact on the premises, I look back at the note and release an airy laugh.

I should have known. It was only a matter of time before he'd try this again. With Kiss Cam and the absence of it still being top news on VlogIt, I should have known he'd be waiting for a vulnerable moment.

I know he watches WereVloggingHere on VlogIt. It's something I liked about him when we met. He seemed to be genuinely interested in me after watching our vlogs. It was like he already knew me.

Kiss Cam has probably made me seem easy in his eyes, like he could easily manipulate me again. Plus, with Jasper paired off with Elaina, he's no longer a threat.

Jasper was always someone Milo would get jealous over. I got so cut off from Jasper while dating Milo that I almost thought we weren't friends anymore.

It should be easy to say no, but then I wonder if I am going to get asked by anyone else. Definitely not Jasper at this point.

Things are going far too well between him and Elaina for him to want to go through with our usual Winter Semiformal antics.

If Milo agrees to be a simple escort, it would make the offer easier to accept, but I don't think that's what he has in mind. Milo doesn't offer anything for free. If he doesn't benefit from me, he won't go, and I'm in no place to pay a price. I'm working on Jasper, and I don't need Milo getting in the way.

The idea of going with him sits heavily on my mind all day, and I'm bursting at the seams to announce my predicament to someone, anyone, just to get their opinion. A lull in conversation at our lunch table gives me the perfect opportunity.

"So," I say. Lenny glances up at me, and I turn my eyes down while I move some green beans around with my fork. "Milo's back."

Jasper clears his throat and leans forward. "What?"

"Yes," Allison butts in. *"What?"*

The hatred Allison has for Milo is mutual. Put those two in a room and they'll have at it. When I refused to do anything with Milo, he decided to get back at me by trying to shag Allison. It was an unsuccessful endeavor, to say the least.

While answers are being demanded, I unzip my backpack and pull out the note and the rose. "He asked me to the Winter Semiformal," I clarify. Lenny's eyes shift to Jasper, who lets out a rather obnoxious snort of disapproval.

"Don't tell me you're considering going with him. The guy's a pervert."

"She most definitely is *not* going with him," Allison says firmly, face stony with disbelief.

"He just wanted me to know he's an option," I continue, despite their immediate disapproval.

"It doesn't matter." Jasper bats the idea away with a flick of his wrist, and Elaina looks between us in confusion. "What does he think is going to happen by taking you to the dance?"

"I really don't know." I shrug, even though I already know how to answer Milo's request. "I just figured I'd see what you guys thought."

Jasper's eyebrows pinch together. "Uh-huh," he mumbles.

I understand why he's upset. He got a real earful after Milo and I broke up. Milo and I had our problems, and I'm very aware that he's trouble. But Jasper's parading around with Elaina all the time, and I don't have to be alone to prove anything to him.

Elaina glances at Jasper uncertainly and places a hand on his arm. Then she turns to me. "Sorry, I'm lost."

It takes quite a bit of restraint not to turn to her and say, "This conversation doesn't include you, so politely back off," but I settle for digging my heels into the floor. She doesn't mean to be annoying, or nosy, that's just how her position is as the newbie to our group.

"Ex-boyfriend," I brief her. "He wasn't exactly a good guy."

"Well then, why bring him up?" she asks, hand still lightly stroking Jasper's arm as if trying to calm him. He pinches his bottom lip between his fingers and stares off past me.

"I just wanted opinions. What happened between Milo and me was a long time ago. Things could have changed," I all but snap. Allison kicks me under the table, and I grip my fork harder to stop from crying out.

"Don't go with him," Jasper mumbles, and hunches over to shovel some food into his mouth. My heart flutters, eyes softening when they fall on him.

Elaina must notice, because she scans Jasper for a moment and then says to me, "Well, you got your answer."

I let a breath out my nose and reply flatly, "Great."

Lenny quickly changes the subject by asking a random editing question, and Jasper takes the bait. Meanwhile, Elaina keeps glancing at me curiously—not in a bitter, suspicious way, but in a way that looks like she's analyzing the situation between Jasper and me.

So the topic of Milo is dropped, and I realize that it was stupid to consider, anyway. He's just another obstacle I have to dodge on my path back to normality with Jasper. And by the way Elaina is staring at me, I figure there's still hope.

Twenty

No Pressure

"DO I LOOK all right?"

Jasper glances between Lenny and me, waiting for us to approve his outfit. I look him up and down, from his nice jeans up to his pale blue button-up shirt and effortlessly styled hair. It's Friday night and he's going out with Elaina. The first-date jitters are really beginning to kick in. I can tell by the way he fumbles with the buttons on his sleeves and bites his lip.

"You look great," I assure him. It's the truth. Normally geeky-looking in a graphic tee and jeans, he looks quite mature and handsome all cleaned up. I can't stop noticing how the first couple of buttons of his shirt are undone. Just a month ago, he wore that open-collared shirt for a different reason. My stomach knots at the memory.

Lenny spins around in Jasper's desk chair and purses his lips when he sees Jasper's formal wear. "Where are you guys going again?"

"Just to the movies, but I'm asking her to the Winter

Semiformal afterward." He sounds a bit flustered, and I can tell he wants this to go as smoothly as possible.

"No pressure," Lenny sings.

"Exactly." He nods. "So I can't afford to screw this up—and I'm so nervous, what do I even say . . . ?" He trails off while his fingers continue to fumble with the button on his shirtsleeves, lip twitching impatiently. After a moment he makes a strangled groan and turns to me, frustration bubbling over. "For the love of God, help me, June."

I'm surprised to hear him beg for my help instead of Lenny's. I think he may have surprised himself as well, because when I stand up, he holds out his arm but turns his face away while I button his sleeve for him. Just because all of us have been hanging out as a group like always doesn't mean Jasper and I have gotten back to our usual selves. We're still being unnaturally careful with boundaries, and I'm guessing his cry for help was an impulse.

My cheeks flush as I finish buttoning the sleeve, and I quietly sink back down onto the mattress. It's hard to say something to him when he's preparing for a date with another girl. And I can't even complain, because it's my fault she's here in the first place.

"Breathe, man," Lenny calls from his spot at Jasper's desk. He's leaning forward now, elbows on his knees. "It's just a movie and a question. Easy."

Jasper scrubs his face with his hands and releases a groan. "What time is it?"

Lenny toes the floor with his socked feet and swivels around to check Jasper's open laptop. "Almost six."

"Shoot," Jasper mumbles, and spins around to his dresser to

spritz himself with cologne and pull socks from the first drawer. "I've gotta go."

Lenny stands up and walks after me as I follow Jasper out of his room and down the stairs. "At least let us know how it goes." His voice sounds eager.

"You'll be the first to know," Jasper calls back to him, and leaps down the last three steps, disappearing down the hall in a jog. "Let yourselves out. I'll see you guys tomorrow. Bye."

Lenny and I stand at the foot of the stairs, listening to him. It's moments after he tells us good-bye that he's slipping on his shoes and sliding out the door.

"Did he look all right to you?" Lenny asks in the silence that follows the slam of the front door. "He left us in his house."

I place my hand on the banister, eyes fixated on the spot where Jasper just stood and feet heavy on the floor. "No," I say, feeling dread settle in at the idea of him going to the dance with a girl that's not me.

Well, not just me. All of us go to the dance together every year and vlog all night. We go shopping at a thrift store and buy crazy outfits, and we dance and laugh and have such a good time the hours turn to minutes. I can't imagine going with anyone else.

"How about you, then?"

I turn to him, eyes narrowing. "What?"

He shoves his hands in his pockets and motions to me by rocking forward on his tiptoes. I've begun to notice he does that when he's being completely serious.

"Are *you* all right?"

"Of course," I say quickly, and push hair from my face. "Why wouldn't I be?"

He shoots me that look that *everyone* gives me these days, and I realize he knows. He knows how I feel about Jasper, and I don't know if Allison told him or if he just figured it out, but it still causes dread to surge through me and make my posture collapse.

I groan and turn toward the staircase, letting my forehead fall to the banister for a moment before pulling away and staring up at the ceiling. I don't know what to be feeling. I'm confused, yet terribly sorted out. I'm happy for Jasper but also feeling strange and disoriented with my own feelings for him. Jasper looks fine and I look fine but *we're* not *fine*. I miss him, but I did this to myself. Nothing feels familiar no matter how hard we try. And I *knew* this would happen to us.

Knowing that he's trying to make things happen with Elaina makes me regret everything that happened, but I know that even if I wanted to take it back, I can't now. I just have to wait. But it's miserable.

"This isn't right," I mutter.

Lenny sighs. "I thought things were off, and then when Allison realized I didn't know, she let me in on the secret." I glance over at him, and he shrugs. "Look, I know this sucks, but you made your bed. Now you have to lie in it."

"I hate that," I say softly, and my face scrunches up while I lean closer to the banister.

"I know."

He sounds genuinely sympathetic, and I know I look about as awful as I sound.

After a couple of minutes of silence, he asks, "Want some ice cream? If I were you, I'd need some ice cream. My freezer is fully stocked."

"Give me everything you have."

When Jasper came back that night, he let both Lenny and me know that the date went great and he now had a date to the Winter Semiformal. That, of course, was followed by a long slew of apologies for not being able to do our usual thrift store stunt.

What Lenny said that night clearly projected itself with the way I handled the situation. I had to lie in the bed that I'd made. So I enthusiastically told him that everything was great and that we didn't mind at all. We were glad he was happy.

I was being too peppy, overcompensating to make things seem like they were fine, but they weren't. They really weren't.

———

"Valentine's Day is next week."

I glance sideways at Jasper as I pack my backpack for the weekend. He's got his back against the locker door next to mine, and his hand is hanging from the back of his head, fingers curling in the baby hairs there.

For the past week we've been struggling to find ways to talk to each other, and I wasn't expecting Valentine's Day to be today's grand opener. I assumed it would be a topic to avoid.

"I need your help, for Elaina."

I shake my hair out of my face and tilt my head toward him, eyebrows pinching together. Jasper Lahey is so smooth that he doesn't need advice from anyone—or so he had me thinking for the past six years. But all this nervousness and uncertainty as of late has me thinking he had me fooled.

"I mean, you're a girl, so . . ." He shuffles his feet from side to side and stares at me pleadingly.

I can't believe he's coming to me. I don't *want* him to come to me. Not for this—especially since I have feelings for him and he's doing this for some other girl. Not to mention he recently had feelings for me and is doing this too casually.

"Gee, what gave you the hint?" I have to force the humor into my voice as I pull my coat on.

He snorts and turns his body toward me. "I've only seen you in your underwear about a million times, remember."

Blushing, I throw my backpack over my shoulder but still manage to say half-jokingly, "Don't tell Elaina."

He makes a face. "Yeah, trust me. I won't. . . . Anyway, back to my dilemma."

Ignoring his insistence that I answer his question, I spin on my heels and merge into the oncoming student traffic. He speed walks to keep up with me as I weave through the endless line of exhausted teenagers. My intent is to try and get out of this conversation. I figure if he can't keep up, he can't trap me into helping him come up with a Valentine's Day gift for his rebound girlfriend—which is my fault, but whatever, it's weird.

It really is no use trying to avoid it, though, because by the time we reach the main office, we're able to walk side by side again, and he's asking the question for the third time.

A little annoyed, I sigh and answer his question with another question. "You're really getting her something? You just started dating."

"So? Girls like gifts."

I laugh. "I don't."

"Yes, you do."

Letting out a deep breath through my nose, I pull back before we reach the doors and turn to him. "Look," I say, "I love you, but I'm not helping you with this."

He looks insulted by my refusal. "Why?"

"Because New Year's wasn't that long ago. And if it's not okay with me, I have a hard time believing that it's okay with you." I don't like the way it sounds coming out of my mouth and immediately want to swallow the words back up and store them away. We try not to talk about New Year's, but it was far too significant in our recent history to not bring up now. I can't help him with this. I can't. I *can't*. Apprehension flashes across his eyes.

Rigidly, he replies, "Oh."

And with that, he pushes through the doors and walks away, leaving me to clench my fists in frustration. If he thinks including me in his relationship with Elaina is going to prove he's over me, it's not fair. How is it *that* easy for him? It's frustrating for me.

But I realize it's not fair. He doesn't know how I feel about him, and I can't just let him walk away thinking I'm holding that night against him. If he let it go, that means it's time for me to let it go, too.

So I throw my weight against the door and burst into the cold February air after him.

"Jas," I call out, jogging up behind him. "Jas, wait."

He's reluctant to stop, but he does and slowly turns to me with an emotionless expression, waiting.

"I didn't mean it like that," I say hurriedly, watching his earlier enthusiasm fade before my eyes.

It's a lie, I did mean it like that, but I can't afford for things to go further haywire between us. I'm just going to have to accept Elaina as another one of Jasper's girlfriends. If he wants to talk about her, fine. It's not my place to be uncomfortable. I can't lose a friend over this. I can't lose *him*.

"You did." He looks down at his feet. The air freezes his breath when he sighs, making it appear as though smoke is curling around his lips.

Students sidestep around us, looking at us confusedly as we stand there awkwardly. I press my hands over my face and release a frustrated groan.

"I know you're trying to act the way we used to—"

He cuts in, "I thought you were trying, too, but then you bring New Year's up." He shakes his head and shuffles in the cold air uncomfortably.

I peek at him through my fingers, seeing his jaw set. My stomach knots. "I shouldn't have said anything. I'm sorry."

He shifts his weight from one side of his body to the other and runs a hand through his hair. "You're confusing me."

"*I'm* confusing me," I admit, and close the spaces of my fingers so I don't have to look at him.

"Well," he says a bit sourly, "I think you need to sort that out, then, because coming to you about my girlfriends has never been a problem before."

I push my hands up through my hair, ready to say something in return, to lie and say it's still not a problem and pretend this incident never happened, but he's already walking toward his car.

We need to stop with this nonsense. We need to get back to the old days when everything made sense.

Twenty-One

Ice Cream and Desperate Housewives

AS VALENTINE'S DAY draws closer, all havoc breaks loose on VlogIt. Kiss Cam was not so easily forgotten. And with a holiday that specializes in romance, it's no wonder new Kiss Cam requests are pouring in. It's been an open-ended segment that we've been ignoring but our subscribers can't seem to let go.

My inbox fills to max capacity with questions I'm not sure I can answer. Jasper says that, like me, he's been getting many Valentine's Day Kiss Cam requests along with demands about what's happened to the segment. At lunch the day before the dreaded holiday, Lenny pulls out his laptop and shows us how Kiss Cam has been affecting him, too.

"We need to do something about this," he remarks.

Elaina looks over Jasper's shoulder curiously to see Lenny's computer screen. She places a hand on Jasper's arm and asks, "Why did you guys stop doing Kiss Cam? Wasn't it really popular?"

I feel Allison's knee brush mine under the table when Jasper's eyes meet mine. She must sense how my heart stops at Elaina's question. The touchiness of the subject won't go away no matter how hard I will myself to become numb to it.

"Jas started seeing you," Lenny replies lamely, as if he's become so used to answering this question that it strikes no urgency in him. The thoughtful look on his face isn't even interrupted. He just continues to stare at the computer screen with his chin propped against his hand and his brows furrowed.

"So?" Elaina laughs. "I watch your vlogs, and I *know* there's more than just Jasiper shippers. Why don't you and June do Kiss Cam?" she asks Lenny.

The hand Lenny's using to prop his chin up drops and slams onto the table while his whole body recoils. "*Excuse me?* You want *me* to do what? *Sure!* Why don't I just jump into a *shark tank*, for God's sake. That sounds like a *great* idea!"

Elaina's small eyes grow and her mouth drops open in surprise as Lenny continues with his tangent. "I *run* ships. I *captain* ships. I don't *become* the ships. I stay in my own lane, Elaina. And my own lane is Eva Longoria and ice cream."

I snort and Allison's shoulders begin to shake with laughter. Even Jasper's cracked a smile, but Elaina is dumbfounded. And Lenny sits there, his face barely holding its serious facade. He catches my eye for a split second, and I know he's succeeded in turning an awkward subject into a joke, because he suddenly explodes in giggles.

"Wait, are you serious?" Elaina asks. Her round cheeks are flushed, like she's embarrassed.

Lenny's giggles slow, and he props his chin back up in his hand. "I don't do Kiss Cam. I run it."

Her thin, nearly nonexistent eyebrows furrow. "How come?"

"June and Jas are okay with that kind of thing, but I think it's kinda gross," Lenny admits. "No offense to either June or Jas, but I will not be the other half of either of those ships." He shakes his head. "Nope."

Jasper clears his throat and shifts in his seat. I glance at him and he looks at Elaina. "He's never been into it. We don't do Kiss Cam anymore."

Elaina spoons some soup into her mouth, her eyes narrowed, thinking. "That's probably a bummer to your viewers, huh? Kiss Cam is *still* on the VlogIt homepage."

Allison shakes the hair from her eyes and leans forward. "Why are you so interested?"

Elaina flushes and her eyes bounce between all of us before she shakes her head and spins her spoon between her fingers. "No reason, I just—"

"Oh, c'mon," Allison says, rolling her eyes. "It has to be *something*."

Elaina catches eyes with Allison and then looks to me, and her blush burns brighter. Jasper looks confused and leans back, blinking while Lenny scoots in. All eyes are on Elaina, and she seems to shrink under the attention.

She struggles with what she wants to say, and then finally she laughs and covers her blushing face.

"Well . . . ," she begins. "I sort of ship Leniper."

We all say it at once. "What?"

"You ship Leniper?" I laugh and turn to Lenny. "She ships us."

Lenny makes a face and allows his head to fall onto the cafeteria table. "Oh, *great*."

Allison is laughing so hard she falls into my lap, and Jasper's raised eyebrows and blank stare say everything. We all sit in awkward, yet relieved laughter.

"This is weird," Allison manages to say when she's caught her breath.

"Uh, yeah," Jasper says stiffly.

"What?" Elaina demands, laughing nervously. "Don't you think they're cute?"

Jasper's face drops, and my eyes widen. Lenny simply bangs his head on the table.

"No," Allison answers for all of us.

Elaina ignores her and looks at me. "You guys are *so* cute. You have to do Kiss Cam just *one time*."

"No," Lenny and I say at the same time, and thankfully, Jasper chimes in. His head has been shaking the entire time, and I have a hard time looking away from his rigid posture.

"I can pretty much guarantee that Kiss Cam will never happen again unless it's with me," he says, and Elaina's face changes into something that isn't pleasant, until Jasper adds, "and I wouldn't do Kiss Cam unless it's with you."

I feel the blood drain from my face. What started off as funny quickly went south, and for me, it's like watching a bad car accident. No matter how horrible it is, I just can't take my eyes off it.

Elaina gives him a skeptical look. "But isn't Kiss Cam only between WereVloggingHere?"

"Who made that rule?" Jasper asks the group. None of us say anything. "Come on." He nudges her. "You say VlogIt wants Kiss Cam so bad? How about we do it?"

And as Elaina's face lights up in awe and disbelief as though she's just won Miss United States, I go numb like I've just witnessed a rolling car receive its final blow by a semi going seventy-five miles per hour.

Lenny glances over at me with the same amount of shock, and Allison grips my knee under the table. Every time things seem hopeful, bad news follows. And I'm still not used to it. Just like I'm still not used to Jasper leaning over and kissing his girlfriend on the mouth in front of us.

There's nothing I can do but sit there and take it.

Even though I was against it, Jasper does end up roping me into helping him with a Valentine's Day gift for Elaina. In the morning I watch across the hall at my locker as Elaina opens up her gift while Jasper films her.

I guess I've been very out of the loop. Friday nights, the nights Jasper and I used to hang out at his house, he has been going to her house. When he told me they share the same taste in music, I offered the idea of making her a mix tape. Jasper and I used to do that all the time when he first bought his laptop. We'd spend hours burning CDs and dancing around his bedroom, singing into deodorant tubes and hairbrushes. He seemed to remember that when I suggested it and tried to say it was "our" thing. But so was Kiss Cam, and he's doing that with Elaina now. So I told him it was fine and left him to it.

When she sees the mix tape and candy at the bottom of the gift bag, a glowing smile stretches across her face, and she promptly pulls him in for a kiss. I walk away then, seeing their attached lips and off-balance poses every time I blink. He's still holding his camera up, capturing the moment for the vlog.

Our viewers know about her, but my inbox still continues to fill up with Jasiper-related e-mails. I've stopped opening them.

Like my house after my mom finished decorating, the school halls are bursting with pinks and reds. Couples hand off gifts and smooch in the corners. Roses are sold during lunch, and boys leave them taped to girls' lockers or hand them off in between classes. Every girl's cheeks are flushed, and every boy seems to have a little lip gloss smeared on the corner of his lips. I've never particularly liked the holiday, but for some reason I hate it even more today and breathe a sigh of relief when the final bell rings.

But that feeling doesn't last long. Jasper and Elaina have the Kiss Cam scheduled for today. And since I'm *supposed* to be okay with this because I'm not *supposed* to have feelings for him, I have to attend. I tried not to think about it all day, but now it's unavoidable. It isn't ideal, and I'd rather go home and flip through channels on my television until I fall asleep, but if I'm going to go along with Allison's advice, I've got to wait it out. Unfortunately for me, waiting it out and being normal about everything is more torturous than it would be for other people.

After school, Lenny and I go to Jasper's with Elaina. She's excited about Kiss Cam, though I don't know what they're going to do. We don't go up to Jasper's room; instead we stay down in the living room. I make myself comfortable on the couch and pull my legs up to my chest in the place where I always sit when I'm over. Lenny falls down next to me and tosses the camera back and forth between his hands.

"What's the deal?" I ask Lenny.

He shrugs and pushes his overgrown blond hair out of his

face. "There was a request on VlogIt from last night, a Kiss Cam one for Valentine's Day. It asked Jasper to kiss the girl he loves. I'm going to read it, and he's going to kiss her."

I resist the urge to roll my eyes. "He doesn't love her. Not yet, anyway."

"Well, he can't kiss you."

I shake my head and hug my knees. "I don't want him to."

I can't detect if the look on his face is disappointment or indifference, so I turn my attention to the incoming couple. Elaina is hanging off Jasper's arm, laughing about something, and he's got a pleased look on his face as he stares down at her adoringly. I look away.

Jasper sits beside me, setting his camera tripod down on the coffee table. Lenny busies himself with attaching the camera, and Elaina sits down on Jasper's lap. She's so small compared to him that she appears childlike, especially when she throws her legs over his lap.

I tuck hair behind my ear and shift my body weight as far from them as I can. Lenny turns the camera on and sits back.

"Happy Valentine's Day!" Lenny waves to the camera. Noticing the little red light, I pull myself together and present a smile to the camera—maybe an exaggerated one, but a smile nonetheless. "Kiss Cam request," he announces, cutting right to the chase. I can hear a collective intake of breath in my head, like those of our future viewers. "Kiss the girl you love."

I feel my stomach knot, waiting to hear the smacking sound of lips being pressed together, but they don't come nearly as quickly as I expected. I feel weight closing in on the side of my body that Jasper is on. Out of the corner of my eye, I see the blurred coloring of his hair nearing my face. My heart begins to pound in my chest.

He's going to kiss me.

Elaina is right there, sitting on his lap. What is he thinking? He can't do this. It isn't right. *Elaina*.

I feel his breath close on my face and pull back, knocking into Lenny.

"Jas," I say exasperatedly, reluctantly turning my head to face him, eyes unable to meet his.

He gives me a goofy grin and chuckles. Then he pecks my flushing cheek before leaning back and firmly pressing his lips to Elaina's. My mouth drops open and I grab Lenny's knee in a death grip, heart hammering in my chest. I feel my face continue to burn, all the while wondering why that just happened.

Confusion is too broad to explain the feelings settling in and weighing me down on the couch between Jasper and Lenny. How could he do that? How could he be so uncomfortable with our recent history, and yet *still* pull that in front of Elaina?

And *Elaina*, how could he do that in front of her? How did *she* feel about that? Was it a tribute to the Jasiper part of Kiss Cam our viewers were used to, or was it a message to me?

How am *I* supposed to feel about it? He doesn't know how I feel about *him*. Maybe he thought I'd find the humor in it. But all I can do is sit there, frozen like a statue.

My knuckles are white with force. I'm staring straight ahead into the camera, trying to keep my face blank even though a blush is spreading down my neck. He shouldn't have done that.

Lenny places a hand on mine uncertainly and tries to pry my fingers off, so I grab his fingers instead and squeeze hard when Jasper's elbow jabs me in the rib cage and Elaina's toes brush my thigh. She makes a noise in the back of her throat, lips still attached to his, and I feel my limbs sink farther into the couch. I want to get up and leave, but the camera is there holding me down.

This moment wouldn't be as uncomfortable if it weren't for his practical joke. A *mean* joke—to both himself and me. But then I hardly know how he feels about me anymore, and I'm the one panicking.

Lenny senses that I'm being pushed over the edge and jumps up, leaning in close to the camera.

"All right, all right. Happy Valentine's Day—WereVlogging Here!" He puts a hand over the lens and turns off the video recorder before turning to Elaina and Jasper, who are just now pulling their lips apart. I stand up and exit the room now that the camera is off. I can hardly believe the feelings flooding my system—not of jealousy, but of hurt. Hurt I don't deserve to feel.

I pull my shoes on and then pull my coat over my shoulders, hoping to make a quick getaway before anyone's even noticed I left. But Lenny rounds the corner before I can get out the door.

"June, wait," he mutters. He rushes forward, camera in hand, and stuffs his feet into his tennis shoes while pulling his coat on. I reluctantly wait for him, even though I want nothing more than to get away. "Come on."

He pushes me out the door and then drags me next door to his house.

"Lenny, no, just let me go home."

I try digging my feet into the snow but slide across the ice despite my wishes. So I end up being pulled onto his porch, shivering in the brisk winter air.

"We don't have to talk," he says, and squeezes my hand. "But

I have ice cream and *Desperate Housewives* on DVR."

I know I hurt him a little bit back there. I think my nails must have dug into his skin, so I know he felt my urgency. I know he wants nothing more than to make sure I'm okay.

I don't know what to say without tearing up, so I give him a tight smile, unable to stop the laugh from tumbling from my lips. "We *knew* you ignored us on Fridays to watch *Desperate Housewives*."

He laughs, too, and releases my hand so that he can unlock his front door. "Eva Longoria." He shoots me a look over his shoulder with a wink. *"Duh."*

I smile and turn my eyes down to my shoes.

"So?" he asks.

I nod, sniffling because of the cold. "Okay."

"That's what I thought," he says, and wraps an arm around my shoulder. "Valentine's Day sucks."

Twenty-Two
Can You Put a Shirt On?

THE FOLLOWING MORNING I arrive at my locker, surprised to see Milo leaning flat against my locker with his hands in his pockets. He grins slyly when he sees me.

I haven't had a conversation with him in some time, but he hasn't changed one bit in appearance. His eyes are a particular shade of green that always seems mischievous and alluring, the kind you can melt right into despite their danger signs. He's short in stature, being only slightly taller than me. Each and every one of his features is sharp and pointed. To punctuate it all, his light brown curls sit atop his head and fall over his forehead in gentle swoops. I remember why I was attracted to him, but that's where it stops.

When I come closer, he licks his lips and his eyes drop. "Hello, Juniper," he says around a smile that displays a set of slightly crooked teeth. It's then that I remember that Winter Semiformal invitation from weeks back.

"Hi, Milo," I drawl, purposely sounding bored, because he'll use any other emotion as leverage.

"Didn't you get my note?"

"Uh . . . yeah," I say, and cross my arms over my chest to force his eyes elsewhere.

He moves his eyes up to stare at me. He holds my gaze for a moment, maybe thinking it'll hypnotize me, and says finally, "So, what do you think?"

I think about everything that's happened recently, and about what Milo put me through. The notion gives me a headache, and I'm tired of feeling miserable. "I don't think going to the dance is a good idea."

I step forward and motion for him to move away, which he does passively to let me into my locker. I begin to exchange books and he turns toward me, purposely invading my personal space.

"I'll make you forget about Jasper," he proposes.

I look at him from the corner of my eye and then turn back to my books, eyes narrowing. "I don't know what you're talking about."

He snorts and pulls one of my notebooks from the crook of my arm. "Don't think nobody's heard about that. Anyone who's been watching VlogIt knows exactly what's happening between you and Jasper." I make a grab for my notebook, but he moves it out of my reach and leans toward me with his face instead. "He's making you suffer and you have nothing to lose by accepting my offer."

"I have a lot to lose, actually," I tell him. If Milo pulls anything at the dance and Jasper sees, my chances to prove myself to him are ruined. It'll look like I'm trying to get even or that I've moved on. I don't want to do either.

He chuckles. "Oh, c'mon, Juniper. He's clearly over you.

Anyone with eyes can see that. If he's said anything different, he doesn't want to hurt your feelings. So stop wasting your time on him."

I rock forward and snatch my notebook out of his hand without a remark. Some of his words sting, but I try to force them from my mind. I know I can trust Jasper more than him, and I won't let him try to change how I feel about things. He just makes my blood rush loud in my ears and anger swell. So I know I won't last a night with him.

"What?" he asks. "Did something I say hit too close to home?"

"You're ignorant."

"News flash, babe." He takes a step forward and sets his hands on his hips, looking down on me mockingly. "But you're hardly the one to talk."

The bell rings to signal the beginning of first period, so I make our last words brief.

"I'm not interested. You can continue to stay away from me now."

"Fine." He shrugs, but his posture is rigid. "Juniper Cooper, Internet sensation, alone at a dance? Kind of pathetic. Says something about you, doesn't it?"

I let out a breath through my nose but don't say anything back. I've got a class to be at, and he's wasting my time by putting me down. Even though I feel flushed, I do my best to maintain my composure as I walk off, purposely swinging my hips as I go.

I can't sleep Friday night. Too much is weighing on my mind. First Jasper psychs me out on Valentine's Day with Kiss Cam, then Milo confronts me about the coming dance. I feel a little sick and confused, and I can't get anything straight in my head. All I want is to vent to someone, but Lenny is babysitting the twins, and Allison is touring a college. I'm desperate enough to want to talk to my parents, but my dad is working and my mom is sleeping. I'm alone, and I can't continue on this way.

So I take a chance on the only person who might be available. And that person is Jasper.

I find everything unlocked and let myself in. It's not surprising. Jasper probably left it unlocked for Leeann. I didn't see her car in the driveway. Once in, I toss my flats aside and throw my jacket down. It's been awhile since I've done this, so I stop on the doormat and stare down the hallway, quieting my breathing so that I can hear if Jasper is awake. It's faint, but I hear enough rustling upstairs to proceed.

I go down the hallway and turn up the staircase, wondering what I'm even going to say when I see him. I have no right to be mad about anything that's been done, but I do need to talk about it.

His bedroom door is wide open, and I can see right in without poking my head in. Jasper sits at his desk in a pair of sweatpants and no shirt. His laptop is open to VlogIt, and I recognize my voice coming from the speakers. He has to be watching one of our vlogs. Maybe it's recent, maybe it's old, but I can't tell because I'm too far away.

I don't really know how to approach him, so I reach in and knock on his door.

He only half swivels around, and his eyes remain glued to the screen. "Hey, Ma, sorry I didn't clean up. I promise I'll get it done before you wake up."

"Not Leeann," I say a little stiffly.

He pauses and then turns around completely, eyes settling on me curiously. "June?"

"Yeah," I say, and drum my fingers on the paneling of the entryway. "Listen. Can we talk?"

He looks back at his computer and hits pause, letting the silence envelop us. We look at each other for a moment, and he scratches his chin.

"Look," he says, hunching forward in his desk chair. "If it's about Valentine's Day—"

"It is . . . among other things that happened this week."

He takes a breath and looks at me with a bit of annoyance. "Could you let me finish a sentence just once?" he wonders.

I get this sense that he doesn't want me here or that I'm irritating him just by being in his presence. It feels like I'm intruding or unwelcome. He looks at me with so much measured patience that I consider walking out.

I think he notices the way my body shifts like I'm going to back out, and he stands, taking a step toward me. Now that he's standing it gives me a better view of his bare chest, and I remember that he's not comfortable with his body in front of most people, yet he still stands like this in front of me like things haven't changed. My eyes drop down to his exposed chest and then I feel silly and turn my head away entirely, because I wasn't expecting butterflies.

"It was for the viewers, okay? I promise it was nothing more," he tells me quickly. "Please, don't leave. I miss you."

I'm standing halfway in and out of his room, looking down the hallway and feeling pressure build up in my chest. "You shouldn't have done it, Jas. Not in front of VlogIt and certainly not in front of Elaina."

"I told her I was going to do it. Don't worry about her." He takes another step toward me. "I just wanted to get back to how we were. Please don't overthink it like you always do."

My jaw clenches and I shake my head, because what does he expect? I didn't overthink for years when I should have. I ignored all the signs, and look where it got me. I'm confused and upset and he's shirtless and it's not helping.

"So what?" I turn to him, trying extra hard to keep my eyes on his face. "They said kiss the girl you love, and you kissed me first, Jas. But I'm just supposed to brush it off like I always have? After New Year's and everything else since then?" I run a hand through my hair and my eyes drop down to his chest again. Squeezing my eyes shut, I turn away again. "God, just tell me what to think, because I can't keep going back and forth with you."

He makes a frustrated sound that could be a laugh or a sigh. "I already told you not to overthink it, June," he says carefully. I feel his presence closer to me, but I can't open my eyes or put my hands down because I know I'll do something stupid. "Hey," he says softly now. "What's going on with you?"

"This mind game is not what I wanted," I say, and my eyes remain tightly shut.

"What are you talking about?" He sounds angry, but not the kind of angry that means he's mad, the kind of angry that means he's irritated with me, and I don't know what to do. I don't even think I'm making sense, and I didn't expect to get so upset while talking to him.

"I just don't know what you want from me," I confess. "And I don't know how I'm supposed to feel about all of it, because none of it is right to me. You act all weird around me one second, and the next you kiss me like everything is fine. I don't know, Jas. I just don't know anymore."

He tugs on my elbow, trying to get me to pull my hands away from my hair. My eyes still remain tightly closed. "Why are you hiding from me?" he asks exasperatedly. "Can we just have a conversation without all the drama?"

"Can you put a shirt on?" I sound stressed, a lot more desperate than I intended, and my cheeks flush. I lean my head back against the wall and cover my face in embarrassment, but he backs away and throws a shirt over his head compliantly.

"Are we good?" he asks when he's dressed, and I pull my hands away from my face and nod, unable to meet his eyes because my cheeks are still glowing.

"Are we?" I ask.

He makes an exaggerated shrug and looks at me helplessly. "I don't know what you want, June. I'm good. Don't worry about me."

"Really?" I meet his eyes hesitantly. "You're over it?"

He lets out a breath. "I mean, it's been over a month. I'm with Elaina. We agreed to let it go."

I bite my lip and nod. So that's it, then. There's nothing left between him and me. The awkwardness needs to stop. Has it just been me? Am I the one who's been stubborn with letting everything go since our last talk?

He's fine. It's just me.

"Right," I say.

It's quiet for a minute, and I hug my arms across my chest. I feel his eyes on me even after I turn my head away.

"Was there something else?"

I glance up at him and run a shaky hand through my hair. "Milo."

"Milo?"

I nod and cross my arms. "He confronted me about the dance today and said some stuff about us that . . . that I didn't want to hear."

He's rigid, the same kind of tense that he gets whenever Milo is mentioned. "Well?"

I bite my lip and shake my head, knowing that Jasper is protective and that I couldn't tell him everything without explaining exactly the reason I'm upset. Jasper has Elaina. I can't do that now.

"You know . . . it was just about us. And he just tried to make me feel bad so I'd go to the dance with him." I play with my fingers and shift my weight onto one hip, dropping my eyes. "But I'm tired of feeling miserable, so . . . you can imagine how that went." I try to laugh, but it comes out closer to a wheeze.

Jasper sighs deeply and shakes his head. "Milo is an ass. I'm sorry I wasn't there—"

"You wouldn't have helped," I tell him, and as an afterthought to all that, I add, "I really messed everything up, huh?"

Jasper tries to disagree, but I stop him. "I was stupid, Jas. About everything."

"June," he asks after some time. He's careful, face soft, and eyes steady. "Do you—you aren't—please say after all this that . . . ?"

I answer him before he can finish his thought. I don't know if it's the right thing to do, but I have to tell him anyway.

My whole body feels like it's on fire when I say what comes out next. "Maybe I was wrong that night."

His mouth drops open like he's going to say something, and he gets this awful look on his face that looks like a cross between disappointment and hurt. "You can't say that now. Not after you put me through all this. And if you think that it's going to make things better—that we can just kiss and make up and everything is fine and dandy—it won't be. I don't want pity love, Juniper."

"It's not pity, Jas."

He shakes his head, and his voice is strangely calm. "I don't believe you. You just want to make things better, but tricking yourself into loving me won't do that. You'll regret it."

"I regret saying no."

"No, you regret the consequences of saying no." He takes a couple of steps toward me and puts his hands on my shoulders.

I feel my teeth grind together and my hands clench. I hate that he's fighting me. I hate that he's trying to talk me out of this. And suddenly, I don't care about Elaina. I just want to make him understand me. I was wrong. I want him. I came here looking for comfort, and now all I want is him. Just him.

I wish I could go back to New Year's and say yes. I wish I didn't overthink everything. And now he's standing before me with his hands on my shoulders, and I'm dizzy with desire. I want nothing more than to prove him wrong, that what I feel for him is true.

It's not like me, and it's against everything I've done in the past, but I reach between us and wrap my hand around his neck, pulling him to me. He doesn't resist and allows me to pull him down to my height until we're breathing the same air and my heart is pounding so hard that I'm numb. He rests his forehead on mine, and my eyes close in anticipation. I've missed this closeness, this intimacy between us.

I move my mouth to his and our lips are close to brushing when he turns his head away.

"I don't cheat," he murmurs.

It hits me harder than expected, the fact that he won't go through with this, that he really is done with me. My lips press together and I hold back sudden tears. My hand drops from his neck, and I lean in to press my face to his chest. He wraps his arms around me and presses his cheek to the top of my head.

"I hate this," I say, tears sliding down my cheeks and soaking the front of his shirt. "Why can't we just go back to being us? Why is it so hard?"

His hands rub up and down the length of my back, and he squeezes me tighter. "Maybe we need to start over."

But I don't want to start over. I just want him to believe me. I just want him to love me again. But I don't say that.

He leans away from me and pushes damp curls away from my face. "Like the first time you spent the night and we told each other everything. Our middle names and our favorite colors. I told you about my dad, and you were weird because you ate french fries with mayo. I taught you how to read a comic book, and you taught me how to braid hair. Maybe we should start over. Like seventh grade."

I wipe stray tears away and nod. He looks eager to try this, and I think yes, we could do this. We could learn to be best friends again.

He leads me to his bed, and I obediently sit down when my knees hit the edge. He goes to his bookshelf and pulls a book from his stack. When he comes back, he kneels down before me and holds the book up.

"Juniper May, this is not a comic book. This is manga, and I haven't taught you how to read this."

I look at the strange artwork on the cover and then at the title written a bit chaotically across the top.

"And how does one read Death Note?" I ask, going along with this the way he wants me to.

He turns the book over and opens to the last page. "You read them backward."

He hands me the book and then stands up and crawls onto his mattress to sit behind me. "So, teach me to French braid."

I show him how and then watch in the mirror above his desk as he works at my hair. Just like seventh grade, he bites the corner of his lip as he pulls strands of hair from one side of my head to the other. When we were younger, I watched in the same fashion as he tried to figure out how to braid. He knelt behind me with long, dark hair and a Pokémon shirt as a thirteen-year-old. Now eighteen, his jaw is wider and is hair shorter. He hasn't shaved recently, and there's a little bit of stubble coming in. Instead of Pokémon, he wears a white shirt that he cut the sleeves off of.

I look different, too. My curls are more defined and my eyes lighter. I still look young in the face, but at least I actually have breasts now, even though they're hidden under a sweatshirt—his sweatshirt, I realize. His Blackhawks one that I stole awhile back. It makes me smile at our reflection.

How could we have lost ourselves so much? How could we have let ourselves get carried away with our feelings?

It feels right to sit here and do things we did when we were younger. But I still wish he would have kissed me. I wish I was gutsy enough to have kissed him before he said stop.

It's not pity love, I remind myself. He just doesn't want

everything he's had to go through to feel like a waste. Maybe that's why he wants to do this with me. Restart. He just wants a clean slate.

Maybe I should let him go. We fight each other too much. We're too scared. We work best as friends. But my stomach stirs when his fingers brush my neck, and I can't help but feel a crippling attraction toward him. It's hurting me, but maybe I should teach myself not to care, to love him anyway. Let him go, but love him anyway. Just like before.

We spend the night doing things we did as kids and talking about things that have been happening lately. I tell him about Lenny and *Desperate Housewives*, and he tells me about the Jasiper drama online, since I've been ignoring it. We watch *Criminal Minds* at midnight, making up for the many hours we've missed together.

Twenty-Three
No Room for Jesus

THAT SATURDAY IS the day of the dance, and Allison and I get ready at my house. Usually we'd get ready at her house and she would drive us there, but since we all agreed to meet up at my house this year, we decided that hitching a ride with Jasper would be best.

Allison arrives at my house with her hair already curled and glitter swept across her eyelids. I'm standing in the bathroom with my dress half-zipped and only a quarter of my hair successfully straightened. After Allison slides into the yellow dress she bought, she takes over my hair straightening, because I can't get the kinks out of the back.

My mother comes in sometime during all of this and begins snapping pictures—as if she won't have enough by the time we leave for the dance—and then continues to get in the way by smoothing my hair down and zipping up the rest of my dress while I'm trying to slip my heels on.

"It *sucks* that we actually have to get dressed up," I groan while my mother struggles to pull the zipper up. It keeps getting caught in the fabric.

My mom clicks her tongue and shakes her head. "You girls look so nice. I'm glad you're wearing dresses instead of those god-awful fur coats."

"Those are hilarious," I insist. Both Allison's and my mother's faces pinch. Okay, so maybe it's only Jasper, Lenny, and me that find our usual thrift store outfits funny during the dance. But they've never stopped us from having a good time, and the pictures are usually priceless.

This year it's all about glitter and dresses and heels, and I'm not entirely happy with the change. Allison, on the other hand— she's having a field day. And my mom . . . Well, you can't stop that woman from cooing over pretty things.

In past years, it's been Allison's mom who's interfered and preened her daughter for the dance. Now it's my mom's turn, and she attacks me like one of her holiday decorating projects. Eventually, I have to shut my mom out of my room while I make some last preparations with Allison.

While Allison stuffs a small handbag with lip gloss and sewing supplies, I trot over to my nightstand and pull the drawer open. She watches from the corner of her eye as I pull out the necklace Jasper gave me on New Year's Eve and then snaps her clutch closed.

I hold the half heart to the place it would hang if I wore it, and turn to my vanity to see in the mirror.

Allison comes over and stands beside me in the mirror. "Not a good idea," she says as though she can read my thoughts. I told her about the necklace, but that was a while ago and she's never seen it. I'm surprised she remembered.

I let out a short breath from my nose. "I know," I reply, and set the half heart down on the vanity top. "I just wanted to see it, I guess."

She picks it up and turns it over in her hand a couple of times and then looks at me in the mirror. "Milo bug you lately?"

I shake my head. Milo has left me alone for the most part. When I do see him, he just gives me a smug smirk. He thinks I'm under him, that I'm missing out or some kind of sorry case who's alone for the first time in forever. But I'm not alone. Lenny promised to save me a slow dance. I'll twirl with Allison, and laugh at Jasper's dance moves, and I won't be lonely or upset. I don't *need* a date for this dance—never have. I'm more than happy with my arrangement this year.

"Great." She smiles and squeezes my shoulders. "Tonight is going to be fun."

I laugh lightly and take one of her hands, pulling her out of the room after me.

Jasper and Lenny are stepping inside just as Allison and I are coming down the stairs. Lenny is accompanied by his parents, and a chorus of oohs and aahs suddenly fills the entryway when they get a look at mine and Allison's dresses.

We meet them at the bottom of the staircase. Both boys are dressed in white collared shirts and black slacks. Lenny bounces the video camera between his hands and smiles at us.

"Miss the fur coats?" he asks, and I nod vigorously.

Allison laughs and lightly slaps my arm. "Let it go, June! We look good."

I shrug and glance down at the midnight-blue dress I'm wearing. It's pretty, sure, but it's not the same.

My dad rounds the corner offering cookies and punch, and

the Davises follow him with Lenny and Allison in tow.

Jasper stays behind and slowly slips off his shoes while waving his hands about, clenching and unclenching his fingers to thaw them.

I remember the many times he warmed my hands for me. So I step forward and hold out my hands. "Hey," I say.

He looks down at my open hands and then back up at me. "Yes, Juniper?"

"Come on," I say, and grab his hands. "You did it for me."

"It's kind of *my* thing," he jokes.

I crack a smile. "I thought it was kind of *our* thing."

A curious look crosses his face, but a playful grin rests on his lips when I rub his hands and bring them to my lips to warm them with my breath.

He wrinkles his nose at me. "Juniper May, sometimes I swear you're in love with me."

It's a weird thing to say after all that has happened, but it reminds me of something he said to me when Kiss Cam started. I wink at him, mimicking the playfulness in his voice when I reply, "Truly, madly, deeply."

Since our talk we've gone back to our playful banter, but I can't quite tell if he's being serious, and I hope he doesn't truly think I'm flirting with him. It's not like that. I don't want to ruin things; I'm just being the kind of friends that we are.

The doorbell rings, and I drop his hands, pushing past him to open the door for Elaina, who wears a light-pink cocktail dress and a brilliant smile. She's so pretty my smile falters, and I step out of the way for Jasper.

We meet the others in the living room. All our parents,

except for Leeann and Elaina's parents, are here and equipped with cameras and chatting with one another on the opposite side of the room from their children. Leeann, as always, is absent. She has only been able to attend one pre-dance gathering, and that was last year. Every other time she's been working. If it bothers Jasper, he's never told me.

Elaina takes a seat beside Jasper on the sofa. The space between the two on the couch is slim, but still more than there has been in a long time. Lenny sits beside Allison, eating the other half of the cookie she doesn't want.

My dad puts a hand on my shoulder and calls the others over to line up for pictures. While they're making their way over, he ducks his mouth down to my ear and murmurs, "Remind me why you don't have a date? You look lovely."

I roll my eyes but still reply, "Thanks, Dad."

"Jas doesn't know what he's missing," he continues.

I shake my head and pull away to look at him. "No, I didn't know what I was missing."

His brows furrow and he shifts back a little, glancing over his shoulder at the lanky boy wrapping his arms around Elaina's petite frame.

Since my dad got mixed up in the Kiss Cam drama that occurred over Christmas, I wasn't sure whether I should update him on anything that happened on New Year's Eve. I figured it was high school stuff he didn't care to know about and was too busy to hear, so I decided not to tell him any further news. When I told my parents that Elaina would be coming here before the Winter Semiformal, my dad seemed a little surprised but didn't say anything. Now I can see him trying to piece this information together, and I really wish I could talk to him about it.

Our discussion before helped me make a decision I regret now, but I don't need advice this time. I just want to talk to someone who isn't a teenager. But I can't right now because of the dance. Maybe if things go badly at the dance I can leave early and see if he's still home. If all my thoughts are out in the open, maybe I can think clearly. I don't think I've made very good decisions up to this point, especially since I've been thinking of the half-heart necklace more and more.

"If you're home tonight, maybe we can talk," I say.

"Did you guys . . . ?" He stops and glances at Jasper again.

"Are you going to be home?" I ask.

He nods. "I've got the night off, June Bug. Besides"—he squeezes my shoulder—"I think you need to catch me up."

"Yeah," I mutter.

My mom calls me over and I stand in the middle of the group, Allison on my left, Elaina on my right, and place my hands on my hips while cameras flash. Despite the sinking feeling in my stomach, I stand with a smile and wait for the parents to finally realize that time is running short.

After that, we all pile into Jasper's car. Elaina rides shotgun, Lenny sits between Allison and me, and we're off. It's tight in the back, and Lenny ends up elbowing me in the ribs the whole drive. Jasper and Elaina don't hold hands over the armrest like I thought they would, which strikes me as odd, since they've done it all the other times that Elaina has driven with us (which really isn't that many). I'm sure that if anyone glanced back they could see right up my or Allison's dresses, because our knees are smashed against the seats in front of us. But Jasper's radio is turned up high, and I lean close to the door and close my eyes, praying that I won't regret coming tonight.

The gymnasium floor is flooded with kicked-off heels and white balloons. Under the scoreboard a DJ is set up behind a table with a black tablecloth over it. The lights are dimmed, with flashing lights sweeping over the filling dance floor. My senses are being struck left and right, starting with that latex smell balloons leave in the air, then a hundred different perfume and cologne scents. My ears throb to the beat of the bass over the speakers. I can't recognize the song playing.

Jasper lifts the video camera he brought in with him and turns it on to scan the room.

"Welcome back to the Winter Semiformal, VlogIt," he says cheerily, and turns the camera back to face him. "I'm gonna tell you right now. It smells like feet already."

"C'mon, Jasper," Elaina begs, and pulls him by his free hand. "It's my favorite song."

"We're vlogging here," he says quickly, and turns the camera back to film his way onto the dance floor.

"Well, c'mon, guys. It's party time," Lenny says, and motions us to follow him.

Surrounded by our peers, we sway back and forth to the music. Every once in a while Lenny grabs my hand and spins me in a circle. Allison and I dance together, and she buckles over laughing when I start to sing along to the music, purposely doing so off-key.

A few songs in, I feel my skin start to get sticky with sweat, and the air is thick now that the gym is nearly full and bodies are bouncing along everywhere. I decide to take a break and push out of the room to the bathroom down the hall. Just stepping out of the gymnasium provides a blast of cool air, and as I make my way down the hall, the music begins to fade.

The cool tiles on my bare feet feel nice compared to the slickness of the gym floor. When I pop open the bathroom door, the room is empty except for a single girl who is drying her hands and preparing to leave. I hold the door open for her and then move to the sinks. I wipe away smudged eyeliner and run my hands under the cold water so that I can wipe away the sweat building up on the back of my neck.

As I'm smoothing my hair back down, the door opens and another girl walks in. I don't realize it's Elaina until she's standing beside me at the sinks, holding her short blond hair up off her neck and puffing out a large breath from her cheeks.

"Hi, June," she says when she catches my eye in the mirror. It's easy to feel strange and out of place at a dance when you're standing next to a girl whose dress is much more glamorous than your own. Add the fact that she's dating the boy you love, and the inadequacy makes you question why you even came.

"Hi," I say back politely. I quickly pat my hair down and make to leave.

"Hey," she says. I suppress a sigh and turn back to the mirror. "Can I ask you something?"

This is really awkward, so I'm going to say no. "Sure."

"You and Jasper are really close, right?"

I feel a rush of adrenaline shoot into my system and dread fills every corner of my mind. It's *the talk*. The talk Jasper's girlfriends give me when they see Jasper and me hanging around too much. But this time it surprises me because I haven't been sleeping over, and Jasper and I keep touching and interacting to a minimum.

"I mean, we're best friends," I say back. "And neighbors. It's kind of hard to avoid each other, if that's what you're getting at."

"No," she says, eyes widening in the mirror. She puts a hand on my forearm with a short laugh. "No, I just mean . . . Were you guys ever anything more?"

I shake my head. "No. I know, with Kiss Cam and everything you must think . . . It was complicated, but I assure you, he *does* like you."

She laughs again. "I know he likes me. But . . ." She shrugs. "I don't know. I'd hate to be someone's second choice."

I frown. "What are you talking about?"

"Lately," she begins, "maybe in the beginning even, he just tries too hard or looks at you like . . . I don't know, I can't explain it. And we got in a fight the other day about it. He's trying to convince me that I'm the only one, but I don't think so." Her eyes have lowered over the course of her talking, but now she glances up at me. "There's nothing more between you two?"

"Our relationship is complicated, you have to understand that," I tell her, and her body shifts away from mine a little stiffly. "But like I said, we've never been together. He'd never cheat on you; he'd never cheat on anyone. He's a good person, Elaina. You're lucky to have him."

She presses her lips together and grabs my forearm again. "Okay. You're right. I'm just paranoid." She smiles and then pats a section of my hair down for me. "You look nice, by the way."

"You too," I tell her with a tight smile. Then, with a certain kind of calculated eagerness, I leave the bathroom and make my way back to the dance, an unsettling feeling following me.

I make it back in time to keep my promise to Lenny about that slow dance. He's shorter than Jasper, but only slightly. I weave his fingers with mine and sway back and forth to the slow love song. There is no room for Jesus between the other couples, whose bodies are pressed close together, heads on shoulders, lips to ears. It's kind of awkward, so I let my eyes sweep over the couples who are close to us.

A few couples away, Jasper has his arms wrapped around Elaina's waist, and her cheek is against his chest. His hands are clasped together in the back, camera dangling from his fingers. He has his chin on top of her head, and his eyes are looking nowhere, face nearly blank.

I turn to Lenny and move our arms a bit. "Jasper look okay to you?"

He shrugs. "Looks tired. Must've worn himself out already."

I hum a little and sway a bit to the music. "Glad he's having fun."

"You're a little bitter," he says with a laugh.

"Change is just hard." I sigh.

Lenny nods and swings our arms. "Hasn't gone unnoticed by VlogIt. They've been suggesting crazy stuff like Operation Save Jasiper."

A smile spreads slowly across my face. "Oh, and what do they propose?"

"Same thing the Jenny fandom proposes. They want to lock you two in a room until you have no choice but to kiss and make up." Lenny's eyebrows wiggle playfully.

"Operation Save Jasiper, huh?" I shake my head and let go of

Lenny's hands as the song comes to an end. "They've got ideas for everything."

The end of the dance approaches with only a few songs left to play. After being pulled into a manic, jumping crowd for a wild pumped-up song that really shouldn't have been played for the occasion, I excuse myself from the group for some fresh air.

In the midst of the crowd, I spotted Milo, who was grinding on some girl with a revealing animal-print dress. He didn't notice me, but it was a relief to see that I didn't have to worry about him. Since I got here I've been a little on edge, worrying about whether he'd try anything. It looks like he occupied himself. So I leave the gymnasium with a satisfied smile.

When I step outside, people file out behind me to get to the restrooms or grab their coats to leave before the traffic rush. Leaning up against the wall near the gymnasium doors, I find someone familiar talking into a camera. His girlfriend is, surprisingly, nowhere near him. Slowly, I walk up to him and lean into the frame to wave.

"Oh," he says, and flinches back, a bit startled. "Hello, Juniper. I haven't seen you all night."

"Hey," I say with a large smile, still looking at the camera. "Whatcha up to?"

"Elaina went to go grab her coat so I could get the car and pick you guys up at the door. She ran off with friends, though. So who knows how long it will take her to get a *jacket*." He shakes his head and then pinches my arm. "Having fun?"

"Yeah, wasn't too shabby," I say. "Missed you, though."

"Sorry," he tells me, but I'm too busy staring at the camera lens to see if he means it. "Did something different for our viewers and hung out with Elaina's friends." He turns to the camera. "Let me know what you guys think of the change. I thought it was fun."

He turns off the camera and lowers it. I sink back against the wall and bump my arm against his. Music from the gym filters out to fill the short silence.

"You good?" I ask. I remember what Elaina said about them fighting, but I don't know if he knows I know. Either way, it's not a bad question to ask.

"Yeah, I'm great." I tilt my head up to look at him and he smiles at me. It doesn't quite reach his eyes, though. He looks down and clasps both hands over his video camera in front of him. "You look nice."

"You don't look too bad yourself," I say lightly.

Jasper and I were planning on only dressing half this formal if we had ended up going together. He wanted to wear an undone tie and sneakers. I wasn't going to wear heels or do my hair. We wanted to get these ridiculous fur coats from the thrift store and show up in them. It was supposed to be fun. It got kind of serious when other plans were made and Jasper started dating Elaina. After that, the emphasis on perfection affected all of us. I mean, things were still fun, but I didn't laugh as much as I have in the past, especially since Jasper didn't do the worm dance. A classic that didn't get a proper high school finale.

The DJ inside announces the final slow dance of the night, and I look down at my bare feet. My stomach does a flip when I realize it's one of my favorite songs and we're all alone in the hallway, trying not to act awkward with each other.

Suddenly, Jasper holds out a hand in front of me. "Shall we?"

I sputter and lean away. "Are you kidding me?" I say, and glance down the hall for signs of Elaina. Things get weird when you've been confronted by a guy's girlfriend regarding your relationship. I don't know if this crosses the line, and I don't want to find out.

"What?" he asks, and sets his camera down on the floor. "It's 'Drops of Jupiter,' June."

"Jas, it's a slow dance."

"Juniper May," he says, aghast. "We danced to this song in the seventh grade on the coffee table in my living room and now you won't dance with me because it's been turned romantic? Who are you?"

"Someone who doesn't want to get beat up by Elaina."

He rolls his eyes and takes both of my hands, pulling me away from the wall. "She's not that type. Dance with me."

I reluctantly let him take me by the hands and sway me back and forth, relishing the feeling of his fingers between mine. He spins me suddenly and pulls me back, closer this time, singing along to the lyrics. I feel my face heat and turn my face away, unable to stop the giggling.

"'Tell me, did you fall for a shooting star, one without a permanent scar?'" he sings, even though he's laughing slightly. "'And did you miss me while you were looking for yourself out there?'"

I pull back and spin him this time, laughing at how he has to duck awkwardly to fit under my arm. When he's upright again, he takes my hands and stretches them high above us, letting them fall at our sides slowly. Then I stretch our arms out between us and let him pull me back in. He spins me out and then back so that his chest is at my back and we're rocking back and forth like this in the empty hallway, singing broken lyrics of the song in short breaths.

I let my head rest back on his shoulder and allow the warmth to fill my body from the place where his breath blows down to the tips of my toes. My eyes almost flutter closed, and I'm prepared to stand in this position for as long as we can. I hardly think he knows how much this moment is making me fall further in love with him.

Then he turns me around and presses his forehead to mine while he sings the final lyric of the song, "'And are you lonely looking for yourself out there?'"

I let out a shaky breath and take a step back, out of his arms. Elaina is coming down the hall with her group of friends, I can hear one of the girls moaning about a tear in her dress, which I assume is the reason they took so long getting back.

I don't know how Jasper and I went from dancing around in a circle, giggling and red in the face, to being wrapped up in each other. I feel bad about it, horrible when I see Elaina send a huge smile in Jasper's direction. If Jasper and I were having a moment, or even if I have mistaken it as one, I know I can't be near Elaina right now, especially now that she's noticed I'm standing there in an empty hallway with him.

Trying not to look guilty about the ever-growing population of butterflies in my stomach, I wave at Elaina and shift my body from Jasper's.

"Did you tell June we're gonna get the car?" she asks him. He takes the jacket from her arm, in a way that I recognize is done to distract himself. I avoid eye contact with all of them.

"Yep," he says. She slides her arms into her coat and he wraps it around her shoulders. "Let's go." Then he looks over his shoulder, not quite looking at me. "Um, could you go get the others? We should try to leave now before the rush."

I nod and kneel down to grab his video camera. I hand it to him as I head back into the gymnasium.

———

The drive back is chaotic. Lenny sits up front with Jasper, and the girls squeeze together in back, thankfully with Allison between Elaina and me. For the first time, we're all too hot to care that Jasper's heater doesn't work. All of our windows are rolled down, the car too full with chatter for Jasper to bother with any music.

The first to be dropped off is Allison, and then Elaina. Jasper doesn't get out of the car to walk Elaina to her door. She just gives him a peck on the lips and gets out without many words exchanged. Nobody says anything about that.

Even though it's logical to drop me off before Lenny, Jasper drives to Lenny's first. Lenny says good night to both of us and takes the camera from Jasper to edit. Jasper backs up across the street and stops before my front door after Lenny leaves.

I push the car door open with the intent of leaving without saying good-bye, but his voice stops me.

"Good night, Juniper."

"Night, Jas," I say back, and scoot off the seat.

"We're kind of pathetic, huh?" he wonders out loud before I can close the door.

"We're something," I say back. He nods and puts his car

back in drive. I close the door and head up the walk to my front door.

We sure are doing a lot of acknowledging without acting on it, and maybe it's because we're afraid. So I guess we *are* kind of pathetic.

Twenty-Four
You Know Why

AFTER SHUTTING THE front door, I lean my back against it and push my fingers into my hairline, releasing a tense breath. The hallway is dark except for a soft blue glow coming from the living room entryway. If I still my breathing, I can hear the low hum of chatter from the television. I remember telling my dad to wait up for me before I left for the dance. Now, after what happened tonight with Jasper and Elaina, I find it hard to hold everything in. Kicking my heels off, I tiptoe down the hallway to peek into the living room.

My dad sits on the couch in his pajamas with his head resting back against the cushions, eyes drooping. When he sees me, he sits up.

"June Bug, how was the dance?"

I shrug, hands smoothing my skirt nervously. "It was a dance. Nothing special. Is Mom sleeping?"

He scoots forward and then pats the cushion beside him. "She is. Want to talk?"

I nod and cross the room to sit beside him. I don't sink back into the cushions, but perch on the end stiffly. He waits for me to say something, and I give myself a few seconds to gather my thoughts. For a moment, there is nothing but silence between us.

Finally, I say, "Mom told me once that she almost didn't marry you. She wanted to finish college, and you wanted to get married. She didn't know if she could balance a marriage and an education—how she'd be able to afford anything. You were relentless, and she wanted to break it off."

My dad chuckles and leans his elbows on his knees, scrubbing his face. "We did break up. Only for a short time, but I was devastated. We found our way back to each other, though. That's how I knew I couldn't let her go again. I had to be patient, and I learned my lesson. It sucked, but I don't regret breaking up. It taught me that I couldn't just expect things from her. I needed to recognize that her concerns were valid. I wanted to be with her, so I waited."

I nod.

"Is this about Jasper?" he asks.

I glance at him and his eyebrows rise. "I pretended I didn't notice his feelings for me. I thought that he was just being his Jasper self—the self without boundaries and harmless flirtation," I start, and wrap my arms across my chest. "He asked me to be his girlfriend on New Year's Eve as the ball dropped, and I choked. I didn't know what I thought of him or how I should feel about him anymore. I could only think about how we would affect VlogIt and Lenny. I've mulled it over a lot since then, and I don't think our relationship would affect them as much as I originally thought. We were practically together, anyway."

"You said no and now you regret it," he says.

"The worst part," I moan, "is that we're both trying to fix things, but I can only feel things getting worse. Sometimes we just . . . say things or do things . . . but we're afraid."

My hands are twisting around in my lap, and my dad puts a hand on my back in an attempt to comfort me as I begin to tell him everything I've been struggling with. I just need to verbalize my problems, and as always, he just listens and doesn't judge.

I explain how Elaina came into the picture and how I went to Jasper's house and confessed. I tell him how Jasper rejected me and how we decided to start over. I decide to include my encounter with Milo, and discuss how he feels about my relationship with Jasper—because sometimes I believe him. My dad sits beside me, quietly absorbing the information. Finally, I tell him about the half-heart necklace and dancing in the school hallway, and he rubs my back.

"Juniper," he says. It always feels weird when my dad calls me by my full name, but it's how I know I need to pay attention, so I lift my eyes to his. "You can't wait on him forever. He knows how you feel, and he's struggling with a decision. On one hand he has you. You hurt him and he feels vulnerable, but from what you tell me, I think he still loves you. You two are important in each other's lives. I know that. Your mom and I are gone a lot, and Leeann isn't around a whole lot for him, either. You guys are each other's family, and he'd be stupid to let you go. But on the other hand, he sees that you've hurt him before, and he's afraid you'll do it again. He's using Elaina as a crutch, but it sounds like she's putting the pieces together. If she doesn't, and he becomes too reliant on her to deal with his feelings, you need to let him go, because that means he won't trust you in a romantic relationship. You guys are best friends; you know each other's quirks. I'm sure you'll figure it out. And even if things don't work out, that doesn't make your friendship worth any less, okay?"

My eyes are watering, and I have no idea when I became so emotional, but I feel my chest tightening in response to my dad's speech. "Thanks, Dad," I manage in a strained voice.

He squeezes my shoulder, and I allow him to fold me into his chest for a hug. There are many things I'm grateful for, and having this man as my dad is one of them.

We sit a little while longer and then my dad decides to hit the hay. Feeling relieved after getting his input, I decide to do the same.

I get out of the dress I wore to the Winter Semiformal and wash off the glitter Allison added to my eyelids. When I go to my closet, my eyes search for something to wear for sleep, but they stop on Jasper's Blackhawks sweatshirt and I can't help myself. So I pick it out and pull it on along with pajama shorts. When I go to my vanity to put my hair up, I catch a glimpse of the half-heart necklace sitting where I left it. I don't hesitate, just pick up the half heart and clasp it around my neck, patting it to my chest when I see myself wearing it in the mirror.

Midday, I wake up to an empty house. My mom left for work earlier this morning, and my dad left me a note on the front door telling me that he's on call today and the ER is being slammed.

I contemplate going to Jasper's, but I don't think it's wise to see him after last night. I don't want to bother Lenny if he's editing, so I stand in the entryway of my house and stare into its emptiness. My mind is loud despite the quiet.

I take a few steps down the hallway to the kitchen, but then there is knocking at the front door. I turn in surprise and smooth my hair as I hurry to answer it, thinking maybe my dad forgot his key or I need to sign for a package my mom ordered.

When I get there and pull the door open, Jasper is standing on the doormat. I pause and my stomach flutters. His eyebrows rise and his lips part when he sees me, and I don't understand the look of surprise until I realize that I'm wearing his sweatshirt and the half heart. My cheeks flush, and I embarrassedly turn my head away and cross my arms, trying to cover myself. He, too, shuffles around and looks away, lips becoming a thin line. The flutters in my stomach turn to stones, and I think about slamming the door in his face.

"I—uh—" He stops and runs a hand through his already mussed hair. I glance sideways at him and notice his eyes are tired. It appears as though he was up all night. "I just really needed to talk to you." I push a lock of hair behind my ear and hesitantly glance at him again. Listening, waiting, a little uncomfortable.

He licks his lips and tries again. "I just came to tell you that I tried. I really tried, but things didn't work, and she was hurt, and you've been so confusing. I don't know what to do because I want . . ." He stops and shuffles around again. My brows furrow in confusion. "I don't know if we want the same things, or if being friends is good enough. . . ." He stops again, and his eyes are on the sweatshirt and necklace. His lips move, trying to form words, but he stops himself each time. Finally, he points to me. "You're wearing it." He scratches his chin with the same hand. He's so jittery.

"Jas," I say. My head can't keep up with him. I'm only picking up bits and pieces, but it's too vague to absorb. "I don't understand."

"Uh." He scratches the back of his neck and inhales deeply before exhaling. "June, Elaina and I broke up this morning."

My heart pounds in my chest, mind reeling. "Oh," I breathe. "Jas, I'm so sorry."

He ducks his head. "I tried really hard to make things work, to have things go back to the way they were." He looks up at me, brown eyes falling on mine. "I just felt like that couldn't happen while I was with Elaina. We are the way that we are, and I'm not gonna let someone get between us, because when that happens, we don't act like us anymore. We're more careful, reserved. It's not us. I want us back."

"Me too," I say.

He nods and looks down at his feet. My hands become restless, and one reaches up to fiddle with the half-heart charm around my neck.

"I want . . . ," he says suddenly, and clears his throat. "I want to clear up some stuff about us."

"Okay."

He looks at the sweatshirt again and watches me play with the half heart for a moment. "Why are you wearing my stuff?"

He knows how I feel about him. He turned me down so that he wouldn't be unfaithful in his relationship. He said no to keep us friends—the way I wanted us to be on New Year's. Above all, he didn't believe what I said was true.

"You know why, Jas," I say softly, and shift away. Now seems like the wrong time to talk about this. He just broke up with Elaina.

He swallows and nods.

"Are you okay?" I ask.

"Yeah, I'm fine," he reassures me. "I'm just . . . letting everything sink in."

"Do you want to come in?" I offer, aware that we've been standing in the doorway this entire time and the winter air is beginning to make me shiver. He looks numb and conflicted. I can't tell what is going on in his head, or why he came here. I don't think he came here for me; if he had, he would have made a move by now. Maybe he just wanted to let me know that there was nothing standing in our way. Now that Elaina is gone, perhaps he believes we can stop being weird about behaving certain ways. I agree, if that's the case. We can stop feeling guilty now.

"Uh." He thinks about it for a second, and then answers hesitantly, "No. I think I should just go."

"Are you sure?"

"Yes," he answers. Then he takes a step forward and loops his arms around me. My arms are crushed to my chest, but it doesn't matter. I close my eyes and lift my chin to fit it into the notch in his shoulder. When he pulls away, we give each other small smiles and he says good-bye.

I feel satisfied, in a terrible way because Elaina was affected through this, and she's a nice person. Along with that, though, I feel disappointed. I want to be with him, and it's understandable that right now isn't that moment, but waiting requires patience, and I'm running out of patience.

Twenty-Five
Your Flirting Sucks

RETURNING BACK TO school after the Winter Semiformal feels like a huge downer. The streamers and balloons that lined the halls on the way to the gymnasium have since been removed, administrators have returned to patrolling the halls instead of absently keeping to themselves in a corner, and the flushed faces of our peers once again turn sunken and tired. Any evidence of the weekend before has completely disappeared, and it makes me feel a little less awkward and a little more normal as Jasper, Lenny, and I make our way to our lockers. The glitz and drama have passed, and there's nothing left but plain old tile floors and familiar company.

I walk between Lenny and Jasper, hands deep in my coat pockets and arms occasionally brushing against theirs. It's funny how people pass by you in an unrecognizable blur until the day you feel like you've done one of them wrong, and then that person seems to pop up everywhere as an ugly reminder of what you've done.

That happens.

As we turn the final corner at our lockers, Elaina pops out, and her eyes grow in what looks like embarrassment when she sees us. It's a slightly uncomfortable exchange. She shuffles a bit to the right, catches eyes with me for a moment, then Jasper, gives us a tight smile, and then trots off.

As soon as she has passed, Jasper lets out a breath and rubs at his jaw with his fingertips. "Well, that wasn't very fun," he comments.

Lenny snorts. "Could've been worse. She could've flipped you off or slapped June...."

I swat Lenny's arm. "I didn't *do* anything."

I say that, but I don't quite believe it. Jasper really didn't do a good job of explaining how the breakup occurred or why, but Lenny has been making jokes all morning about my part in the breakup—which doesn't exactly make a person feel so good.

"You exist," he replies, and shoots a look at Jasper, who rolls his eyes.

"You know what?" Jasper says. "You try getting over someone by means of another girl, and tell me how that works out for you."

"You know," Lenny starts, "I told you it was a bad idea, but you didn't listen to me, so don't go throwing that in my face. If I wanted to get over someone, I would do it the right way." He crosses his arms and nods a little at his statement.

I raise my eyebrows. "And what exactly would that look like?"

Lenny laughs under his breath like I've told a joke. Then he wraps an arm around my shoulder and holds his other hand in front of my face. "One," he says, sticking out his thumb, "binge watch every season of *Desperate Housewives*. Two"—his pointer finger juts out—"eat my feelings. And three," he says while his middle finger joins the others, "fall madly in love with Eva Longoria all over again because she can't break my heart. *Fin*."

"That's not healthy," Jasper mutters.

"Uh-huh." Lenny shakes his head and motions between the two of us as he breaks off from our group to find his locker. "And you two are just a prime example of *healthy*. I think I'll take my chances."

He turns on his heel and disappears into a mass of students near his locker, leaving Jasper and me.

We take a few strides in silence, and then he takes a sidestep and follows an invisible trail to his locker. I pause for a second and then decide to follow him. When he sees I've joined him, he checks over his shoulder and then looks back at me with a raised eyebrow.

"Is Milo over there or something?"

I shake my head. "No, I just wanted to ask you something."

He shrugs. "Shoot."

I feel weird asking this, because it sounds self-interested and snobbish, but I need to know so that I can treat the situation accordingly. I don't want to make Elaina feel uncomfortable when she sees me. She was nice to me, and I don't want to feel like I betrayed her.

"When you and Elaina broke up—"

"She told me she didn't want to be my second choice. She knew, June, but it wasn't your fault."

"It just doesn't make sense," I insist, mind stuck replaying the conversation I had with Elaina the night of the Winter Semiformal. "I told her there was nothing going on between us.

She looked relieved. She even said she was being paranoid."

Jasper stops picking at books in his locker and grabs my hand to stop it from tangling in one of my curls. "We had a fight, and then she found you and me too close for comfort in an empty hallway. She wanted to believe you, but I'm the one who ruined it, okay? The whole thing was my idea, and it was never honest. I finished it. It's all over now."

"We did a bad thing," I mutter, pulling my hand from his. "We involved another person. Elaina was nice, Jas."

Jasper puts his hand on my shoulder instead and takes a deep breath. "She's okay. I called her last night. It's just a little . . . Well, you know how breakups go."

"I'm not on good terms with my ex-boyfriends," I remind him.

"You have bad taste," he counters.

"Not entirely."

His eyes meet mine for a second and my stomach flutters. Then he ducks his head and releases an airy chuckle. Pushing my shoulder back, he mutters, "Get ready for class, Juniper. Your flirting sucks."

I bite my lip to stop a smile from spreading across my face. "Sure it does," I taunt, and nudge my shoulder into his arm as I walk away.

———

After school on Thursday, we pile into Jasper's room and prepare for our Q&A video of the week. Lenny immediately flops down onto Jasper's mattress and pulls out his cell phone. I sit down beside his feet and watch Jasper cross the room to grab his laptop off his desk.

We've all been getting back into the swing of things since

Jasper and Elaina broke up. Jasper was right about Elaina being a roadblock even in our friendship since New Year's. Since they've broken up, it's easier for us to be together without feeling guilty. He's been throwing an arm around my shoulder more casually, talking to me more freely, and just being more Jasper as a whole.

VlogIt has been informed of the breakup as well. Jasper vlogged about it, making it clear he didn't want to hear any more hate toward Elaina, which I guess has been a trend since they started dating. She threatened Jasiper, so our fans naturally hated her and blamed her for ruining Kiss Cam.

We've all been feeling really bad lately. We've been doing a lot of lying in our vlogs to hide our personal lives. Lenny pointed out how we started WereVloggingHere as a video diary to log our lives for our future selves, and how our videos have stopped following our original intentions. So that pushed us to clear things up for our sake.

So things finally feel like they did a few months ago. Like the first time we got a kissing request: Thursday, an ask day. Lenny and I are staying out of Jasper's way. He's setting up the camera to face his bed. It kind of looks like we're going to film cheap porn. Jasper smiles at me like he knows what I'm thinking. I wink back.

This is us. This is WereVloggingHere.

Lenny sits up suddenly and scoots to the edge of the mattress. "What's today's ask theme?"

"Twenty questions," I say, and pull my legs up, crossing them neatly under me. "Hopefully all innocent questions."

"Yeah, right." Jasper rolls his eyes at me. "We're too hot to get innocent questions."

Lenny's eyes crinkle as he chokes back laughter, and he buries his face in his hands.

"You're so full of it," I say, shaking my head at Jasper.

Jasper lets out a short laugh and steps back from the tripod. "Check your e-mails more than once a week and you'd see the love letters they write us."

I watch him turn on the box lights and shake my head again when he looks back at me. "I have *never* gotten a love letter. The only e-mails I receive are ones asking if I can confirm Jasiper or whether Lenny is single."

"What?" Lenny squawks, sitting up. "They ask *you* that? Every e-mail I get tells me I'm adorable. Try feeling manly after that."

I smile at him, but then my eyes hood. "They totally just use me for information." I gasp, offended. "I am the third wheel on this channel. You guys get the love and I get the buffer questions."

"Our viewers are eighty-seven percent teenage girls, actually," Jasper says offhandedly, spinning about as he collects the remote and avoids wires in his path. "So it doesn't surprise me."

I sigh and flop back onto his mattress. Lenny leans over me. "You're only good for Kiss Cam, really," he teases. "You can only save yourself by bringing it back."

I push his face away and sit back up to point at him accusingly. "You two are out to get me," I whine.

Lenny giggles, and when I glance over at Jasper, he simply bites down a grin and shrugs.

"Trouble," I say. "You both are trouble."

Jasper falls down on his bed between Lenny and me, laptop

in hand. "Oh, Juniper." He sighs. "You're paranoid."

I lean over to eye them up. Both are wearing mischievous grins, but I can't tell if they're just doing it to mess with me or if there's something going on that I don't know about. "Just remember, boys," I say, "the last time you two tag-teamed, it did not end well."

Jasper bumps my shoulder with his. "Relax." He laughs. "It's really easy to get you going."

"Yeah," Lenny says. "You've made it crystal clear that Kiss Cam, or anything related to it, is never happening again."

"The subject just needed a new tone, one that doesn't make you and me cringe," Jasper adds. "We can joke about it now."

I glance between them skeptically one last time, then lean back. "Uh-huh," I reply slowly, "sometimes a girl has to make sure."

"You sure you're sure?" Lenny asks through a smile.

"Yep." I pop the *p* and place my hands in my lap. "Let's start this video, then."

Jasper nods and then hits the record button.

After the video, Lenny leaves and I stop at the bottom of the staircase to wait for Jasper. I haven't stayed at his house in a while. Lately, I've been leaving at the same time as Lenny, just to ease Jasper and me back into our routine. Today I want to stay, though. I'm tired of waiting to make sure we're all healed, but I want to make sure it's okay with Jasper first.

Jasper notices me halfway down the stairs and grins. "Are you staying, then?" he asks.

"Is that okay?"

When he reaches the bottom, he grabs my wrist and pulls

me along after him. "It's always okay."

He leads me into the living room, where I immediately find my spot on the couch and make myself comfortable. He sits down beside me for a moment, and then he stands back up.

"Actually," he says, "I want to show you something."

Then he darts out of the room. I sit a little straighter and duck back to see where he went. I don't know if he meant for me to follow him, so I stay put, fingers restless in my lap. The last time he did this he came back with a love declaration and jewelry. The memory makes my stomach uneasy, and I pinch my fingers together in my lap.

I can't think about that now.

He returns after a minute with an envelope in hand. He tosses it in my lap and sits down beside me, watching as I turn it over and slide my fingers under the flap. What I pull out is an invitation to the next VlogIt meet-and-greet.

"It's this summer," he says. "Lenny already knows."

The last meet-and-greet we did with the VlogIt family was fun. Lenny's parents chaperoned since it was held in L.A., and we got to meet our viewers and other vloggers. It was a three day thing full of speeches and pictures and ding-dong-ditch on our hotel room door. But with that came viewers who asked us to kiss for the camera or shout out to their friends and family. Lenny would be there to politely turn some suggestions down, but that didn't mean it wouldn't be any less awkward— especially this time.

"Oh," I say, and purse my lips as I read the remainder of the invite.

"Yeah . . ." He trails off. I hand the invite back to him.

A silence settles between us, not an awkward one like I

would expect, but a silence that begins when both parties are lost in thought.

I love that we're back to having our regular old friendship. It's comfortable and it's fluid, but the thing is, it's not the same. We've changed, but since this past weekend we've been pretending we haven't, and I don't know why. I guess we've been so eager to get around the roadblock that was Elaina that now that we've gotten around it, we're ignoring the fact that we have to take a new route to do so.

We can joke all we want, tease as much as we like, and beat around the bush for as long as we want, but at the end of the day, I know this change is on our minds and we need to do something about it while we have the chance. Otherwise, everything we went through will have been for nothing.

He's worried about pressure at the meet-and-greet, but what if there wasn't any pressure? What if we stopped hiding from each other, from our viewers?

My patience has reached its end.

"Jas," I say, turning my head to look at him

"Hm?" he hums but doesn't look up from the envelope he is now twirling between his fingers.

"What if we stopped being pathetic?" I ask.

He stops playing with the envelope and looks up to meet my eyes. "What?"

"Our viewers only pressure us because they're in fantasy Jasiper land," I tell him. "They'd stop pressuring the moment Jasiper became real. They try so hard because they believe in us, but the hard work would be done if we believed in ourselves for once."

"June." Jasper squeezes his eyes shut. "Don't be rash."

"I'm not being rash, Jas. I'm being serious," I say, voice steady.

"You know I love you," he says, eyes snapping open. He places a hand on my wrist. "But being together for the sake of the fans or because you're lonely doesn't do anything for us. You don't love me, June. Sometimes I think you do, but then your reasoning doesn't match up."

I make a frustrated noise in the back of my throat and stand up to pace in front of him, hands scrubbing my face and legs weak but unable to stop moving. I don't know what more he wants from me. I've tried to make him see how I feel in every way that I know, and he shoots me down every single time. He's still scared of me.

"What do you want me to say, huh?" I ask as I push my hands through my hair and turn toward him. "What do you need to hear from me? You don't believe I love you? Okay," I say, and clench my teeth. "You sing in the shower, but not cool guy songs. You sing Adele, and you sing her music really off-key. I love that. I think it's hilarious. You never eat the crust of your pizza, which is really weird, but I kind of think it's adorable. You have one hundred and eighty-four comic books, I've counted. Sometimes I steal them from you and read them so that when you talk to me about them, I can keep up. Freshman year, you told me you liked the new perfume I was wearing. I haven't stopped buying it since. You don't wear body sprays if you can help it, but you smell good anyway and I've never understood that. I'm the only girl you've ever let see you shirtless. I don't know why that matters, but it makes me feel important. You never pick up the phone when your dad calls; you stopped caring about him the moment he left. You're good at that, forgetting people. Oh, and do you want to know why 'Drops of Jupiter' is my favorite song?

Because you used to sing 'Drops of Juniper' to me to be obnoxious, but I secretly fell in love with that version of the song. Actually, I just secretly fell in love with you, but you never seemed interested. You'd always chase after some other girl after I convinced myself that maybe you had a thing for me. So don't blame me for not picking up the memo. I've been paying attention all along. You've been the tease, and I learned how to convince myself that I was imagining things. You love me? Okay. Well, I love you, too. Believe me, I do."

I'm shaking, and I don't realize I've been talking fast and tripping over my words until I'm finished speaking. Jasper sits tensely on the couch in front of me, eyes wide and a little startled, jaw unhinged, looking like he just got slapped. When he doesn't say anything, I decide I'm done waiting and march out of the room, eyes stinging.

I've done everything I can. There's a hundred ways to show someone you love them? Well, screw that. You can show someone you love them, shout it at them even, but sometimes they still ignore you. Sometimes they still convince themselves you're lying to them. With some people, a single heartbreak can ruin your chances completely. That's when you need to force yourself to walk away, no matter how much it hurts, because if you hang around waiting, you might be there forever.

At his door, I pull my shoes on and grab my jacket off the rack, hoping to hear him call my name or appear around the corner, but he doesn't, so I yank open the door and slam it shut behind me.

Halfway across the street, I'm beginning to jog, anxious to get home and cry tears of frustration into my pillow, when I hear Jasper yelling my name from his front door. But for me, it's already too late. I don't stop.

"Juniper!" he calls again.

I shake my head angrily and step over the lip of the curb, just a few feet from my front door.

"Hey!" This time his voice is closer, this time a hand yanks my arm back, stopping me from climbing the steps to my porch.

I turn and yell right back, "What?"

"You *really* love me?" he asks.

I wipe away a tear that managed to escape my eye and sniff back a sarcastic answer. I could say, *Were you not there two minutes ago? I said that, you idiot!* or *Are you hard of hearing these days, Jasper, darling? Because I'm getting really sick of repeating myself like a broken record.* But I don't say either one of those things. I know what he's looking for.

I say it slowly, enunciating each word. "Truly, madly, deeply."

"Okay," he mutters, nodding. "Okay . . ."

He looks at me for a moment, eyes sweeping over my face. Then I extend my hand out to reach for him, and he ducks forward, pushing my hair between his fingers and cupping the base of my head to brace me as he presses his lips to mine. We pull each other closer, kissing like we've been without each other for too long. Finally, we pull back a few inches to catch our breath.

"If you say Kiss Cam, I swear to God . . ."

"It's real."

Epilogue
When the Fandom Takes Control, There's No Going Back

FIVE MONTHS LATER

WE DECIDE TO come out as a couple at the VlogIt meet-and-greet.

After dating for five months and seeing how strong we are together, I gave Jasper the okay. It was becoming harder and harder to keep our relationship a secret. Lenny had purposely been leaving Jasiper moments in the vlog when editing.

Jasper's hand squeezes mine over the armrest of his car while I stare out the window, letting L.A. become a blur as we drive through traffic. Lenny's crammed in the back, laptop out, grumbling about how little legroom he has.

We come up to a giant white building with grand windows and an arch over the doorway. We've finally reached our hotel. For a bunch of silly Internet people, this hotel feels like too much for VlogIt to provide us.

"This is it," Jasper says.

"This is it," I repeat. I feel my stomach knot. I make myself smile, and it helps. I can feel the tension, the nervous flutters dissipate.

Lenny pulls himself up between Jasper and me and stares out at the hotel. "Guys . . . we're actually here again."

I glance back up at him and smile. "I know. Crazy, right? Who would've thought we'd be here again?"

We all go silent and reflective, looking back at all the things that have gotten us here. Suddenly, Lenny's arms slide between the car seats and squeeze our shoulders. "I love you guys."

After we park, we enter our hotel behind a group of vloggers. When we pass through the tall, weighted doors, we are immediately overwhelmed by loud squeals and clapping rising from every corner of the lobby. The hotel is bustling with incoming vloggers. Some fans are sitting in the lounge, videotaping us. Like the previous meet-and-greet, this feels unreal. Seeing so many people who look at all of us vloggers as inspiration, hope, friends— it makes a person feel very small and humbled.

As I'm taking it all in, my stomach flutters in excitement and my face heats. Suddenly, there is a high-pitched shriek. A group of girls a few years younger than Jasper, Lenny, and me ambush us, cameras bouncing off their fingertips.

"Kiss Cam!" a short, dark-haired girl gushes. Her face is flushed, and I can tell it took quite a lot of courage to confront us by the nervous glint that flashes across her eyes when we look at her. Her friends giggle and clutch at one another behind her.

Lenny looks between us with a slight smirk.

"Well, isn't that funny," Jasper muses. "They're taking matters into their own hands now."

"When the fandom takes control," I say with a wide grin, pushing my confidence, "there's no going back."

One of the girls behind the dark-haired one pipes up, her nose wrinkling when she says, "Kiss Cam!" She points to Jasper and me. "Kiss each other and it confirms Jasiper is *real*."

I see the look in her eyes; it's something close to daring. They're done with the games we've been playing. As our relationship became harder and harder to hide, it turned into a running gag for WereVloggingHere. We turned to teasing them and purposely displaying our half-heart jewelry. Lenny took that as his cue to become the ultimate fangirl.

These girls are waiting for cannons.

"Well, in that case," Jasper says. He points to the camera in the dark-haired girl's hand. "Ambush Kiss Cam—Kiss June, confirm Jasiper. Status . . . pending." Then he turns to me. I raise my eyebrows, and he raises his back.

"Status," I say to him with an impish grin, "in progress."

With that we meet each other halfway to confirm Jasiper in a firm lip-lock that sends warm jolts of excitement throughout my body, pushing goose bumps to the surface of my skin.

The girls before us begin shrieking and jumping up and down, and somewhere in there Jasper and I start laughing through our kiss.

"It's real!" they repeat over and over.

As we pull away, Lenny pushes between us, wrapping his arms around our shoulders with a victorious grin. "All right, girls, I *own* this ship. I claim captain!"

"We're vlogging here!" Jasper tacks on, waving at the camera. I bury my face in Lenny's shoulder, trying to mask my blush. It comes into my mind suddenly that this all started with Kiss

Cam. We started with Kiss Cam. Twice. The first time gave us the push we needed; the second announced it to the people that started it all—our viewers. I shake my head a little and glance past Lenny at Jasper, who is already gazing at me with a soft smile. He winks like he knows what I'm thinking.

"Status," I yell over the madness, "completed with success."

It's one of our better ideas.

Acknowledgments

First and foremost, Jean Feiwel, thank you so much for the opportunity to write for you. I can't express enough how grateful I am. You've made my biggest dreams come true. For that, I'd probably do anything you asked (no, seriously).

This book would not be as pretty and perfect as it is without my editor, Holly West. I might have written the story, but she helped buff and polish it to the manuscript you have before you now. All of my people on Wattpad, you will see and understand that firsthand. So thank you, Holly! Really. Where would I be without your keen eye and incredible support?

Also, Lauren Scobell is the reason you have an extra Kiss Cam scene in the back of the book. So thank her for that extra-brilliant idea. Alex Rodriguez and A. Olivia Smith, thank you for the prompt that inspired the bonus scenes.

All of you who helped make this story what it is over at Swoon Reads, I cannot thank you enough. From the wonky word fixes to the cover to the marketing, I am extremely amazed by your dedication and love for each and every single book that has required your attention. I couldn't ask for a better team of people.

Thanks to my little sister, Isabel, who read anything and everything I threw at her. Sorry for the "does that sound okay?" question a hundred times in ten minutes. You're a star. You deserve an Oscar for all those dramatic readings you presented me with. Mom, she is the real MVP. You were right about us being friends someday. You were also right about putting myself out there. Thank you for giving me the confidence to go after whatever I dreamed. As all the adults in my family say, "Storytelling runs in the family."

As for my writing family . . . my Wattpad people . . . you are the reason this book exists. You are the reason I finished it. You are the reason I took a chance on Swoon Reads. I am eternally grateful for that. I've grown up with you. You've seen my writing mature. You've always believed in me. I have the best writing family in the world. So, big hugs all around. And an especially big hug for Stephanie, my first fangirl and best friend. She truly understands how much I hate editing, and she got an earful every time I hit a wall. I would be a head case without her. So thank you, Stephanie, for your unfailing support and kindness.

And finally, a giant thank-you to all the fangirls, fanfiction, and ship wars that have ever occurred on the Internet for my eyes to see. It inspired this crazy story, and you've given me more than enough material to work with. Never stop supporting the things you love.

Turn the page for some

Sw♥♥nworthy

Extras...

Kiss Cam *started out as a little story I posted on Wattpad, and WereVloggingHere's viewers were based almost entirely on my own readers as they became invested in the story of Jasper and Juniper and their kissing escapades. So what better way to thank you for all your support than one last Kiss Cam? And an extra-special thanks to Alex Rodriguez for this ship-tastic Kiss Cam request!*

"I Miss You"

I flop onto the lumpy bed in my dorm room with a defeated sigh and pull the covers over my face. Few Valentine's Days will ever compare to the one I experienced last year with Jasper and Elaina, but that doesn't mean this one has been much better.

It's one thing to look longingly at the person you love be with another person, but it's another thing entirely to *have* the person you love and *still* not be able to be with them. Long distance really sucks.

I guess the worst part about it is that Jasper was supposed to be here. He was supposed to come see me this weekend. But when you live six hours away from each other, things don't always go according to plan. Jasper got stuck in a group project that's due tomorrow, and there's no way he can spend twelve hours traveling to see me *and* get that done. Even though he assured me that we will be able to see each other *next* weekend, it didn't make today any easier.

You know how Valentine's Day is. It felt like every boyfriend on campus was giving his girlfriend flowers or oversize teddy bears. I have to have seen *every* couple sharing kisses and holding hands. And now my roommate has come in to get ready for her date.

"Hey, June," she sings as she waltzes by, searching for the heels I said she could borrow.

"Hi, Alex," I mumble, sitting up.

She glances over, noticing my frizzy hair and tired expression. Her dark eyes soften, and she stands, my heels dangling from her fingers by the straps.

"Oh," she says sympathetically. "Rough day?"

I shrug. I really like having Alex for a roommate. We've gotten close, and I consider her to be one of my best friends. And being this far away from home, I *really* need one of those. But it's nothing like having Allison, or Lenny, or . . . Jasper.

"I'm sorry," she says, sitting down beside me. "Here I am being all chipper and you're having a bad day—are you sure I can still borrow these?" She lifts up the shoes.

I nod, and she sets them in her lap.

"I'm fine, really," I insist. "Just miss my boyfriend. He was supposed to be here."

She places a comforting hand where my shins are under the blanket and squeezes. "You guys video-chat a lot. Why don't you call him up?"

"He's got this huge thing he's supposed to have done by tomorrow. I don't want to bother him," I tell her. "I watched his last vlog about ten times yesterday just to hear his voice. All of us vlogging separately for the channel was a really good idea, but it's not enough sometimes. I miss Lenny, too. I just wish I could actually *see* them again. Everyone's just so busy. . . ."

"I'm sorry, hon," she says, and I know she means it.

When I met her for the first time, she immediately knew

Swoon Reads

who I was from WereVloggingHere on VlogIt. That was bizarre, but cool, too, because she completely understood what it was like for me to be away from Jasper and Lenny. And she was the first viewer I met in real life who treated me like a real person, and not a celebrity. I could talk about them and she didn't try to pretend that she knew everything about our lives.

"Gosh, I'm such a Debbie Downer," I scold myself, and wave her away. "Go, get ready for your date!"

She grins and stands up to change into a skintight red dress that complements her olive skin. While she's touching up her makeup, I check my phone to see if Jasper has tried to get ahold of me. Nothing. Alex notices in the mirror.

"C'mon, June. Do you honestly think Jas is *too* busy right now? He's up to something." She smiles reassuringly.

I shake my head, wanting to believe her, but knowing the truth.

Alex yanks on my shoes and grabs her purse off our futon. "Well, in any case," she says at the door, "you have the room to yourself. I won't be back tonight." She winks at me, and I can't help but laugh at the insinuation.

"Use protection," I warn teasingly.

"I'm not stupid," she reminds me as she slides out the door. "Oh." She pokes her head back in. "If he doesn't call by ten, you call him. There's no excuse at that point."

"All right, all right," I say, motioning her away with an airy laugh. "I gotcha. Go have fun."

The door clicks softly behind her, and I fall back against my pillows with a groan. I check my phone again. Still nothing, but it's only six thirty.

So I try to do what most people without a date do on

Valentine's Day. I avoid romantic movies on Netflix and watch a good sitcom instead. I have half a mind to loot Alex's wine stash or finish off the opened box of Pop-Tarts, but I'm too lazy to get out of bed. So I bury myself deeper under my blankets and start to drift off, ignoring the urge to blast a Taylor Swift CD.

I'm not *that* sad yet.

I jump so violently I nearly fall out of bed when my phone starts to ring, blaring the chorus of "Drops of Jupiter." I haven't been asleep for very long—my alarm clock says it's only five past ten. Knowing that "Drops of Jupiter" is Jasper's ringtone, I quickly answer.

"Jas?"

"Why, hello, Juniper darling. How was your day?"

There's a sense of relief at hearing his voice, and my heart flutters excitedly. The little things matter when you're in a long-distance relationship.

"Now? It's perfect. I'm so happy you called. I didn't want to bother you," I ramble. "God, I miss you."

I can hear the smile in his voice when he speaks next. "Of course I called. It's Valentine's Day, and I *love* you."

I feel my face warm and my skin tingle. I just want to jump on him, *The Notebook*-style, and never let go. It has been nearly two months since we've seen each other in person.

"I love you, too. I really wish you were here," I tell him longingly.

He chuckles and then clears his throat. "Juniper, look out your window."

My brows furrow, and I sit up in bed, throwing the covers off. "What?"

"Look out your window right now."

I feel my heart begin to pound so hard it's making my legs shaky. I'm suddenly very aware that my curls are chaotic and my makeup is probably smudged and that my clothes are rumpled from sleeping, but it doesn't stop me from walking to the window and yanking the curtains open.

My mouth drops open when outside on the lawn Jasper is standing with his phone at his ear and his video camera in hand, staring up at me with a huge grin while Lenny is bouncing up and down beside him with a sign that says in big, bold letters I LOVE YOU TRULY, MADLY, DEEPLY.

"Oh my God," I say, and I hear Jasper's laughter in my ear.

Adrenaline and excitement are bubbling up inside me, and the next thing I know, I'm ending the call and making a mad dash out of my dorm. I don't think I've ever run so fast in my life—not during gym class, not when Lenny and I were being chased out of the school by Jasper, not when I thought I was being followed on my way home from a party.

My head begins to spin with unanswered questions—did he lie about the group project, did he get done early, is he ditching, did Alex know, how did he get Lenny here, too, *am I dreaming?*

But then I'm running across the lawn, and they are both so close, and I'm laughing and crying a little bit, too. Lenny has the camera now, and Jasper's arms are wide open, and when I collide with him, it's a running jump. Then he's spinning me around and we're kissing. I'm squeezing so tight I don't think I'll ever be able to unwrap myself from him. Lenny is cheering like a fangirl, and I feel like I could live in this moment forever.

When Jasper and I pull away, we're out of breath, and I begin giggling. I point toward the camera.

"Is this a Kiss Cam?"

Lenny nods vigorously.

"Kiss Cam!" Jasper announces suddenly, like he forgot. "Also, I love you! Happy Valentine's Day!"

"We've been planning this for *weeks*. Transportation was the easy part. Jasper went back home to grab his car and then pick me up. The hard part was coming up with a believable lie so that we could surprise you," Lenny says. "We even got Alex in on it."

"Ah! This is so crazy!" My voice is strained from the excitement. "I've missed you so much."

Jasper loosens his grip on me, and I immediately go to wrap my arms around Lenny. He gives me the best bear hug he can manage while holding a sign and a camera.

"I'm so happy right now," I say contentedly as I release Lenny and back up into Jasper's arms again. He presses a kiss to my cheek. "WereVloggingHere is reunited."

"It's magical," Lenny agrees.

Jasper nuzzles his face into my neck. "I've missed you like crazy. You smell so *good*. I'm never leaving."

I laugh and turn my face so that he can kiss me again.

"All right, while these two get a room, I'm gonna end this vlog . . ." Lenny laughs. "Thanks for tuning in. We're vlogging here!"

Forget what I said. This is the *best* Valentine's Day.

A Coffee Date

with author Kiara London and her editor, Holly West

"Getting to Know You"

Holly West (HW): What was the first romance novel you ever read?

Kiara London (KL): I never read anything that was exclusively romance when I was younger, because I was always worried about getting teased by my peers for reading "kissy, girly books." So, it wasn't until *Twilight* that I read anything specifically centered around a romance—and I definitely tried to hide it, ha-ha.

HW: Do you have an OTP? Who do *you* ship?

KL: I ship Bellarke (Bellamy and Clarke from *The 100*) *so hard*. It's the only ship I actually track on Tumblr, ha-ha. Those characters deserve nice things, and I just want to lock them in a room together until they figure out that the nice thing they deserve is each other. I also ship Dramione (Draco and Hermione), but that's another thing entirely. . . .

HW: Where did the idea for *Kiss Cam* start?

KL: I admit it, I've got my obsessions when it comes to YouTube and vloggers and blogging. But *goodness*, has anyone ever read the comments underneath this stuff? You put a couple of friends together in a video, and all of a sudden there are ship wars going down in the comments. It is *chaos*. And, oh my God, do *not* insult someone's ship unless you want to be publically dragged on the Internet.

All of this got me thinking. Hey, I wonder what all this looks like from the vlogger's perspective. What do they think about all this shipping? Would they be willing to humor their viewers? Is there something *secretly* going on between some of these people? And that, my friend, was what inspired *Kiss Cam*.

HW: Have you ever had a vlog yourself? Where can your fans find you online?
KL: I've actually *never* had a vlog. Lots of people assume I do because of *Kiss Cam*, but the truth is I may have been living vicariously through my characters. (Whoops!) You can always stalk me on Tumblr, though (wink wink)...
daydreams-to-neverland.tumblr.com...

HW: What's your favorite way to spend a rainy day?
KL: Movie marathon! Grab a friend or a sibling, pop some popcorn, make your favorite drink, and turn the TV room into a blanket fort dream! May also include various face masks and nail polishes. Thunder makes the movie *extra intense*.

"The Writing Life"

HW: When did you realize you wanted to be a writer?
KL: I think I've always wanted to be a writer. I'm a daydreamer, and I'm always stuck in my own little world. I've been a storyteller since I was little, and I would act out my stories with dolls. However, it wasn't until I was fourteen and I had finished my

first book that I knew for sure that writing was the only thing I *really* wanted to do.

HW: Do you have any writing rituals? Like, do you always write in a specific place?

KL: I have to be in a writing *mood*, you know? I mean, I can force it, I can get those creative juices flowing. But it's always more natural when I'm in that *mood*. I love writing when it's gloomy outside. I'll make myself some coffee or tea and I'll get cozy. It doesn't have to be anywhere specific, but I *have* to be alone. I tend to mouth out dialogue and get super intense in the face, and that's just embarrassing, so . . . yes, I must be alone.

I can only type. I used to be able to handwrite, but I've gotten way too used to how fast my thoughts get down when I type. So it's a must now.

And, funnily enough, I prefer to be a little sleepy.

HW: What's your process? Are you an outliner or do you just start at the beginning and make it up as you go?

KL: I cannot, for the life of me, outline. I wing everything. I know how I want to start, I know how I want to finish, but the middle is a bunch of question marks. I figure it out as I write.

HW: What was it like getting the edit letter?

KL: In one word: overwhelming. I remember going through it the first time and thinking *whoa*. I was so excited, but I was also freaking out a little bit because there was so much to be done. And, more than that, it finally hit me that this was real. *I just got an edit letter. From a real publisher. Oh. My. God.*

But, really, I was so happy and excited to start working on my book.

HW: How does the revision process work for you?
KL: The same way my writing process works. I wing it, ha-ha.
I start from the beginning and work to the end. But because I was revising that way, I had to backtrack a hundred times and make a ton of notes everywhere to remind myself to fix something later in the book.

It was messy. And I worked in large clumps instead of bit by bit. If it weren't for those edit notes, I would have been super frustrated.

I really need to find a better system, ha-ha. I can only get better.

HW: What's the best writing advice you've ever heard?
KL: I know people get caught up in perfection—and that's why a lot of people never finish their first drafts.

The best writing advice I've ever heard is to write without ever hitting backspace. Just focus on getting your ideas and dialogue down. You can go back and clean it up, I promise.

ALL IS FAIR IN LOVE AND FANDOM.

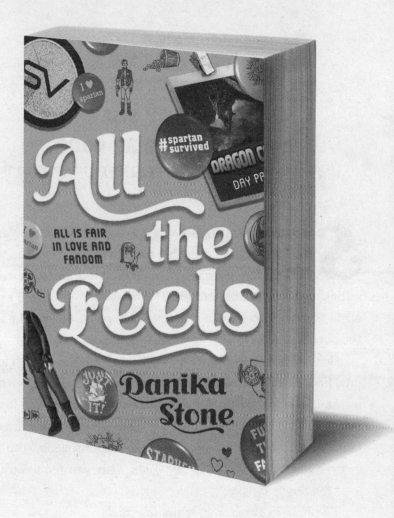

When über-fangirl Liv's favorite character is killed off, she
and her best friend, Xander, an aspiring actor and steampunk
enthusiast, decide to fight back—and end up changing everything.

3

"I SOLEMNLY SWEAR
THAT I AM UP TO NO GOOD."
(HARRY POTTER AND THE PRISONER OF AZKABAN)

Saturday morning Liv woke to the sound of the garage door closing. Her mother had the day off, but she went in for a few hours each weekend and had done so for as long as Liv could remember. The house was cold, and an icy wind rattled the bedroom windows. Liv rolled over and pulled the covers over her head, waiting for sleep to retake her.

Heady warmth spread through her limbs. Behind closed lids, images flickered: the video she'd done for her final project last semester, the girl in the audio lab who always asked Liv for help with the anticrackle effect, Xander dragging her through fabric stores so he could pick out "the right brocade," the new ONLY ONE MAN CALLS ME DARLIN' T-shirt Liv wanted to buy.

"You ready, darlin'?"

The alien bug crouched, ready to attack.

"G'bye, Spartan."

Liv's eyes snapped open. With a groan, she whipped off the covers and swung her legs off the bed. No point in sleeping if *that* was what she'd dream about. Twenty minutes later, she was back in bed, albeit showered and dressed, with a cup of tea on the bedside table and her laptop balanced on her knees. Out of habit, she opened her e-mail.

Three hundred eighty-seven messages.

Liv blinked in confusion. "What the . . . ?"

The hundreds of messages had one source: her Spartan post from the previous night. With shaking fingers, she scrolled through them. Tweets, replies, likes, and, most exciting of all, "evidence posts"—at least fifty of them—filled the screen. These were getting their own reposts and replies, too. She leaned back against her pillow, heart pounding.

#SpartanSurvived had taken off.

Liv fumbled for her phone and flicked off airplane mode. It began to vibrate in her hand, four separate tweets from Joe, Brian, and two other fangirls appearing.

@JoesWoes: @LivOutLoud OMG Liv-GET ONLINE! Something's going on with Starveil. O_O

@StarVeilBrian1981: @LivOutLoud Check out the new manip I just posted:

New Spartan post, btw. You should do a vid or something.

@SpartanGrrl: @LivOutLoud Liv! LIV! LIIIIIIIVVVVVVVV!!!! Where ARE you??? There's a Spartan revolution about to begin!

@VeilMeister: @LivOutLoud Check out this post, bb. http://tinyurl.com/Starveil3

"Oh my God!" Liv gasped as the realization hit her. "I'm trending."

Liv started to type an answer to Joe's tweet, then stopped and deleted it. It felt important she keep anonymous, at least for now. It wasn't supposed to be a joke. It was a call for action. She flicked back to VeilMeister's tweet. Not just a call to arms, a Spartan revolution.

Grinning, she finally decided on Xander. Besides being her friend, he had absolutely no connection to the *Starveil* fandom. Even if he accidentally said something online, it wouldn't matter. The only people who really knew him were the steampunk crowd. Besides, he *needed* to be in the know, since they had a vid to film. She wrote half a page of text, then deleted it after all, calling instead. The phone rang three times before a sleep-laden voice answered.

"Liv?" Rustling echoed in the background. "You all right?"

"I'm fine. I just need to talk to someone."

"So text me," Xander mumbled. "Goodness. What century were you born in?"

"But I need to talk to you *now*, not three hours from now!"

"I cannot imagine anything that can't wait three hours."

The sound of yawning came through the phone. "There are reasonable ways to wake a person in the morning, you know."

"From someone who prefers an inkwell to a Sharpie," Liv said, giggling, "you are a surprising technology snob." She peeked down at her computer screen. Forty-six new notifications had arrived in the time since she'd woken. "So are you awake yet?"

"Mrrrph. I'm trying . . . I really am."

"I'll take that as a yes. I need you to go online, Xander."

"As in right now?"

"Yes, now."

"But I'm so tired," he moaned. "Can't this wait?"

"No."

"Honestly, Liv. How are you awake at all?"

"Please, Xander," she pleaded, "just do it."

"All right . . . let me grab my tablet." He yawned again. "Okay, I'm online. This better be good."

"I need you to go to the *Starveil* wiki."

There was a pause. "Are you joking? You know how I feel about *Star*—"

"Just GO."

"Fine . . . But only because it's *you* asking, dearest." Liv heard him moving around, the phone being shifted. "All right. I'm over on the dark side. You'd better have the cookies I've been promised."

Liv giggled. "Now find the list of Spartan forums."

"Where? I don't see it," Xander grumbled. "This is really the *worst*-designed fan page I've ever—"

"They're over on the left side of the page. You see them now?"

"Um . . . yeah. Yeah, I got it. Which one?"

"Just click on the search box at the top of the list and type in Spartan Survived."

There was a pause.

"Okay," Xander said. "I've got about a hundred different results. Which one?"

"All of them!" Liv laughed. "That's me! I'm trending."

There was a pause of several seconds.

"That's . . . *you*?"

"Yes! That project I was telling you about last night? I kind of started it on my own. I put out a post. It should be the first one on the list."

Liv heard him moving about, sheets rustling. Xander's voice returned, brighter than before. "Is this the Spartan Rescue Mission post?"

"Exactly! It's trending. I've got like . . ." She refreshed her e-mail browser, eyes widening at the new list. "Close to five hundred replies already."

"Are you kidding me? This is for freaking *Starveil*. Unbelievable!"

Liv choked back laughter. "Don't be mad," she teased. "I'm sure steampunk will have its day."

She could hear the grin in Xander's tone. "It already does, Liv dearest. You just have to meet *real-life* people at cons to truly experience it."

"So you keep saying."

"Then why don't you come with me this summer? Dragon Con is something you must experience to understand. Arden and I are already planning our dual cosplay."

Liv rolled her eyes at the mention of Xander's girlfriend. "Wouldn't that be . . . kind of weird?"

"Why would it be weird?"

"I dunno . . . With Arden and you, and then . . . me?" Liv laughed. "I'm not excited to be a third wheel."

"Pfft! Arden adores you. Besides, every room is packed that weekend. That's just how Dragon Con works. My cousin's coming, too. We could find room for you, if you wanted."

"I don't think so. But thanks."

"Not a problem," Xander said. "And seriously, Liv, this whole thing you did with the *Starveil* post is fantastic. Bravo, dearest! Five hundred overnight is . . . It's amazing! I'm in awe."

"Thanks, Xander. That means a lot." She grinned. "So are you ready to start a revolution?"

He chuckled. "I think it's already started."

Kiara London is the Internet-savvy, hopelessly romantic alter ego of Bethany Novak-Tveten, who in real life is part of the US Air Force. She started writing on the online writing site Booksie when she was thirteen and then transferred to Wattpad, where her debut novel, *Kiss Cam*, was originally posted. She spends most of her time scrolling down Tumblr, attempting to read everything she can get her hands on, and drooling over fictional men.

daydreams-to-neverland.tumblr.com